THE TROUBLING DEATH OF MADDY BENSON

THE TROUBLING DEATH OF MADDY BENSON

Terry Shames

**SEVERN
HOUSE**

First world edition published in Great Britain and the USA in 2024
by Severn House, an imprint of Canongate Books Ltd,
14 High Street, Edinburgh EH1 1TE.

severnhouse.com

British Library Cataloguing-in-Publication Data
A CIP catalogue record for this title is available from the British Library.

ISBN-13: 978-1-4483-1182-8 (cased)
ISBN-13: 978-1-4483-1183-5 (e-book)

All Severn House titles are printed on acid-free paper.

MIX
Paper | Supporting
responsible forestry
FSC
www.fsc.org   FSC® C013056

Typeset by Palimpsest Book Production Ltd., Falkirk,
Stirlingshire, Scotland.
Printed and bound in Great Britain by TJ Books,
Padstow, Cornwall.

Praise for the Samuel Craddock mysteries

About the author

Award-winning author **Terry Shames** is the author of ten previous Samuel Craddock mysteries. As well as winning the Macavity Award for Best First Novel, *A Killing at Cotton Hill* was also shortlisted for The Strand Critics Award. *The Necessary Murder of Nonie Blake* won the RT Critics Award for Best Mystery. Her books have also been shortlisted for Left Coast Crime Awards for Best Mystery.

Terry grew up in Texas, and her Samuel Craddock series is set in the fictitious town of Jarrett Creek, which is based on the fascinating people, landscape, and culture of the small town where her grand-parents lived. She is a member of Sisters in Crime and was formerly on the board of Mystery Writers of America.

www.terryshames.com

ONE

Jarrett Creek is a small town, and I know most people who live here, or at least have heard of the ones I don't know personally. So when a call comes in from a woman asking the police department to rescue someone I've never heard of, I'm puzzled.

'What did you say her name was?'

The woman on the phone is agitated. Maybe angry. 'Maddy Benson. She's my sister.'

'She lives here in Jarrett Creek?'

'Of course she does. Otherwise, why would I call the police? Who am I speaking to?'

'This is Samuel Craddock, Chief of Police.' I already identified myself when I answered the phone, but she was too worked up to listen. 'What does she need to be rescued from?'

'I'm not sure. The call was so odd. It may be nothing. She tends to be dramatic.' Pot, meet kettle.

'Why don't we start with you telling me who you are.'

She sighs as if I'm making her suffer. 'Eileen Currey. Mrs Jack Currey, from San Antonio?' Sounds like she thinks I should have heard of her.

'Why did she call you?'

'She didn't call me; I called her because I hadn't talked to her in a while. But when she answered her phone, she sounded – I don't know – out of breath, so I asked her where she was. I thought maybe she was out on a walk. She told me she was on a road off the main highway. And then she said she couldn't talk, she had to get away.'

'Get away from what?'

'I asked her, but she said never mind, she'd call me back.'

'For the first time, she sounds more desperate than annoyed. I'm wondering if Maddy Benson has dementia and has wandered away from home.

'Did she sound scared?'

The woman is silent for a moment. 'I believe she did, but maybe she was just out of breath.'

My deputy Maria Trevino has been listening. She was working on her computer, and she's stopped and is looking my way, alert.

'I'll be glad to go out and check on her. Is her car broken down maybe?'

'If it was, she didn't mention it.'

'Does she live near there?'

'I don't know. I'm not familiar with the town.'

'Do you have her address?'

She makes an exasperated sound. 'Hold on a minute. Let me get my book. I don't remember the address right off. She hasn't lived there long.' Which would explain why I don't recognize the name.

She's gone a minute, and while she's gone, I tell Maria what the woman is phoning about. 'You ever heard of anyone by that name?'

'Maddy Benson, no. But Jack Currey in San Antonio? Sure, if it's the same one.'

Before she can enlighten me, Eileen comes back on the line and gives me her sister's address. It's north of town in a section of new homes that have sprung up over the last few years. The thing is, if Maddy is actually where she told her sister she is, she's several miles from home.

The only road in town that leads off Highway 36 is farm-to-market 1362. There are a few houses out there, but it's mostly pastureland with big lots of twenty acres or more. So what was she doing there? And how are we going to find her?

'How long ago was this?'

'Not long. Fifteen, twenty minutes. Like I said, it's probably nothing, but when she didn't call back, I decided to phone again, and she didn't answer.'

'Does your sister live alone?'

'No, she lives with her son and daughter-in-law. Her husband died of cancer last year.'

'Did you call them? Maybe she told them where she was going.'

'That would make sense, wouldn't it? But I doubt she did. They're so wrapped up in their own lives that I don't know how much they talk to her. I thought I'd get better results calling the police. Besides, they already think I'm a busybody.'

I ask her to describe her sister, although if she's actually where Eileen Currey says she is, it's pretty deserted. There likely won't be more than one woman needing help along the road there.

'Ma'am, one more question. Does your sister have any mental issues? Maybe dementia?'

'Good Lord, no. She's sharp as a peacock.' A peacock?

I get off the phone and fill Maria in on the call. 'Why don't you come with me to pick her up? She might feel more comfortable with a woman in the car.'

We take the squad car instead of my pickup, which I usually drive. And we leave my dog Dusty at the station. He doesn't like it, looking as always as if he is crushed at the idea of being left behind.

We step outside to find that a north wind has come through as predicted. It was nearly eighty degrees this morning and the temperature has dropped at least twenty degrees, the wind making it feel even colder. I retrieve my jacket from my pickup, and Maria gets one out of the trunk of her car.

We drive across Highway 36, over the railroad tracks, and out on to the farm-to-market road. The sky is gray and wintry, even though it's only mid-October.

'You said you know who Jack Currey is?' I ask Maria. 'Who is he? The woman acted as if I ought to recognize the name.'

'If it's the same one, he owns several car dealerships in San Antonio. He's always advertising on local TV. Sort of an arrogant guy.'

We drive east, a couple of miles past the railroad tracks, and we only meet a couple of cars coming from the other direction. It's a sparsely populated area, poor scrubland with just a scattering of post oak trees. Although people do raise cattle out here, the land can't support many cows. There's no sign of the woman.

'What was she doing out here?' Maria asks. 'She could be anywhere.'

'Maybe she's off the road somewhere,' I say. We turn around and go back the way we came, this time driving slowly and looking past the road on either side in case we missed her the first time.

When we are even with Tom Gainer's property, I spy something that makes me slow down and pull on to the gravel verge leading up to his place. 'Why is that gate open?' I ask. 'Gainer usually only comes on the weekends.' The gate has Gainer's name etched on to a wooden plaque, attached to it.

'Maybe the wind blew it open,' Maria says.

She's right. The north wind is kicking up sand and dead brush. 'Not if it was locked,' I say, pointing to the heavy padlock hanging off the hinge of the gate.

'We should go in and see if anyone's around.' She sounds uneasy.

'It can't hurt.'

We drive through the entrance and proceed slowly down the rutted road that leads to a clump of post oak trees in the distance. The only living things in sight are cactus, some low bushes, and a couple of listless cows who stare at us the way cows do when confronted with the unexpected. I'm getting uneasy, although I couldn't say why exactly. It seems strange that the woman would be out here in the middle of nowhere.

'Hold it. Oh dear.' Maria's voice drops to a whisper.

I look at where she's pointing. Thirty yards to our right, I see someone lying on the ground. We're both out of the car and running in seconds. Maria gets there first, of course, being younger and more spry. She crouches down next to the body – a middle-aged woman, sprawled out on her stomach, dressed in tan slacks and a sleeveless white blouse. I'm hoping she's just passed out from dehydration or exhaustion, but when I step closer, I see that's not the case. There's a bullet hole square in the middle of the woman's back. A green backpack was slung over one shoulder, and it's lying half under her.

Maria whips a pair of gloves out of her pocket, puts them on, and feels for a pulse. She shakes her head. 'Still warm. Can't have been dead long.' She shivers.

I hunker down next to the body. This didn't happen long ago, so where did the shooter go? Did we meet him on the road? Is he still around here somewhere? Are we in danger?

Maria stands up and looks around in every direction. When I get up, the wind almost takes my hat off.

Maria nods toward the only place where someone, or a car, could be hidden – the clump of trees a quarter of a mile away.

I happen to know that Gainer has a snug two-room cabin there among the trees. 'I'm going to check it out,' I say. 'You go ahead and put in a call to Hedges.'

Alvin Hedges is the county sheriff in Bobtail. He'll either come out himself or call the Texas Department of Public Safety, who will send out a team of highway patrol officers to assess the scene along with an ambulance and the medical examiner.

Maria squints up at me, her face stony. 'Be careful. Could be somebody holed up there.'

I nod. Back in the squad car, I drive slowly toward the stand of trees, which are shivering in the wind. I'm on alert, wondering if at any second somebody will take a shot at my car. But nothing happens, and when I get there, I find the place deserted. There's no sign of a car or any human. I get out and check the cabin. It's locked up tight. I peer in the windows and can see that no one is inside. At the front of the house, Gainer maintains a tank that he stocks with fish. I walk over to it, keeping my eyes out for footprints, but the bank around the water is undisturbed.

I head back to where I left Maria and find her prowling around the area several yards away.

'I was looking for shotgun shells or footprints.' She's gloomy. She's never a ray of sunshine, but she is more serious than usual. Nobody likes finding a dead body.

'No luck?' I ask.

'Nothing. Not even sure how far away the bullet came from.'

I look toward the road. 'From what she said to her sister, it sounds like someone was after her,' I say. 'She said she had to get away.'

'So why was she out here in the open if she was trying to get away?' Maria asks.

'Good question.' We walk back to the body.

'Hold up,' Maria says. 'She doesn't have a purse with her, but she must have had a cell phone since she answered her sister's call. It must be in the backpack.'

'Or in a pocket,' I say. We can't move the body to look. That will have to wait until the medical examiner gets here.

'I'm curious how she got here,' I say. And why here? I try to put myself in the place of a woman running from someone. Did she know Gainer's cabin was here? Did she run here to try to get help?

'I'm going back up to the cabin to look more closely.' Maybe find tire tracks, although they probably won't show up unless there's a patch of clay that would hold an impression.

Sure enough, there's no sign of car tracks, but when I go around the back of the cabin, I see that the weeds have been disturbed. And there, lying among the weeds, is a cell phone. I put on a glove and pick it up and stow it in an evidence bag.

TWO

It has gotten colder in the short time we've been here, and since it might take a while for the ambulance and Department of Public Safety crew to get here, I retrieve my rain gear from the car and send Maria back to headquarters. She can pick me up when I turn over the crime scene to the patrol officers.

I stand out by the open gate to wait for them and think back to exactly what Maddy Benson's sister said, that Maddy lived with her son and his wife. I wonder if they even know she's gone. I need to notify them, and I should call Eileen Currey to tell her we found Maddy. I'd rather tell her in person, but that won't work. I don't have the manpower to send anyone to San Antonio.

Two highway patrol officers arrive first. I recognize one of them, Arnold Mosier, an affable guy in his thirties. The other one is even younger. They seem to get younger every year. We shake hands, and I climb into their car to drive to the body. When we arrive, they put on booties and gloves to examine the scene.

Mosier looks to the north, where dark clouds are forming. 'We have to get this scene processed soon. Looks like this norther is going to bring some rain.'

'Medical examiner should be here before too long,' I say.

They peer down at the body but don't make a move to get closer. They'll leave the close work to the forensic team. 'How did you know she was out here?' Mosier asks.

I explain about the phone call and seeing the gate open. 'From what she said, she was running away from someone.'

'On foot?'

'I don't see a car.'

'Maybe up there among those trees.' He gestures toward where Gainer's cabin is.

'I was up there, and there wasn't a car. Could have been she was a passenger in somebody's car, and they had an argument and she got out and ran.'

'Makes sense.' He gazes out at the road, his brow furrowed. We're all troubled by the idea of this middle-aged woman being gunned down. 'So she's from Jarrett Creek,' he says. 'You know anything about her?'

'No, only that she and her family live out in a new part of town. According to her sister, she hasn't lived here long. I'll see what I can find out from her son when I notify him what happened.'

Mosier nods. 'I appreciate you doing that.' He checks his watch. 'I don't know what the forensics team is going to find since she was shot from a distance away.'

I want to notify Maddy Benson's son right away, so I call Maria to come and get me. She arrives in ten minutes. I'm glad to get out of the wind. She hasn't brought Dusty with her. 'If it starts thundering, he'll go crazy,' she says. 'He'll be better off at headquarters. Brick will be there this afternoon.' Brick Freeman is one of my other deputies. I'm glad it's him in today. He's good with Dusty. My other deputy, Connor Loving, isn't a dog person.

I have Maddy Benson's address, but I don't know her son's name.

The house is on a winding road north of the lake, with large homes on big lots. It's set back a hundred feet from the road at the end of a gravel driveway. It's a colonial style, two-story, white, with pillars and a large front porch with a swing and potted plants. The architecture looks odd out here in the scrubby Texas landscape. It looks like it belongs in a Deep South setting with a green grass lawn and big shade trees. Instead of a green lawn, the front yard has a cactus garden planted in gravel. There's also a small pond in the yard with a birdbath in the middle of it, surrounded by stonework animals – a family of three frogs, a rabbit, and a squirrel presided over by a large statue of St Francis of Assisi. Next to the birdbath is a metal stork surrounded by reeds.

'Must be Catholic,' Maria says. 'You don't get many Protestants with a saint's statue in the yard.'

The garage doors are open, and inside there are two cars: a light gray Toyota Camry and a small black BMW SUV.

When we get out of the squad car, Maria tells me to wait a second. She walks into the garage and puts her hand on the hood of each car. She comes back. 'Toyota was driven recently.'

Could mean whoever owns the vehicle drove Maddy Benson to where she was killed.

We ring the doorbell, and I can tell by the way Maria clears her throat that she's as nervous as I am. It's awful to have to tell someone that a loved one has died.

A woman answers the door, mid-thirties, trim and attractive, with long light brown hair. She's wearing jeans and a T-shirt. 'Brrr,' she says, shivering. 'I didn't realize it had gotten cold. Can I help you?'

'I'm Samuel Craddock, Chief of Police here in Jarrett Creek, and this is Deputy Trevino. Is this the home of Maddy Benson?'

'Yes.' She searches our faces.

'May we come in?' I ask.

She glances behind us and then frowns. 'What is this about?'

'Are you a relative of Ms Benson?'

'I'm her daughter-in-law.'

'And your name?'

'Krista Benson.'

'Is her son here?'

She hesitates and I see alarm rising in her eyes. 'Let me . . . yes, please, come in.' She opens the door wider and hurries away.

We step into the large foyer, closing the door behind us. At the end of the short hallway is a stairway to the left. Krista Benson runs up the stairs, calling out, 'Josh? You need to come.'

I hear a muffled reply and then a door opens. 'What is it?' Impatient.

'There's . . . the police chief. He's at the door.'

'Police? What do they want?'

They both come down the stairs, their footsteps muffled by deep carpeting.

Josh Benson walks toward us, taking off his glasses. 'Hi, I'm Josh Benson What's the trouble?'

'You're Maddy Benson's son?'

'That's right.' His voice is impatient. His clothing is rumpled: a plain gray T-shirt with a wrinkled short-sleeved blue shirt over it, and khaki pants so wrinkled they look as if he slept in them. His hair is short but sticks out like he's been running his hands through it. 'Why are you here?'

'I'm afraid I have bad news for you.' I wait a beat for that to register. 'Your mother has been shot.'

'Shot?' His eyes go wide. 'How did that happen? Is she OK?'

I shake my head. 'I'm sorry. It was fatal.'

'That can't be right!' Josh staggers as if he's losing his balance.

His wife makes a sound of distress and grabs his arm. 'Josh, let's go sit down.'

She leads us down a short hallway to a generous-sized living room. It's furnished with two plump leather sofas flanking a massive fireplace, and several armchairs, furniture that looks expensive. We sit down on opposite sofas, with a large iron-and-glass coffee table between us.

'I can't believe this,' Krista says. Her voice is shaky, and a tear makes its way down her cheek. She brushes it away. 'Who shot her?'

'We don't know, and I need to ask you a few questions,' I say.

'Wait,' Krista says. 'Can you just tell us where this happened?'

'And when?' Josh adds. 'I mean, she can't have been gone that long.' He glances at this watch. 'It's only nine o'clock.'

'Your mother was out on the farm-to-market road on the other side of Highway 36. It's a few miles from here. Do you have any idea why she might have been there?'

They look at each other, and their expressions are so shocked and baffled that I believe them when they both shake their heads. 'Who found her?' Krista asks.

'Maria and I did. We got a call an hour ago from an Eileen Currey. Your aunt?'

Josh grimaces. 'Yeah.'

'She said she had talked to your mother. Your mother said she was trying to get away from someone. Your aunt asked me to find her.'

Josh puts a hand to his forehead. 'This makes no sense. Get away from someone? Who? And why?'

'That's what we need to find out. At any rate, Ms Currey told us her sister was out on FM 1362. We went out there and we found her.'

'Oh, my God.' Krista puts a hand to her mouth. 'She's really dead?'

'I'm afraid so,' I say. 'Were you aware that she was gone?'

'I was,' Krista says. 'But I thought . . .'

Josh looks at his wife. 'What do you mean you knew she was gone?'

'I . . . I hadn't seen her this morning. I was going to the grocery store, so I went to ask if she wanted anything, and she wasn't in her apartment.' Maria and I exchange glances. If Krista went to the grocery store, that explains why the car in the garage had been driven.

'You said her apartment?' I ask.

'Yes. They have their . . . well, not they, her husband died a few months ago . . . she has her own wing of the house. It's an apartment, really.'

'Were you alarmed when you found that she wasn't here?'

'No, she sometimes goes for a walk. I didn't think anything of it. But . . . you said you found her several miles away?'

'Yes. So we're wondering how she got there. We didn't find a car nearby.'

Krista seems to be in a trance. Her voice has dropped to a whisper. 'She doesn't have a car. She uses ours when she wants to go somewhere.'

'Could a friend have picked her up?'

The two exchange helpless looks. 'We don't really know anybody around here. Like I said, Luke, Josh's dad, died a few months ago, and Maddy was still not ready to be very social.'

'And you have no idea why she would say she was running away from someone?'

Krista looks past us, as if trying to picture it. She shakes her head. 'No idea at all.'

Maria clears her throat. She asks, 'Was there any problem between you? You have a spat or anything? It can be hard living with relatives.'

'No! She was . . . I mean, since Luke died, she was sad sometimes, but she was very independent. We didn't . . . we didn't . . . have big arguments or anything.' Krista suddenly gives a sob and puts her hands to her face. 'I'm sorry. I can't believe this. It doesn't seem possible.'

'I know it's a shock. Josh, you said you were working. What kind of work do you do?'

He looks for a moment as if he can't quite comprehend my question. 'Oh. Oh, we're both writers. I write history books. And my wife writes . . . well, novels.'

An odd look passes between them, and Krista glances away, her lips pursed.

'Can you think of any reason someone would have targeted your mother?'

He shakes his head and looks toward his wife, as if she might have a clue.

'None. And I don't understand why Eileen called you instead of calling us,' Krista says.

'She said you were probably busy and she didn't want to disturb you.' That's not exactly what she said, but I'm being diplomatic.

Krista gives a sharp bark of laughter with no humor. 'Translation, she didn't think we'd care.'

'So there's no reason for her to think there were problems between you.'

Josh shakes his head. 'That's just Eileen stirring up trouble. There weren't any problems with Mamma. We got along great. She was very independent. We hardly ever had disagreements.'

'It's odd that she called Eileen, though,' Krista says.

'Why wouldn't she?' Maria asks.

'They didn't get along all that well. Eileen is conservative. You know, politics. And Maddy was the opposite.'

'Actually, it was the other way around. Your aunt called her to check in. She said she hadn't spoken to her in a while. And Ms Benson told her she was trying to get away from someone.'

Josh looks stricken. bites his lower lip. 'Who could have been after her?' He gets up. 'I could use some coffee. Anybody?'

'I'll get it,' Krista says.

I tell her I wouldn't mind a cup.

'I'll have a glass of water,' Maria says. 'I'll come in and help you.'

And have a look around at the same time, I expect.

When the two women walk out, I say, 'Josh, do you own any weapons?'

'Weapons? A rifle. We keep it for snakes. I don't think we've ever used it.'

'Where do you keep it?'

If he knows I'm checking to see if he could have used his weapon to kill his mother, he doesn't let on. 'It's out in the garage.' He shrugs. 'We store it in a locked box. You want to see it?'

'On our way out. First, I'd like to take a look at your mother's room if you don't mind.'

'Apartment,' he says. He's distracted again.

'If she had her own living quarters, did you have meals together?' I ask.

'What? Oh, sometimes.' He smiles sadly. 'Mamma was a vegetarian.

She didn't eat with us often because it bothered her to see us eat meat. So once a week or so, we'd have a vegetarian meal so we could eat together.'

When Maria comes back with Krista, I tell her we're going to take a look at Maddy's living quarters.

Josh leads us down a long hallway, past a bathroom to a door that looks like it could lead to outside. But when he opens it, it's into exactly what he said: an apartment. We step into a good-size living room furnished very differently from Josh and Krista's, with a hodge-podge of furniture that's crammed in, as if it was brought from a larger place. The maroon sofa is too big for the room, as are the side chairs. Next to each of them is a big side table, with lamps and collectibles – ceramic bowls, figurines, and framed photos. A large coffee table has been pushed under a window and is stacked with books and magazines.

Josh stands at the doorway, his expression dismayed.

'Oh my goodness. All her things,' Krista wails. 'She loved all this stuff.'

'She brought it with her when they moved,' Josh says. 'She had to get rid of half of her furniture, and it almost killed her.' He stares up at the ceiling as if he can't bear to look at the room and all it contains.

Off to the left, there's a compact kitchen painted in bright colors, separated from the living room by a bar that's cluttered with more ceramics and a few plants. One thing catches my eye. I walk over and see that there's a small plate with some crumbs on it, a half-eaten muffin, and a few grapes. There's a coffee cup with an inch of coffee in the bottom. So whatever happened, she didn't take time to clean up her breakfast dishes.

'What did your mamma spend her time doing?' I ask.

'Oh, she had projects,' Josh says. 'Come on back. I'll show you the rest of the apartment.'

We follow him into the next room, a bedroom even larger than the living room. It has a king-sized bed, a large dresser, again too big for the room, and two large bedside tables. On every surface, there are photos, the records of a life. I walk over to the dresser. You could read the photos like a book, beginning with a young couple grinning at each other, a man in an army uniform, a couple of them with a backdrop of a Middle Eastern country, and then photos of the couple with children. Two of them. 'You have a sister?' I ask Josh.

'Yes, Hannah is in Los Angeles.' He bows his head. 'Oh, God, I have to call her. She's going to be devastated. And my grandparents.'

'Where do your grandparents live?'

'They're in a retirement community in Houston.'

The later photos progress from a plump, smiling man to a gaunt man with a haunted look. I recognize that look as the one on my wife Jeanne's face before she died. It makes me want to lay the photo facedown.

'This is where she spent most of her time.' Josh moves to a door off the bedroom and opens it on to a cozy office filled with plants. One wall is bookshelves crammed with books. There's a large desk with a wooden desk chair and a wicker side chair. The desk is piled high with folders and brochures. I walk over and pick one up. It contains glossy brochures of Hawaii.

'Mamma was a travel agent when she and my dad lived in Houston, and she kept some of her clients. She told me she was cleaning all that stuff out of her desk.'

'Did she travel?'

'Not after my dad got sick. They had some good trips together before that, though.'

Behind the desk, there's a shelf with two sets of books on it. Two books bear Josh's name as author. There are also a couple dozen paperbacks, all by a name I recognize, Olivia Cartwright. I've seen some of her books in Loretta Singletary's house. Romance novels. Loretta is an avid romance reader. She once told me she reads one a day.

'Your mamma was a fan of Olivia Cartwright?' I ask, gesturing toward the books.

Josh's lips tighten, as if he's tasted something sour. 'You might say that.'

'They're mine,' Krista says. 'I write them. Olivia Cartwright is my pen name.'

'Really?' Maria says. I know she's thinking she'll have to tell Loretta.

The atmosphere in the room is peculiar. Krista is looking at her husband with defiance, and he has two bright spots of color in his cheeks. Some subtle war is going on here.

'By the way, I found your mamma's cell phone. I'd like your permission to go through it.'

I notice the slightest hesitation, but then Josh says, 'Of course.'

'Do you know her password to the phone and computer?' Maria asks.

He glances at Krista and shrugs. 'I don't. Krista?'

'No, but she probably kept it in the desk somewhere. She was always afraid she'd forget her passwords, so she kept a list.' She opens the middle drawer. It contains nothing but pens, paper clips, tape, and scissors. In a side drawer, she finds a printout. 'Here it is.' She smiles faintly. 'Not much of a security system.' I jot down the information I need.

'I came over here to notify you right away what happened, but now I need to go back to the scene. After that, I'll have a clearer idea of what happened. We'll come back then. I'll phone before we come.' I don't have to rush back to the scene. It always takes longer than I think it will for the medical examiner and the ambulance and the forensics people to arrive, but I know these two have phone calls to make, and they need time to come to terms with the death of Josh's mother.

'That's fine.' Josh hardly seems to register what I've said. He's still staring at the desk. He sighs. 'I can't believe she's not going to come back here.'

Krista puts a hand on his arm and squeezes. He looks at her as if she's a stranger.

'At some point, I'm going to need one of you to make a formal identification of the body. Once they've transported her to Bobtail.'

'I'll do that,' Josh says.

We head for the door back into the main house. As Josh opens it, I notice a bag near the back door. 'Looks like she might have packed a bag. Did she mention that she might go away?'

'That's her go-bag,' Krista says. 'She always kept a go-bag. She said it was in case she needed to leave in a hurry.'

Maria and I glance at each other, taking a second to process what she said. 'Why would she need to leave in a hurry?' I ask.

Krista shrugs and looks at her husband. 'We don't know. We used to tease her about it. It's not like we have earthquakes around here, and in a tornado, who has time to grab a bag?'

'Did she ever use it?'

'I don't know,' Josh says. 'I don't think so. But she usually took a backpack when she went walking. I don't see it here.'

'She had it with her,' I say. 'But she didn't have a purse.'

'It might be in the bedroom,' Krista says. 'She rarely carried one. It was always the backpack.' Her smile is rueful. 'Like she was a teenager.'

She goes into the bedroom and is back in a few minutes. 'I found the purse.' It's a small black bag. 'There's nothing much in it.'

Maria slips on a pair of gloves and takes the bag. 'We'll need to go through it,' she says, and Josh tells us to do what we need to.

We go back through the front part of the house, and are at the front door when Josh says, 'Look, this might be asking a lot, but would you mind calling Eileen and telling her what happened? I don't think I can do it.'

I tell him I will. 'And when you call your sister, if she has any concerns or questions, she can call me.' I hand him my card. 'Now, before I leave, you were going to show me that lockbox with the rifle?'

'Oh, right.'

The four of us go out to the garage. Krista follows, like a puppy who doesn't want to be by herself. I gesture to the two cars.

'You said your mother didn't have a car,' Maria says. 'Did she use yours often?'

'All the time. We don't go anywhere much, so it was no problem.'

'Did she usually tell you if she was going to take one of the cars?' I ask.

Josh shakes his head. 'It wasn't necessary. 'You have to understand. Krista and I are both writers. We start first thing in the morning and write for a few hours, maybe take a break for a cup of coffee or to walk outside if we're stuck on something. But my mother knew we were busy, and she didn't make a habit of disturbing us.'

'Not that we would be mad if she did,' Krista adds hastily. 'It's just that it was our routine. The three of us.' She takes a shuddery breath.

Josh shows us the locked gun safe where the rifle is kept, the only firearm in it. I check it; it hasn't been fired in a long time, if ever. I tell him if he plans to use it, he needs to maintain it.

Krista says, 'Or we could get rid of it.'

'Probably best,' he says. He's distracted again. They both are. If they had anything to do with Maddy Benson's death, I'd be surprised. But something isn't quite right with them.

On our way back to headquarters, Maria says, 'Funny family. I don't mean they seem suspicious, but the husband and wife aren't getting along, and they hardly seemed to know his mother at all.'

THREE

B ack at headquarters, Dusty greets me as if I've been gone for months. I wonder if I ought to take him home where he can hide under the bed if it starts raining, but I need to get back out to the crime scene. Before I go, I call Eileen Currey. She doesn't answer her cell phone, but in her voicemail message she leaves another number to call.

'Yeah.' The man who answers the phone is brusque.

'Did I reach the Currey residence?' I ask.

'Yes, who is this?'

I give him my name and tell him I'm chief of police in Jarrett Creek. 'May I speak with Eileen?'

'What do you want with her?'

If this is an example of the car dealership mogul's salesmanship, I'm surprised he's a success.

'Is this her husband?'

'Yes. I can have her call you.'

'I spoke with her earlier today, and have some bad news. Her sister, Maddy Benson, has been killed.'

'Huh. How did that happen?' An underwhelming reaction to news of his sister-in-law's death.

'We're not sure. I'd like to ask your wife some questions. Do you know when she'll be in?'

'She's actually on her way to Jarrett Creek. She doesn't answer the phone when she's driving, which is the way it ought to be.'

'OK. If she contacts you, would you ask her to call me?'

'If I'm here.'

I call Eileen's cell phone again and this time leave a message for her to contact me as soon as she can. I hope she calls before she gets to the Benson house. Her nephew seems to have some animosity toward her, and the news of her sister's death might be better coming from a neutral party.

While I've been on the phone, Maria has gotten a call about an altercation at the Two Dog Bar, so she's off to handle that. It's not even noon. Seems early in the day for a bar fight.

When I drive back out to the site of the shooting, the ambulance and Junior Addison, the assistant medical examiner, have only just arrived, saying that they were late because they were called out to the scene of a bad wreck south of Bobtail. Addison and I follow the ambulance as it trundles over the barren ground to the body. Now it's Addison's show.

'Where are the forensics people?' he asks.

'You know how that goes. DPS will get to it when they get to it.'

When Addison approaches the body, he takes his hat off and spends a moment gathering his thoughts. Finally, he puts his hat back on. 'You know this woman?' he asks.

'I don't, but her name is Maddy Benson.'

'Short for Madelyn? Margaret?'

'I don't know. I don't have a formal ID, and I didn't think to ask her son.'

'No ID?'

'Probably in her backpack.' I nod toward it.

'Purse?'

'She left it at home. We have it.'

'Is this how her body was found?' Addison asks.

'Yes. Deputy Trevino and I found her right after it happened.' I tell him that we didn't move her, that Maria had gloves on when she touched the woman's arm to determine if there was a pulse.

He's still standing up, getting a sense of the scene. I like Addison. He hasn't been on the job long, but he's serious and competent.

He crouches down and inspects the entry wound and then turns the woman's body on to its side and looks at the front. That's where the blood has gone. Pooled under the body and into the dry soil. He stands back up. 'This was a long-range shooting, so whoever did it knows how to handle a rifle.'

He doesn't have to expand on his statement. There are no powder burns or other indications of a close-up shooting. And a rifle is more accurate at long range. Not impossible that it could have been a shotgun, but unlikely.

'And the exit wound is big,' he continues. 'We're talking a high-powered rifle. Deer hunter.'

He's frowning as he looks back down at her body. 'Something unusual. It was a straight-on shot. Usually, there's some kind of angle, but this was *straight*. I can't be sure, but my guess is the bullet is around here somewhere and didn't stay in her body.'

'The area will have to be searched.' I'm hoping the DPS will do that; I don't have the manpower. 'I don't suppose you can give me any hint how far away the shooter was?' We both look off into the approximate direction the shot must have come from to hit her straight on.

'Find me the bullet and tell me how far away it is from her body, and I might be able to get you what you need.'

I sigh. Even if he has the bullet, it means scouring a large area for jacket fragments. That might be a job for Maria. She has an uncanny ability to spot clues.

We both turn at the sound of a vehicle. A paneled truck is lumbering toward us with the DPS logo on the side. The forensics team.

Two men get out and introduce themselves. 'You fellas could have picked a nicer day to invite us to a crime scene.' One of them looks up at the gathering clouds.

They confer with Addison, who tells them what he has ascertained. He particularly asks them to look for the bullet. They go back to the truck to get supplies.

We watch them go, and then Addison turns back to me. 'Who called this in? Who found her way out here?'

I describe the phone call I got from her sister. 'Apparently, she was running from someone.'

'Why would she be out in the open, though? Why not up in those trees, to hide?' He gestures toward the stand of trees.

'She was up there. There's a cabin. I found her cell phone outside, where she must have dropped it. I don't know why she came out into the open, though.'

'People panic when they're cornered,' he says.

'Or she thought her pursuer was gone. If he knew he was accurate at a long distance, he could just hang back, let her think she'd gotten away.'

'Either way, he flushed her out.'

'I don't like that thought.' It gives me a chill to think of her assailant hanging back and her breaking out into the open, hoping maybe she could get somewhere safe. What kind of grudge must somebody have to hunt down a middle-aged woman?

He nods. 'I don't either.'

A gust of wind blows up and he zips up his jacket. 'You turning the investigation over to DPS?'

'May have to. I don't know the woman or her family.' Which is a drawback. In a small town, it's likely that if someone is shot, it wasn't a random event. It was probably done by someone close to the victim. Not knowing the family, I don't know who that might be other than her son and daughter-in-law, and so far I don't get the idea they were involved. Still, I hate to turn over the investigation too fast. It's my territory, if not exactly my jurisdiction. Homicides in small towns are technically the responsibility of the Department of Public Safety.

'Do I need to notify the family?' he asks.

I tell him I did that. 'She lived with her son and daughter-in-law. Seemed like a good enough arrangement.'

'Still. That can create problems.' His mouth clamps shut. Tells me about his relationship with his in-laws.

We watch the ambulance drivers take the gurney out of the back of the ambulance.

'I'll let you know if there's anything unusual in the autopsy, but it looks straightforward.'

'I'd like to get my hands on the backpack as soon as you're done checking for fingerprints,' I say.

'I'll get it to you by tomorrow. Maybe sooner. Depends.'

I know what he means. It's a small county, always short-handed. An auto accident can throw off a whole day's schedule.

'You mind opening it so I can see what's there?'

He unzips it and opens it wide enough that I can see she had her laptop with her, a wallet, and some stray notes. Interesting that she brought her computer with her. Why?

I stand back while he instructs the ambulance drivers to load the body. It's a lonesome feeling being out here in the middle of this scrubby territory, seeing a heap of a body loaded up and the ambulance door slammed on it. A hard way for somebody to end up. To add to the atmosphere, the first fat drops of rain blow out of the clouds.

One of the forensics guys comes over and fetches us. 'Found the bullet. Wanted you to see it before we bag it.'

Hands on his hips, Addison eyes the bullet on the ground and shakes his head. 'I'll have to do some calculations. You want to measure it?'

The forensics guy nods. 'I'll do that. We're almost done here. Pretty sparse info.'

'I hate to ask this,' I say, 'but any chance you can get some people out here to search for jacket fragments so we can pinpoint where the shooter was? It's going to rain, and that's going to mess with the chance of finding anything.'

'That's why they pay us the big bucks,' he says. 'I'll put in a call to get a couple more fellas out here.'

'I'll send my deputy, too. She's got an eye.'

'The more the merrier,' he says. 'Tell her to bring her raincoat.' The rain spatters are getting more frequent.

I'm getting into my car when the call comes from Eileen Currey. 'Did you find her?' Which means she hasn't talked to her husband.

'Where are you?' I ask.

'I'm on my way to Jarrett Creek. I didn't like the way Maddy sounded so I decided to visit her. I stopped in Bobtail to get a few groceries. Maddy never has anything worth eating in her kitchen.'

'Mrs Currey, are you in the grocery store now?'

'No, I'm in my car. I'm just leaving. I'm trying to get to Maddy's place before it starts raining. Is Maddy back home?'

'I'm afraid I have some bad news for you.'

She's so silent that I wonder if she's still on the line.

'Mrs Currey?'

'Call me Eileen.' Her voice is tight. She's trying not to process what the bad news must be.

'Eileen, I'm so sorry, but your sister is dead. We found her where you told us she would be, but she had been shot.'

'Shot? Who shot her?'

'We don't know. I'd like to talk to you in person. Can you come to the police station here in Jarrett Creek? Are you OK to drive?'

'Well, I guess I'll have to be, won't I?' she snaps.

'No, not at all. One of my deputies and I can come to you and drive you back to headquarters.'

'That's not necessary,' she says. 'I'll come there.'

I give her directions and she says she'll be here soon.

Maria is back at headquarters, having smoothed things out between two men who hadn't actually been drinking; they were just arguing and it got out of hand.

'You up to going back to the scene to look for bullet fragments?' I ask.

She gives me the stink eye. 'Have you seen the weather?'

'You don't have to. The DPS guys can do it.'

'You know I have to go out there, don't you?'

'I figured.' Forensics is her favorite part of the job.

She's been gone ten minutes when a big white SUV wheels into the parking lot. I go out to meet it. Rain is still holding off, just the occasional flurry of drops blown sideways with the cold wind. Eileen turns out to be a smaller version of her sister. She practically has to climb down out of the SUV.

I introduce myself and we hurry inside.

'I can't stay long,' she says. 'I have to get the groceries in the refrigerator.'

'I understand.'

Dusty has been sleeping under my desk and he wriggles out to meet her.

'Oh! A dog.'

'I can put him in the other room.'

'Is he friendly?'

'Maybe too friendly.' I take him into the room where we have two jail cells and close the door. He whines, but I know he'll settle down. This isn't the first time he's been in there.

Eileen Currey looks like her sister, but a more stylish version, with short salt-and-pepper hair that looks like she just stepped out of a beauty salon. She's wearing a crisp blue blouse with black slacks and a black jacket, and pearls with matching earrings. The diamond on her left hand is one of the biggest I've seen, set on a platform of small diamonds. Her nails are manicured with light pink polish. All in all, she oozes wealth and security.

I get her seated and bring us both cups of coffee to warm us up. 'Have you spoken with Maddy's son? Does he know you're here?'

'I didn't think that was necessary,' she said. 'I was coming to see Maddy, and I didn't think I'd see much of him. He's always standoffish. Like that wife of his. We hardly say two words to each other when I'm here.' She pauses and I can see her process the fact that things are different now. 'I suppose I'd better call and let them know I'm coming to their house.'

She touches her pearls and says, 'Can you tell me what happened to Maddy?'

I describe finding Maddy's body. 'Do you know if she was having problems with anyone?'

'I don't live nearby, so I wouldn't be aware of something like

that. But it certainly sounds like it. I mean, somebody killed her.'
She's got a sharp tongue; I'll give her that.

There's a clap of thunder, lightning flashes, the sky opens up,
and right on cue Dusty lets out a howl.

'Oh, poor thing,' Eileen says. 'He's scared. You can bring him
in here.' The rain is so loud that I can barely hear her. She moves
up a notch in my estimation by being kind to my dog.

I go in and get Dusty. He's trembling and whimpering, and I
tuck him under my desk. I'll have to take him home as soon as
Eileen leaves.

'Just a few more questions,' I say. 'Did your sister ever mention
anything troubling her?'

She looks outside and shivers. 'I should have brought my umbrella
inside.'

'I can lend you one.'

She brings herself back to the moment. 'Maddy and I don't phone
one another often. I mean, maybe once a month. And we never
discuss things that are bothering us. We aren't close that way.'

'And yet you called her this morning.'

She brings a hand to her mouth, and I realize she hadn't really
thought of it. 'Now that you mention it, that was a strange coincidence. She popped into my mind, and I decided to give her a call.
Maybe it was ESP.' She shakes her head. 'I'm glad I did. I wish I
had paid more attention to what she was telling me when she said
she was running from someone. She could be dramatic sometimes,
and I got impatient with it.'

'What would she get dramatic about?'

'Oh, she was always working on some political thing, and she
could get worked up.'

Speaking of dramatic, there's another long roll of thunder and
Dusty moans. 'It's OK,' I tell him.

'I don't blame him,' she says. 'Look how dark it is out there. I
hope we don't get a tornado.'

She's right: it's dark.

'Let's finish up here and let you get on to your sister's place. A
couple more questions. Did your sister get along with her kids?'

She raises her hands and drops them to her lap. 'I think so. She
never complained. They were self-absorbed – you know, always
working – but she didn't seem to mind that. She had her own
interests.'

'How often did you see her?'

'Oh . . .' For the first time, she looks distressed, her voice wobbling. 'I hadn't seen her in a few months. I guess I wasn't a very good sister.'

'Which of you is older?'

'I'm older by two years.'

'Other siblings?' I'm hoping there may be someone Maddy confided in.

'No. Just us two.'

'Your parents are still living.' That's what Josh said anyway.

A sneer threatens. 'Oh Lord, yes. They live in a fancy retirement community near Houston.' She rolls her eyes. 'We hardly ever see them because they've got tennis and pickleball, and bridge club and book club, and trips here and there. It goes on and on. You call them and they hardly have time to say hello.' She sounds resentful. But then she collects herself. 'Someone will have to tell them what happened to Maddy. She was their favorite.'

'Josh said he'd call them.'

She clasps her hands in front of her, knuckles white. 'Good. I don't think I can do it.'

'One more question. Is Maddy a nickname?'

'Yes. Madelyn. She hated the name. Said it sounded like a name out of a Victorian novel.'

She thanks me for breaking the news to her and stands up. 'I guess I'd better get out to their house to find out what they want me to do. Call friends, plan the funeral.' Her voice wobbles when she says 'funeral' and tears spring to her eyes. 'This is just awful.'

'I'm so sorry,' I say. 'I wish we'd gotten to her in time.'

I walk her out to her car, holding an umbrella over her. 'By the way, I called your husband after I tried reaching you and asked him to tell you I had called. So he may get in touch to tell you.'

'I doubt that,' she says sourly.

'Did your husband not get along with your sister?'

'They were fine. He just wouldn't be bothered to call me.'

I have no reply to that.

She drives away just as Maria pulls up.

Maria jumps out and sprints inside. Her raincoat is drenched and drips on the floor when she takes it off. 'The forensics team had to call off the search. We couldn't see anything for the rain and figured we'd grind any evidence into the mud.'

She sits down at her desk with a cup of coffee and one of the kolaches I brought in this morning. 'I have to catch my breath and get warm.'

'Before too long we need to get back out to the Benson place. And maybe we ought to take Dusty home, too.' While she gathers herself, I tell her about my conversation with Eileen.

FOUR

Although it's the job of the Texas Department of Public Safety to investigate major crimes in small towns, the local DPS has a wide territory to cover and they're always pressed for time. The new district head, Leeland Reagan, talked a big game when he was first on the job, but he learned fast that he has a bigger job than he first imagined. He'd like to have his say on every crime in the district, but he simply doesn't have the manpower for it. A small-town murder could languish on the back burner until the clues dry up. Because of that, Reagan is mostly happy for me to take on an investigation. And I am, too. After all, I generally know the victim, or know something about them. So I end up investigating and am usually successful because I know my community.

But I don't know this victim or her family, and I hardly know where to begin looking into the crime. It might be that for the first time, I'll turn it over to the DPS. Or rather, bow out when they declare that they're going to investigate.

But as soon as the thought enters my head, I start considering why I don't want to do that. The officers sent to investigate would take it seriously, but they don't have the same sense of urgency that I do to solve crimes in my town.

Another reason not to relinquish control of the investigation is that it would disappoint Maria. She and I have our spats about procedure, but I have a high regard for her. She's a good officer and she feels a keen responsibility to investigate crimes in our community.

So ten minutes later, when the inevitable call comes in from Leland Reagan, I tell him I'd like to handle the investigation.

'No surprise there.' His tone is dry. He likes control and it's hard for him to relinquish it to me. The first time we met, we started on a bad note because he was arrogant and thought I should step aside. But he has learned that his area is wide and his manpower sparse. He also knows I've got enough sense to not make a mess of the investigation. 'Keep me informed,' he says brusquely. 'You're not always good at that.'

'I'll do my best.' I hesitate. 'And I may need some help on this one.'

'That's a new one,' he says. 'But just say the word.' He hangs up.

'Reagan?' Maria asks. She hasn't forgiven him for treating her like she was a clerk the first time they met.

'None other.' I tell her she needs to cut him some slack. 'He's learning.'

Now that I've committed to the investigation, I've got a few things to do right away. I want to return to the Benson house and take a thorough look at Maddy Benson's office. But first I Google her name. Madelyn Benson. She still has her travel agent website. It's got a photo of her, and the lead line is 'No matter where you need to go, we can guide you. Trust us.' The menu includes 'Travel Quotes,' which is a questionnaire on where and when the customer wants to travel; 'National and International,' with pictures of beaches and hotels; 'Resources,' which includes general insurance information, travel dos and don'ts, and packing suggestions; and 'Contact Us.' Under the last one, it says, 'We ensure complete discretion,' followed by an email address and a phone number. Seems like an odd assurance. Did she have clients who didn't want anyone to know where they were traveling?

I dial the number on the website from my cell phone. Her cell phone doesn't ring, so it isn't her personal number. Maybe it's an old office number from when she worked before she came to live in Jarrett Creek. But in case someone picks up email in the office, I send an email to the address listed. When I get her backpack, I'll check her laptop for further information.

I show Maria the website.

She looks it over. 'Professional.' Then she laughs and points to the phrase 'We ensure complete discretion.' 'These days people are so paranoid that their movements will be tracked that I guess they need to be reassured that no one will know where they're going.'

'You ready to go back over to look at Maddy Benson's office? I think we've given the family enough time to absorb the blow.'

She glances at the front windows, where we can see the rain still coming down in earnest. She shudders. 'I guess we have to.'

'It's lunchtime. I'll run over to Town Café and pick up some food. Maybe the rain will slack up by the time we eat.'

I bring back enchiladas for me and a hamburger for her, our usual fare.

Brick Freeman, my newest deputy, comes in as we're finishing up. Ridiculously good-looking, Brick is tall and muscular, with jet-black hair, twinkly blue eyes, and a dimple in his chin. I found that having him along on difficult interviews with young women makes things a lot smoother.

He eyes the remains of our lunch with a frown. He goes home for lunch because he insists on a healthy diet and thinks Maria and I eat too much junk food.

'Don't say a word,' I say. 'We've had a tough morning.'

I give Josh Benson a call to ask if it's OK for us to come. His voice is strained. 'Any time. There are a couple more things I'd like to ask you.'

I had intended to take Dusty home, but Brick says he doesn't mind watching him.

With the rain showing no sign of letting up, when we arrive at the Benson place, Maria and I dash from our squad car to the front door. Krista greets us at the door. Her eyes are red and her face blotched. She's the one who seems most affected by her mother-in-law's death.

I hear raised voices in the living room. Josh and his aunt Eileen.

'I don't know why she left or where she was going, OK?' Josh shouts. 'We didn't fight. She didn't say a word to us about leaving.'

'Why does she have to be so nasty?' Krista whispers. 'I mean he just found out his mamma was murdered.'

'Let's talk to them,' I say. We walk toward the living room.

Eileen's reply to Josh is acid. 'That's because you're always locked away in your room.'

'My door isn't locked.' Josh sounds desperate.

'But she knew you didn't like to be disturbed.'

Josh is standing at the fireplace and Eileen is sitting stiffly on the edge of the seat in an armchair. The coffee table is strewn with plates of half-eaten sandwiches. There's a bottle of wine in the middle of the table and three wine glasses, two of them empty.

Josh greets us with obvious relief.

'Sorry I caught you at a bad time,' I say.

'No, we were just . . .' His voice trails away.

Eileen jumps to her feet. 'Have you found out any more about what happened to Maddy?'

'Not yet. Josh, we need to search your mamma's apartment to

see if we can find any clue as to why she left and where she intended
to go.' And if she knew she was in immediate danger.

'I'm not sure you should be going through her things,' Eileen
says.

'Why not?' Josh asks.

I try to keep my patience. 'It's the best chance we have to find
out what happened to your sister.' Does she know something she
doesn't want us to find out?

'Maddy was a very private person. I don't think she would want
you poking around in her life. Anyway, don't you need a warrant?'
Eileen's voice is shrill.

'Not if Josh consents,' I say.

'Which I do,' he says, glaring at his aunt.

'Eileen, can you help me in the kitchen?' Krista sounds desperate
to divert her attention.

'What is it you need help with?' she asks sharply.

'Cleaning up. Could you bring in the dishes from the living
room?'

'I suppose if I must.' She glances from me to Josh.

'Have you gotten in touch with your grandparents?' I ask Josh.

He shakes his head. 'I called, but they didn't answer their cell.
I left a message for them to get back to me as soon as they can.'

'They're off flitting around, as usual.' Eileen says. The woman
is full of resentment.

'Let's go back to your mamma's apartment,' I say to Josh.

I can see that Eileen is torn between helping Krista and going
with us to keep an eye on what we're doing.

'Eileen?' Krista says. There's an unexpected firmness to her voice,
and Eileen reluctantly heads to the living room to gather dishes.

When we get into Maddy's apartment, I say to Josh, 'On the
phone, you said you had questions. I'll tell you what I can.'

'Where exactly was Mamma?'

I tell him she was on Tom Gainer's property. 'Do you know Mr
Gainer?'

'Never heard of him. What kind of person is he? Did he see what
happened?' Josh is suspicious.

'I've known Tom for a long time. He lives in Galveston and
usually only comes up on weekends. He has a little place out where
your mamma was found. I'll certainly look into why your mamma
was there.'

'Was she shot up close? Would she have known someone was going to shoot her?'

'It was a long-range shooting. But I got the impression from what she said to your aunt that she knew she was being pursued. Have you had a chance to think of anyone who might have been a threat to her?'

'I've gone over everyone I can think of, and no, I don't understand who would kill her.' He draws a deep breath and glances around the room. 'Everyone liked her. She was a good person.'

'Just keep it in mind.'

'One last question,' he says. 'When do you think they'll release her body? We need to plan her funeral.'

I tell him that will be up to the medical examiner. 'The autopsy shouldn't take too long. They'll call you.'

'OK, I guess that's all. Do you need anything else? I didn't come back in here after you left. It's too . . . I can't face it.' He glances around the room and then looks down at his shoes.

'You can leave that to Maria and me. We'll be searching for a while if you'd like to go.'

'If that's OK. You can come upstairs and find me if you need anything.'

I feel a sense of release once he's gone. It's a high-strung family. In Maddy's office, I'm struck again by how pleasant the room is. The plants, the photos, the books all give a feeling of peacefulness and content. So what happened to make her leave this cozy room this morning and end up dead?

I sit down in the desk chair and open the side drawers. They're full of folders in addition to the ones piled on her desk. 'Why don't you go through these?' I say to Maria. 'I want to take a look at her phone calls.'

While Maria searches the desk, I go through recent calls on Maddy's phone. Many of the numbers have a name attached to them, but several don't. There's one number that she called and received calls from frequently, in a Houston area code. Her folks lived in Houston, so maybe it's their number. No one has reached them, and if they answer, I'll have to break the news to them about their daughter's death.

The phone rings several times before a woman answers.

Without greeting me, she says, 'Yes, what do you need, Maddy?' Her voice is quiet, cautious even.

'This isn't Mrs Benson. I'm afraid I . . .' Before I can finish, whoever it is hangs up. I dial the number again, but it rings until the automatic operator comes on telling me that no one is answering.

'Strange.'

'What?' Maria asks. She's sorting file folders into stacks.

I tell her what happened. 'The woman asked what Maddy needed. I wonder if it was some kind of helpline? But when she answered my call, she didn't identify herself.'

Maria shakes her head. 'That is odd. You'll have to get the phone company to identify the number.'

I go back into the main house to ask Josh and Krista if they recognize the numbers and who they belong to.

Halfway up the stairs, I call out for Josh and Krista. Krista immediately comes down to see what I want. She goes back to the living room with me so I can show her the phone.

She is able to tell me that most of them are people Maddy was close to in Houston. 'She missed her friends,' Krista says. 'Talked to them a lot.'

Then I show her the number for the call I made that was shut down. 'Any idea who she'd be phoning at that number? Whoever it was, they exchanged calls several times over the last few days.'

She looks puzzled and shakes her head. 'No idea. Maybe it was somebody she was helping plan a trip?'

Krista could be right, but why would the woman hang up when she found out it wasn't Maddy on the line? And before I could tell her who I was and what had happened to Maddy?

'Would you say Maddy enjoyed working as a travel agent?'

Krista settles back on the sofa and ponders the question. 'I don't think she was doing much of it anymore. She stepped away from it when Luke was sick and needed so much care.'

'Was it possible she was getting back into it?'

'If she was, she didn't mention it to me.'

'In general, what were her interests? What did you talk about over meals?'

Krista bites her lower lip. 'You know, the usual. She'd want to know how our work was going. She'd describe things she'd read. Articles about all kinds of things. Science. Health. But her biggest interest was politics. She got riled up over court rulings and Texas politics.'

'Were there any disagreements about that? It can cause bitter disputes in families these days.'

'No. We all pretty much had the same opinions. Josh was maybe more conservative in economics, but nothing dramatic.'

'Did the three of you do anything together as a family? Go out? Go on trips?'

Krista sighs. 'Not really. Every now and then, Maddy and I watched a movie together and we had a few series that we watched. Mostly fem jep stuff.'

'Fem jep?'

She smiles. 'Females in jeopardy. You know, things where the wife thinks her husband has committed a crime or is cheating on her, and then she gets in trouble when she starts looking into it.'

I grin. 'Fem jep. OK. And your husband doesn't watch with you?'

'Josh doesn't like TV, except for the History Channel and not much of that. He gets wrapped up in his work and spends a lot of hours at his desk.'

'The two of you ever take a vacation with Maddy?'

'Not since Luke died. The last time was a couple of months before that. Luke loved New Orleans and he said he'd like to go one more time. So we drove down there and spent a couple of days.' She shakes her head. 'It was a tough trip. He was really too sick to travel, but we tried to make the best of it.'

'Would you say Maddy was happy?' I'm wondering if Maddy was calling a helpline, since the woman who answered asked how she could help.

She considers the question. 'Luke hasn't been gone that long, and there were a few hard months before he died. Maddy stayed right with him all that time, which wore her down. So she was burned out. After he died, she seemed to feel some relief. We all did. He was suffering. Since then, she hasn't seemed unhappy exactly, but sometimes she seems serious.'

I refer to the calls on her phone again. 'Who would you say was her closest friend?'

'There were two women she was close to. Carol Warren and Joan somebody. Vincent, that's it. Joan Vincent.'

I thank her and go back to Maddy's study apartment. Maria is standing in the office with her hands on her hips. 'OK, I've got the files sorted.'

'Anything that jumps out?'

'Most of them are household bills for the house she and her husband lived in before they moved here; some about a previous car they owned, old tax filings, that sort of thing. And, of course, there's a giant file containing her husband's medical information and a smaller one for herself. But there are a few that might be interesting. I've set them in that stack.' She indicates a few folders much smaller than the stacks.

'I'll take a look at them.'

'Honestly, I imagine if there's anything helpful, it will be on her computer. I'm itching to get my hands on it,' Maria says. 'For now, I'll tackle her bedroom to see if she stashed anything there that might help.'

I'm happy for her to do that. She has a meticulous eye. She'll do a good job searching the dresser drawers, the bedside stands, and the closet to look for things Maddy might have stowed away.

'Good. I'll take the kitchen.' That's often where people jot down phone numbers, addresses, reminders that might help. I'm just getting started when my phone rings. It's Brick.

'What's up?'

'Dusty is having a nervous breakdown with the thunder, but other than that, it's quiet. I wondered if you needed any help.'

'We're almost done here. It's not a big place. Do you mind taking Dusty to my place? He'll be better off there, even if he's by himself. He'll crawl under the bed.'

'This storm is so loud I might crawl under there with him,' Brick says. He's right. The storm is raging outside. It even sounds like hail is mixed in with the rain.

In the kitchen, I find a printout of names and phone numbers and I put it aside to match later with her phone. There's a junk drawer, but no stray notes in it; just the usual clutter. I then look in the living-room side tables. One drawer is full of travel pamphlets, everything from South America to Europe. The other contains decks of cards and a couple of board games – Monopoly and Scrabble.

I peek in on Maria and ask how she's faring.

'Nothing so far. I'm going to go through her pockets to see if she might have left any notes to herself or business cards.'

I go in to take a closer look at the books on Maddy's shelves, shaking out every book for stray notes. Josh's books have pride of place, big hardcover books published by a university press. One is called *THE INEVITABLE WAR: A Turbulent March into the Twentieth Century*. The second is *UNEASY PEACE: The Stumbles of Weary Adversaries*. Dry subjects. I open the first. It's dedicated to his mother and father. There's a Table of Contents, a Foreword, and an Index. A scholarly book. I read a few lines and it's clear he writes for someone other than the casual reader. The blurbs on the back cover are by scholars at various universities, and they attest to the worthiness of the book.

The second is the same, but dedicated to his wife.

Then I turn to Krista's books, written as Olivia Cartwright. Twenty-two paperback books in all, what the blurbs on the cover call 'contemporary romance.' *Tomorrow We Love, A Taste of Love, Never Love Again, The Mystery of Tanya's Love.* The covers feature smartly dressed young women who look purposeful but have a good bit more skin showing than is probably true in real life, and young men with roguish leers, wearing jeans and T-shirts that show off unlikely muscles. She seems awfully practical-minded for someone whose imagination runs to such fanciful subjects. I wonder how she gets her ideas for her books.

The other books on Maddy's shelves are sober-minded – books about social issues, politics, and biographies of political figures. There are a few current titles concentrating on feminist concerns and one concerning the current Supreme Court. As Krista said, there's no question where her political opinions lay.

Finally, I sit down at her desk to look more closely at the file folders Maria indicated were more interesting. One of them contains information relating to Josh and Krista as authors. Flyers for reading events featuring their books, copies of and printouts of newspaper reviews, things I'm sure both Krista and Josh will want to see. They may not know she kept these things, and it gives an indication of her pride in them.

Then I hit gold. Given what happened to her, it's no surprise, but the contents are shocking. The slim folder is dubbed 'Correspondence' and contains notes and letters. Some are handwritten on stray pieces of paper, some on stationery, and a few are printed out from a computer or typewriter. They're threats and admonitions. They're as baffling as they are hateful.

You think you've been clever, but I know who you are, and I know what you do. God knows, too. Unsigned.

I saw you at the march and I hope you burn in hell. You're dead to me. I thought you were a good person, but you're not, and you're not welcome in my home again. Libby Robinson.

Some of them are so vile I can't imagine the kind of person who felt compelled to write. They refer to town hall meetings she attended, marches, and articles she wrote. But there's nothing specific enough for me to understand the vitriol.

I find another folder with copies of articles Maddy wrote. They are mostly for online publications that favor women's choice. But she did have one in a prominent women's magazine and another in a newspaper opinion piece.

Maria comes in holding a slip of paper. 'I found something that might be interesting,' she says. 'I don't know what it means.' She hands it to me and I read the scribbled note – 'new clinic' – and a phone number.

'I looked up the area code and it's in New Mexico.'

'Nothing more?'

She shakes her head. 'Could it be that she has some kind of medical issue and she's found a clinic?' Maria asks. 'And then I found this in one of her jacket pockets.' It's a business card for an organization called The Time Is Now. The name on the card is Isabella Lopez.

'We'll give this woman a call,' I say. 'Look at these.' I hand her the folder containing threats. While she reads it, I go through the other drawers in the desk. The only thing I find of interest is a small collection of business cards in a plastic bag. I add the card Maria found to it.

'Wow, these are some awful letters,' Maria says. 'Most of them anonymous, of course.'

'I'm going to have to talk to some of her friends to see if they know what stirred people up so much and if they know why she was threatened.'

We pack up Maddy's phone, the folder of hate mail, the note Maria found, and the business cards. It's enough to get us started on finding out who Maddy really was. We need to find someone to tell us who might have targeted her. I keep going back to the phone call I made where the person who answered hung up. I hope we don't find ourselves stonewalled by others.

FIVE

Just as we're about to walk back into the main house, Eileen comes into Maddy's apartment. Rain mixed with hail is making a racket on the windows and she raises her voice to be heard. 'Have you found what you're looking for?' As if we're burglars.

Maria makes an exasperated sound. Eileen's getting on both our nerves. 'Not yet,' I tell her. 'We don't want to be any more intrusive here, so we're taking some of the things back to headquarters to go through more thoroughly.'

'You'll need a plastic bag,' she says. 'This rain . . .' She goes over to Maddy's kitchen and retrieves a garbage bag. I tuck the things in it.

'Let's sit down for a minute,' I say. 'I have a few questions.'

We sit at Maddy's small dining table in an alcove off the kitchen.

'Do you know any of your sister's friends in Houston?' I ask.

'No, I never met any of them. But I know she and Luke had couples in Texas they did things with. They lived there a long time. You think one of them might know something?'

'I'll be contacting them. Did she ever say whether she made friends here in Jarrett Creek?'

'She never said, and I guess I didn't ask. I suppose Krista would know if anyone does. Josh certainly wouldn't know. His head is always in the clouds.'

Maria says, 'I have a question. Do you know why the family moved to Jarrett Creek? It seems sort of out of the way.'

'Tsk. That's exactly what I said when Maddy told me she wanted to move here. I guess it was all right with Josh and Krista because they can work anywhere, but I was still surprised that Maddy thought it was a good idea. I thought she'd be in Houston forever.'

'Wait,' I say. 'You're telling me it was your sister's idea to move here?'

'That's right. I thought it was foolish, because Luke was very sick and there were no big hospitals close by. And they were leaving their close circle behind.'

'What did she say?'

'She said she had done her research and she thought this was a nice town. She said there was a good hospital in College Station associated with the university, and it's not that far away, so Luke would have good medical care. And the real estate was cheap, and there was that lake . . . I personally didn't get why she'd want to leave Houston after all those years, but she was stubborn.'

'And you said the kids came with her, not the other way around?'

She throws up her hands. 'No accounting for the way some people decide to do things. It was none of my business, so I kept my mouth shut.'

I doubt that. But she's right; it seems like an unlikely move. I had assumed Josh and Krista were the ones who wanted to come here and that Maddy and her husband went along with it.

'Maddy has a daughter. How did she react to their moving here?'

'I have no idea what Hannah's thoughts were. That whole family has their own way of doing things. Josh called her, and she'll be coming tomorrow, so you can ask her yourself.'

'Younger or older?' I ask.

'Several years younger. Maddy had trouble getting pregnant the second time, so Hannah is only twenty-two.'

'What does she do in California?'

'Something in the movies. I don't know what. Film editing, I think somebody said. Don't ask me, they never tell me anything.'

I get up. 'I'd like to talk to Josh again. Can you ask him to come down?'

She puts a hand to her heart. 'And disturb his precious work? I wouldn't dare.'

'I'll go,' Maria says. She has no patience for such fake drama.

'His office is the first door on the right at the top of the stairs,' Eileen says.

When Maria comes back with Josh in tow, he's in his stocking feet. Casual.

'We've had time to take a look at your mamma's desk and didn't find anything helpful. But I do have a couple more questions.'

Eileen looks alert, as if she has every intention of staying right with us while we question him.

'If you'd give us a minute,' I say to her.

'Can I bring my things in here?' she asks. 'I'd like to stay here in Maddy's apartment.'

'That's up to Josh,' I say, 'But it would have to wait until we're finished here.'

She looks predictably annoyed.

'Aunt Eileen, why don't you sleep in our spare room upstairs? You know where it is.'

'Well, I suppose, if you insist.'

'I do. You're welcome here. We've all had a shock.'

Her expression softens. 'I guess that will be OK.'

When she leaves, Maria, Josh, and I settle in Maddy's living-room area, Maria and me on the sofa and Josh in an armchair.

'I had the impression that your folks moved in with you when your daddy got sick, but Eileen said it was the other way round.'

'She's right. Krista and I were renting in Houston near my folks, and we were thinking of buying a place, but we were tired of living in the city. When my daddy got sick, Mamma said she wanted to move here. So we bought this place. It had the apartment, and she said it suited her. She knew Daddy wasn't going to live long.'

'How long ago was that?'

'Little over a year ago.'

'So your daddy has been gone six months?'

'Eight months. He didn't live long after we moved. I think the move was hard on him.'

Jarrett Creek is my home, and I like it, but it seems like an unlikely place for a young couple, and I'm not altogether sure he's telling me the whole story. 'Do you know how your mamma decided on Jarrett Creek?'

He chews the side of his lip. 'Not exactly.'

'Did she know anyone here?'

He's tapping his fingers on the arm of the chair and looking off as if trying to remember. 'Look, I don't pay as much attention to everyday matters as I should. When I'm working on a book, I get deep into it. I vaguely remember Mamma saying she knew somebody here. Or maybe she'd met somebody who told her it was a nice town.' He shrugs. 'Maybe Krista remembers.'

'So who owns the place?'

'Krista and I do. Like I said, we'd been planning to buy, and I have to say this place was a lot more affordable than things we'd looked at in the city.'

'You like it here?'

'Chief Craddock, I don't really care where I am. I like it quiet, so I can write and do research and not be bothered by much. It's quiet here, so it suits me fine.'

'I noticed the two books you wrote cover the time between the two world wars. What are you working on now?'

His expression undergoes a change, more alert, as if he's on firmer footing. 'The first one was about Germany after World War I, the second covers the rest of Europe after the war, and this third one will be about how the United States developed afterwards. How it became more isolationist, and the effect that had on our allies and . . .' He pauses. 'Anyway, you don't want to hear the details, but that's the gist of it.'

'How much of it is written?'

He shrugs. 'I'm halfway through my outline, although things always come up that change the narrative.'

'Do you do all your research on the computer, or do you go to a university setting?'

'A lot of it is on the computer, but Texas A&M has a good library. I go over there from time to time.'

I've gone off on a tangent with him, probing for anything that might give a hint as to what happened to Maddy Benson. Time to reel it back in. 'What did your mamma think of your books? She must have been proud.'

'I think she was. My daddy was the one who was really pleased. I'm so glad I got them published before he passed.'

'You said you like it here in Jarrett Creek,' Maria says. 'And Krista? Is she happy?'

He makes a sound of distress. 'You'll have to ask her.'

He tells us he'll have her come down to the apartment.

Of the three of them, Krista is the only one who looks truly shattered by Maddy's death. She's composed, but pale and haggard-looking, as if she's been up for days.

'Sorry to bother you again, but we're still trying to get a handle on the details. Josh thinks you might be able to tell us more about Maddy than he can.'

'Probably.' Her mouth twists wryly. 'Josh doesn't exactly live in the world of other people – unless they are from the past. So, how can I help?'

'I understand that it was Maddy's idea to move here. Do you know what prompted that decision?'

'It was . . .' Pink appears high on her cheeks. 'She . . .' She sighs. 'Josh didn't tell you?'

'He said he wasn't sure.'

'Oh, he was sure. He was just being discreet.' She crosses her arms across her chest. Protective stance. 'It was because of me. I was having an affair, and Maddy thought . . . no, it was actually Luke who thought that if we moved out of the city, into a less "provocative" environment, I'd be less tempted to stray.' Her chin lifts in a show of defiance.

I'm surprised by her candor, but I'm not sure what this might have to do with Maddy's death. 'How did they know you were having an affair?'

'Josh told them. We were considering a divorce, and he told his folks. I have to give them credit. They didn't come off as judgmental, although I'm sure they would have preferred to think it was all my fault. But they asked if we'd tried marriage counseling and asked if we thought there was any way to heal the marriage. It was Luke who suggested we might try moving to a small town.'

'And you were OK with it?'

She suddenly tears up. 'Not really, but I adored Luke – and Maddy, too. My own parents were . . .' She hesitates. 'Let's just say they weren't great people, and Maddy and Luke made me feel cared for. In a way, I almost think I married Josh because I liked his folks so much. They were always wonderful to me. That's why when I knew Luke was really ill and likely to die within the year, I wanted to give him that gift, to think that Josh and I might stay together. Seemed like a small price to pay.'

'Has it worked out better?'

She shakes her head. 'Not really. I don't hate Josh; we just want different things.'

'So you ended your affair.'

She hesitates. 'Yes.'

I'm not sure I believe her.

'Do you think you'll divorce now?' Maria asks.

It takes a few seconds for her to answer. 'We're taking it a day at a time. And right now, with Maddy being killed, I can't really focus on what comes next. I want to support Josh. He's more fragile than he seems. Lives in a different world than most of us. Plus . . .' She hesitates. 'He might have money problems when we split up. I don't know whether Maddy had money to leave him. We'll find that out.'

'Why would he have money problems?'

'Well, his books sold well, but they're scholarly works, so they take a long time to write, and they don't make as much money as mine do.'

'I counted twenty-two of your books on Maddy's shelf. That's quite a few.'

'Actually, those are just the paperbacks. I've also published another twenty online. They've been successful.' She smiles a tired smile. 'I'll offer Josh alimony. I don't want him to have financial worries.'

This is news to me. I didn't realize romance writers would make enough money to support a family. But then, I've heard of her, so probably her books are widely popular.

'Back to Maddy. Do you know why she chose Jarrett Creek in particular? Did she know anyone here?'

Krista considers the question. 'It's funny, I hadn't thought about it in a while, but I remember she said she had met someone from here and that she thought it might be a nice town to live in.'

'Did she say who it was or how she met them?'

'No.'

'Do you remember a name?'

She shakes her head.

'Did she belong to a church? Any other kind of social activities? Playing cards . . . anything?'

She glances between us. 'Maddy wasn't really a churchgoer. In Houston, she played bridge and was in a couple of book clubs, but she hadn't gotten involved with that here. She borrowed Josh's car to go back to Houston a few times, and I think she met her friends at an outlet mall between here and Houston. But we haven't been here that long. I expect eventually she would have met people.'

'Have you met any of your neighbors?' Maria asks.

She nods to the north of us. 'Kay Springer next door invited me to have coffee with some of the neighborhood ladies last month. They were nice.'

'Was Maddy included?'

'Yes, but she begged off. Said she thought they might all be younger women and she wouldn't have anything in common with them.'

'Have you made other friends?'

'I've met a couple of women I like, but my social life has been limited. It sounds funny, but if you don't have kids, you don't necessarily get to meet other women.'

'Have you joined a church?' Maria asks.

'No. I said Maddy wasn't a churchgoer. I should have said none of us are.' She cocks her head. 'Why do you ask that?'

Maria shrugs. 'I'm Catholic and I was curious about the statue in your front yard.'

Krista smiles. 'The statue was here when we bought the place and I sort of like it. It's peaceful, so we kept it.'

I tell Krista that we're done in the apartment. 'We'll let you know if we have any more questions.'

'I'll be here. I'm not going anywhere in this weather.'

'One more thing,' I say. 'Do you want me to keep quiet about your being an author? I know some women in town would be thrilled if they knew you lived here, but I don't have to blab it.'

She smiles. 'That's nice of you, but I don't care if you tell people. I didn't intend to hide behind a pen name; I picked out a different name because I thought it sounded more like a romance writer's name.'

She walks toward the door to go back to her part of the house, turning back at the last minute to look at the room as if she's saying goodbye.

It's still raining heavily, casting a dark gloom even though it's only five o'clock, so when we get back to headquarters, I send Maria and Brick home. I'm driving to Bryan to see my girlfriend Wendy tonight, but I don't have to leave until seven. But no sooner are Maria and Brick gone than I get a call that there's been a wreck out on the dam road, and someone has been hurt. The highway patrol is on its way, but ETA is a half hour and I can be there in five minutes.

By the time an ambulance has arrived to care for the injured party, and I've sorted out who to ticket for the accident – a couple of teenaged boys joyriding who failed to stop at a stop sign and clipped a car pulling out on to the road – it's time to get home to change.

At home, I find my dog cowering under the bed. I'm glad we're off to Wendy's because he adores her, and it might take his mind off his misery with the nasty weather. The rain is still coming down, although the sky is lightening to the west.

Wendy greets me, as always, as if she's thrilled to see me. We've been together for almost two years and none of the thrill has abated. Although Dusty is wet and has muddy paws, Wendy hugs him and scratches his ears. He's in heaven. Tonight we don't linger on the porch like we sometimes do, because the rain is slashing in sideways.

'It's like a biblical flood,' she says once we're inside with the door closed. We go into the kitchen where she says she's trying out a new recipe. She makes the best lasagna in the world, and I'd be satisfied with that every time she cooks, but she likes to try new things. That's who she is in every way – a woman who likes to explore new things.

I sit at the kitchen table with a glass of merlot while she puts the finishing touches on what she calls Chicken Marengo. She gets some old towels for Dusty and gives him a fresh treat from the freezer that she keeps for when we visit.

'Tell me about your day,' she says. 'I can't talk while I'm cooking a new recipe, but I can listen.'

'Unfortunate day,' I say, and I tell her that a woman was shot and killed.

She pauses and gives me a concerned look. 'How awful. Who is she?'

That's the question, isn't it? I tell Wendy that Maddy and her family are relatively new to the area, and I don't know much about them.

'Interesting point, though,' I say. 'The woman's daughter-in-law is a romance writer. Ever heard of Olivia Cartwright?'

She laughs. 'Of course I have. Anyone who's ever been in an airport would have heard of her. That's the woman's daughter-in-law?'

'Yep.'

'What is she doing living in Jarrett Creek? Not that there's anything wrong with Jarrett Creek,' she adds. 'It just seems a little out of the way.'

'I thought so, too. Apparently, they had their reason for moving here. The woman's son is a writer, too. But his books are historical.'

We carry the food into the dining room. I'd be happy eating in the kitchen, but Wendy insists on serving meals in the dining room, even when it's only the two of us. We don't go back to the subject of Maddy Benson, and instead discuss a weekend getaway we're planning, to attend a bluegrass festival in west Texas next month. I know she loves bluegrass music, and I like the fiddle tunes. This is the first time we've decided to attend a festival.

I usually stay over, but I have to be up early tomorrow, so we call it a night early and I'm home by ten.

SIX

Thursday morning

My neighbor Loretta Singletary comes by most mornings with baked goods that she makes for folks in the neighborhood. It used to be every day, but she has branched off into other interests. I'm not surprised to see her sitting on my porch when I get back from the pasture where I see to my cows every morning. I'm sure she's heard about the murder; she may even have been the first to hear. She'll want details.

She's brought coffee cake this morning, laced with cinnamon and nuts. We sit in my rocking chairs on the porch and drink coffee and eat the coffee cake. Or rather, I eat and drink. Sometimes I wonder what Loretta exists on, as I hardly ever see her eat. But she's energetic, so she has to get sustenance somehow.

'You going to tell me about this woman that got killed?' she asks. 'It's upsetting to think about somebody being gunned down like that.'

'How did you hear about it?'

'You know Ruthie Beal? Her cousin is married to Junior Addison, the medical examiner over in Bobtail, and he told her what had happened. And Ruthie is best friends with Jolene Ramsey, and you know Jolene can't keep a secret for anything.' There's no stopping the grapevine. One way or another, things get out.

'The woman's name was Maddy Benson. Have you heard of her?'

'Not at all. First time I heard the name was when Jolene called. I don't even know what church she belonged to.'

'She and her family haven't been here long. Maybe they haven't had a chance to join a church.' That's vague enough.

'So what have you found out so far?'

'Hardly anything. But I do know one thing that might interest you.' I tell her that the woman who writes under the pen name Olivia Cartwright is the dead woman's daughter-in-law. 'Krista Benson is her real name.'

Suddenly, Loretta's flustered, hands fluttering to her chest, her cheeks getting pink. 'Really? Oh, my goodness. I love her books! I wish I could meet her. Not to bother her or anything, just to tell her how much I enjoy them.' She pauses. 'I guess this isn't a good time to be gushing all over her with her mother-in-law just murdered.' She cocks her head. 'Why in the world did she move here?'

'Somebody told her mother-in-law it was a nice place. Maddy's husband was dying, and I think she wanted to settle down where it was quiet.'

Loretta blinks. 'Just because the mother-in-law wanted to move here doesn't mean Olivia Cartwright had to move, too. They must be a close-knit family.'

'Not particularly, but I think with the daddy being so sick, the kids wanted to help. And they bought a place in that new subdivision that had an in-law apartment.'

'It sounds like a practical arrangement. But it's still odd that they landed here. Who was it who told her it was a nice place to live?'

'The daughter-in-law didn't know who it was. Maybe you can find out.'

Loretta frowns. She likes to know what's going on in town, and I expect it bothers her that someone knew Maddy Benson and she doesn't know who it is. 'I'll ask around,' she says. She hops up. 'I'd better get going. You tell Krista and her husband to call me if they need anything. I'll be happy to arrange some meals for them.'

I tell her I'll let them know, but I have a strong sense that they aren't people who would like to have ladies bringing them hot dishes.

There's a lot to look into today, and when I get to the station, I make out a list of assignments. While I'm doing that, Maria bustles in, looking more energetic than usual. She likes a challenge, and Maddy Benson's shooting presents one.

I set her to work combing through the files more closely, looking for anything that triggers her curiosity. 'Even the ones with household expenses information. Just keep an eye out for anything unusual.' She'll know what to do. She has an eye for detail.

'What are you going to do?' she asks.

'I'm going to talk to the neighbors to find out if anyone saw any strangers hanging around, or if they saw Maddy when she left the house yesterday morning.'

*   *   *

I start with Kay Springer, who invited Krista for coffee with the neighborhood women. I called first to be sure she was home, and she said to come on by. 'I'm reorganizing my kitchen cabinets, so I'm glad to have an excuse to stop and sit down.' It's only nine o'clock so she must have gotten an early start.

She's a tall, bony woman in her forties, with short dark hair shot with gray. I've seen her around town but don't know her. 'Excuse the way I look,' she says, as she leads me into her kitchen. 'I don't usually wear this old T-shirt, but I figured there was no need to dress up for this job.' She waves a hand at the countertops stacked with dishes and pots and pans.

'I admire that you tackled it,' I say. 'My wife died a few years ago, and goodness knows what's in my cabinets.'

She laughs and pours us a cup of coffee. 'Let's sit out on the back porch. After that rain yesterday, it's cooler.' Which means it's eighty degrees instead of ninety-five.

We sit in sturdy wooden chairs around a wooden table. She sighs as she sits down. 'I thought reorganizing the kitchen would take my mind off missing my kids, but no such luck. The older two are on summer jobs, one in Houston, one in Dallas. The youngest one starts college in the fall, and she's gone off for the summer working in Guatemala, helping to build a school. I'm proud of her, of course, but I wish she'd thought of a do-good project closer to home.' She gives herself a shake. 'OK, I'll stop feeling sorry for myself and chewing your ear. I suppose you're here about my neighbor.'

'That's right. Trying to get some idea of who she was.'

'I'm afraid you're not going to get it from me, or anyone else in the neighborhood. None of us knew her at all. Well, that's not quite true. Giselle Russell down the street said she saw her out walking from time to time and they'd stop to say hello.'

'You never saw her around?'

She shakes her head. 'I work in Bobtail at the courthouse, so I leave early most days and get home late. The only reason I'm home today is that I took the week off to take my daughter to the airport in Houston the day before yesterday. I squeezed in a couple of extra days to tackle some projects.'

'You work at the courthouse. Do you know Jenny Sandstone?'

'Of course I do! She's a force of nature, that one. You know her?'

'She lives next door to me.'

'Like I said, I'm not around much during the week.' She frowns.

'Seems like I would have seen my neighbor on the weekends, though. Different patterns, I suppose.'

'Let me try you on this. Have you noticed anyone hanging around the neighborhood that you don't know? Strange car?'

'I really haven't. I wish I could help you. They say she was shot out on FM 1362. What in the world was she doing out there?'

'That's what I'm trying to find out.' I get up. 'Time for me to let you get back to your cabinets. I'd appreciate it if you'd keep your ear tuned in case anyone mentions seeing something out of the ordinary.'

'I'll sure do that.' She stands up and groans, stretching. 'I'm too old for hauling all these dishes around.'

She has no idea.

I continue to knock on the doors of houses closest to the Benson house, but no one is home. But when I get to the house where Kay Springer told me Giselle Russell lives, a man answers the door and introduces himself as Ray Russell. He's in his sixties, bright-eyed and congenial. He invites me in and immediately asks if I'm here about Maddy Benson.

'That's right. Did you know her at all?'

'I didn't, but my wife says she talked to her a few times. Let me get her.'

I hear grumbling from the interior of the house, but when Giselle Russell comes bustling in, she's all smiles. 'Sorry, you caught me trying to wrestle a chicken into submission.' She giggles. 'I mean, a dead chicken.' She laughs harder, and her husband and I can't help joining in. 'No, that sounds wrong. I mean I'm trying to figure out how to spatchcock a chicken. That's what the recipe says, and I don't even know what that means.'

'I can't help you with that,' I say.

'I googled it, and I have to say the YouTube video isn't much help. But you don't need to hear that. Let's go into the living room.'

'Want me to give the bird a try?' Ray Russell says.

'Be my guest. You can become the spatchcock champion.'

He laughs and disappears in the direction of the kitchen.

Giselle offers coffee, but I've had plenty, so she sits, directing me to the sofa. She's a woman in her fifties with her hair in a ponytail and wearing shorts and a bright pink blouse. I could have imagined from her sunny disposition that the room would be decorated in bright colors, and I'm right. Splashes of yellow and orange and red accentuate the sofa and chairs. There's a big fireplace that this time of year has decorative greenery in front of it. A pleasant room. The sofa is comfortable.

'So you're here about that poor woman who got killed,' she says, suddenly sober.

'That's right. Your neighbor Kay Springer said you talked to her a bit.'

'Just to say hello. I must say she was never particularly friendly. I don't mean she was rude, just didn't seem to want to get to know me. I asked her over for coffee, and she said she was too busy.'

'Did she say what she did that kept her busy?'

She shakes her head. 'She didn't seem to welcome questions. I told her a bit about myself, hoping she'd open up, but she didn't.'

'When did you usually see her?'

'Early morning. That's when I take a walk. I try to walk as far as the lake and back most days. It's a couple of miles.'

'Did you walk with her or meet her?'

'I think of myself as an early bird, but she was usually coming back from the lake when I was leaving for my walk. Around seven thirty.'

'Did you happen to see her yesterday morning?'

'I wouldn't have. I had to go to Bobtail for a dentist appointment, so I didn't walk yesterday.'

'Did you ever see her walking with anybody?' It's a stab in the dark.

'As a matter of fact, I did. She was with another woman a couple of times.'

'Did you recognize the other woman?'

'No, she didn't look familiar. And I didn't stop to talk because they seemed in serious conversation.'

I ask her to describe the woman. She says she was younger than Maddy, tall and thin, with long hair. 'Pretty. But I'd say intense looking. She gestured a lot with her hands while she talked. Like I said, I didn't stop to say hello, just nodded.'

'So it wasn't her daughter-in-law.'

'No, I met her daughter-in-law when Kay Springer invited some of the neighborhood women over for coffee one morning to introduce her.'

'When was the last time you saw Maddy with this woman?'

She blows out a breath. 'Gosh, it's hard to say. Couple of weeks maybe.'

'You walk past the Benson house on your way to the lake. Did you happen to notice any cars in the driveway – like if the young woman had driven here?'

'I'm sorry, I don't remember.'

'Ever notice any strangers in the neighborhood recently?'

She sits up abruptly. 'As a matter of fact, I did. Last week. I told my husband when I got back from my walk that I'd seen somebody parked on the side of the road. A man. It kind of seemed creepy, but I don't know why. He didn't get out of his car, or look at me funny or anything. It's just that we're out of the way here, and you don't usually see strangers parked on the road.'

'Did you get a good look at him?'

She laughs nervously. 'I didn't want to stare. I was afraid he'd . . . I don't know what. Saying it out loud makes me sound paranoid, but I've heard about men attacking women, and there was nobody around, so I thought it best to scoot on past. But I do remember he had kind of long hair. Not like a hippy from back in the day, but down to his collar. Brown hair. Youngish. Perhaps thirties, but I may be wrong. Hard to tell. The older I get, the younger everybody else seems to get.'

She tells me he was on the side of the road across from the houses, bordering on a wooded area, and facing south, as if he was ready to leave the subdivision.

'What kind of car was he driving?'

'Nothing fancy. So many cars look alike these days. And it was gray. Half the cars on the road are gray.'

'You didn't get a license number?'

'Wouldn't that have been a smart thing to do! But I didn't.'

'I did.' Her husband comes around the corner, wiping his hands on a kitchen towel. 'Sorry, I wasn't eavesdropping; I was coming in to say the chicken has been beaten into submission.'

They exchange a delighted look and laugh.

'I'll go get the information,' he says. 'I stuck it in the kitchen drawer.'

'If you can find it,' Giselle says. 'That drawer . . .'

While we wait, I ask if she had ever seen the car before.

'Not that I recall. The only reason I noticed was because he was sitting at the side of the road. Just seemed odd.'

Ray Russell comes back with a piece of paper that contains the make and model of the car and the license number.

'Sure makes my job easy,' I say. 'What compelled you to make a note of it?'

'Detail-oriented. My wife and I own a couple of motels outside of Houston, and when we used to work on-site, I made a habit of noticing the details of the cars that came in. Wanted to make sure there was never any trouble, or that if there was, I'd know who had been there. We decided to hire a manager and retire somewhere quiet where I can fish and my wife can do her pottery. She has a nice studio in the garage,' he says with pride. I make a mental note to ask to see her work once I'm done with this case. 'Anyway, when I saw the car sitting there, I wrote down the information. Force of habit.'

I thank them for their help and tell them if they hear anything that might add to my knowledge of what happened to give me a call.

SEVEN

Back at headquarters, I run the plates on the car that the Russells noticed parked along the road. It belongs to a Gunther Schrage in Houston. But I find that Gunther Schrage died three months ago of a heart attack at the age of sixty-seven. His obituary lists a thirty-nine-year-old son, Jason, and a thirty-six-year-old daughter, Karen. I look them up and they both live in Houston. Could be that the son was using the car. What would he have been doing in Jarrett Creek?

I hadn't wanted to go to Houston, but with Maddy Benson's closest friends living there, and now this car's owner located there, it seems best for me to make the trip. It's a little over an hour's drive, so I can make it there and back by late this afternoon.

Maria is still going through Maddy's folders. 'Lot of paper here,' she complains. 'And nothing interesting.'

'I need to go to Houston to question Maddy Benson's friends.'

'I could come along.'

'I don't think both of us need to go. You hold the fort in case somebody else gets shot.'

'That's not funny.' She cocks her head. 'You think Maddy's kids called her friends and told them she was killed?'

Somehow I doubt it. 'I'll find out. I'm going to call them to see if they're available today for me to talk to. And I guess if they haven't heard, I'll have to break the news.'

'You're going now?'

'The sooner the better. And there's something else.' I tell her about the man watching from the side of the road, and the information I found on the car. 'I could call, but if it was this Jason Schrage who was sitting outside the house, I want to see in person how he reacts to questions.'

I only reach one of Maddy's friends, Carol Warren. Unfortunately, she hasn't been told that Maddy was killed, and I spend some time consoling her. She sobs that of course she'll talk to me. I ask if she knows Joan Vincent, and I tell her I couldn't reach her.

'I'll keep calling her,' Carol says. 'This is the worst news. She'll be so upset.'

I'm on the road by eleven. As always, the traffic in Houston slows me down and I don't get to Carol Warren's house until one o'clock. She opens the door so fast it's as if she is on the lookout for me.

'I was sort of hoping you were a crank caller and that Maddy really wasn't dead,' she says. A plump, matronly woman, with hair dyed a dark brown, her eyes are red from weeping. She leads me into her living room, a mishmash of old and new furniture that somehow looks like it belongs together. 'I'll bet you could use a sandwich,' she says. 'You OK with turkey? That's all I've got.'

'That's nice of you, but you don't have to feed me.'

'Yes, I do. I have to do something. I'm too upset to sit around. What do you want on it? Mayonnaise, mustard, tomato, pickle?'

'Whatever you want to throw on it,' I say. 'Maybe easy on the mustard.'

She attempts a smile. She's back before long with coffee and a pile of sandwich halves. 'Eat first, and then you ask me whatever you want.'

I'm grateful for the coffee and only take a few bites of the sandwich before I wipe my mouth and sit back. 'How long have you known Maddy?'

'I was thinking about that before you got here. We met when our kids were in grade school together. That's well over twenty years. Josh was in the same grade as my Travis. They were pals when they were in grade school, but as they got older, they had different interests. Trav was into sports and Josh was sort of a nerd.' She smiles fondly. 'But Maddy and I stuck. We got along from the minute we met.'

'Did you share interests, or what?'

'Mostly, we shared an off-beat sense of humor and got annoyed by the same things at the school. You know, teachers we thought were smart and those we thought were idiots. And parents who thought their kids were the only kids ever born and could do no wrong.' She raises her eyebrows.

'Maddy was a travel agent, I understand.'

'She didn't get into that until the kids were teenagers. Before that, she was active in school support activities – PTA, fundraisers, that kind of thing. But you know, kids get older and more independent, and I think she and Luke were struggling for money, so she got a job because she wanted to be able to pay for their college.'

'Maddy also had a daughter. Did you have a child her age?'

'I did have a girl a few years older,' she says sadly. 'But my daughter was a special needs child and she died in her early twenties. It was a tragedy, but she was suffering. I try to be philosophical, but sometimes . . .' Her voice trails away.

'I'm sorry to hear it. I know it's tough.'

'Anyway,' she says firmly, 'Maddy was such a source of strength to me during that time. I think that's why I was mad at her when she decided to move away.'

'You tried to talk her out of moving?'

'All her friends did. But she said she had her reasons, and there was nothing we could do to stop them.'

'Did you know the reasons?'

Carol chews her bottom lip and looks away. 'I don't like to gossip, but I can tell you that her son and daughter-in-law were having problems. I could have killed them for making her feel like she had to choose their lives over hers.'

'How did her husband feel about the move?'

She grimaces. 'Well, that was another story. I don't want to speak ill of the dead, but he made her life hell that last year. Demanding, bad-tempered. I know he didn't feel good, but he took it out on her.'

That's a different story from what I heard from Josh and Krista.

'Were you and your husband friendly with them?'

She sighs. 'You're really getting into it. My husband Robbie and I divorced a few years ago. I think it was the strain of our Anna dying. My husband Robbie and Maddy's husband Luke were peas in a pod, demanding and self-centered, so I understood what Maddy was going through when he was ill.'

'Carol, do you have any idea who might have had a grudge against Maddy, or had some reason to kill her?'

She thinks before she says, 'She was a good person.'

That doesn't answer the question. I wonder what she's holding back.

'Her neighbors say they didn't get to know her at all, that she was standoffish.'

She blinks and sits up straighter. 'That doesn't sound like her.

She was outgoing when she lived here. I don't know anything about
the town. Maybe people weren't easy to get to know.'

'How often did you see Maddy in the last year?'

'She came down a few times, but . . .' She pauses. 'To tell you
the truth, when I suggested coming there, she put me off. Not that
it bothered me; I figured she was still getting settled.'

I didn't get a satisfactory answer when I asked earlier if anyone
had a grudge against Maddy, so I give it another go. 'Did you ever
know Maddy to have a problem with anyone? Anybody threaten
her?'

For the first time, she looks uneasy. 'She did get into some things
that bothered a few people.'

'Like what?'

'She got into civil rights marches – you know, that Black Lives
Matter thing – and some other political stuff.'

'And that got her into trouble with somebody?'

Her lips start to tremble, and then her face crumples. She buries
her face in her hands and sobs. 'I told her she was going to get into
trouble if she kept that up. People are so mean. She got spit on and
yelled at.'

'Where was this? On a march?'

'No, it was outside the Planned Parenthood clinic. She was a
counter-protestor, and those anti-abortion people were vicious. They
pretend to be all lovey-dovey, but they're mean as snakes.'

'Was there any incident in particular where she was harassed, or
did she identify anybody who threatened her?'

She sniffs. 'If anybody threatened her, she never said who. She
didn't want her friends to worry.' She frowns. 'You think one of
them found out where she was living and killed her?'

'I don't have any evidence of that.' From what she said, I wonder
if the Schrage father or son might have been one of those who was
put off by her activism. 'Let me pass a name by you. Ever hear of
somebody named Gunther Schrage or Jason Schrage?'

She ponders the question and shakes her head. 'Doesn't sound
familiar.'

'Did you ever go on these protests with Maddy?'

She shakes her head, looking mournful. 'She knew I wouldn't
approve.' She purses her lips. 'I loved her and tried to understand
why things upset her so much, but it was hard. I didn't share her
commitment. I'm on the fence about the subject. I mean I understand

how young girls can get scared when they're in trouble, but . . .'
She trails off, shaking her head.

'You were on the fence. Did Maddy make enemies over her
activism?'

'One or two people might have gotten huffy with her, but I don't
know of anybody who got really riled.'

'I want you to give that some further thought.'

'I'll do that. She was such a good friend to me, I owe her that.'

'Did she know people who protested with her?'

'Well, that would be Joan Vincent. If anything, she was more
outspoken, but then she's a lot more interested in politics than I
am.'

'Anybody else you can think of who might have had a conflict
with Maddy about her activism?'

'Oh, yes, that would be Isabella Lopez. She's a piece of work.
That woman could chew your ear off with her opinions.'

'And they didn't get along?'

'No, which was strange because they were on the same side. I
think it was mostly a matter of both of them wanting to be the boss.
But if you're asking if Izzy would have hurt Maddy, absolutely not.
I just mean they butted heads.'

'How did they know each other?'

'They were on some committee that organized marches. I don't
know Izzy that well, but Maddy said she was bossy. Always wants
things her way and thinks she knows better than anyone else.' Her
smile is forlorn. 'Of course, you could say that about Maddy, too.'

I thank her for her time and ask her to call if she thinks of
anything else that might be relevant.

I still haven't heard back from Joan Vincent, so I head over to the
address I have for Gunther Schrage. It's several miles away and
takes me a half hour to get there. In a neighborhood that looks as
though it's seen better days, it's a modest house, with chalk-colored
asbestos siding and a tired-looking yard. There's a car in the
driveway, the car the Russells reported seeing in Jarrett Creek. I
ring the doorbell. When I don't hear it ring, I knock on the door.

The young man who answers is lanky and good-looking in a
slick sort of way. He's wearing jeans and a ragged T-shirt. I identify
myself and he says he's Jason Schrage.

'I'd like to ask you a few questions.'

He hesitates. 'What kind of questions?'

'Can I come in? It's hot out here.'

He blinks and looks behind him. 'Place is a mess, but sure, come on in.'

He's right, the place has been torn apart. Furniture has been pushed to one wall and there are piles of goods and some boxes.

'I'm cleaning out my daddy's house. He died a few months ago, and we're selling the place.'

'We?'

'My sister and I. Of course, she's working in Seattle for a few weeks so this move falls to me. She always did manage to get out of the hard work.'

'Do you live here?'

'No, sir. Come on in the kitchen. We can sit at the table there.'

The kitchen is in the same state, but there is a table we can sit down at, and two chrome kitchen chairs.

'Is that your daddy's car out there in the driveway?'

'Was. It's mine now. I'll be selling it, though.'

'But you drive it from time to time?'

'Once or twice, but I've got my own car, so it usually sits here.'

'I told you I was police chief in Jarrett Creek. You ever been there?'

'I was there once, a few years ago. Went to the lake and camped out for a few days with some friends.'

'You been there recently?'

'No, why?'

I don't get the sense that he's lying.

'Ever lend your car to anyone?'

He laughs. 'Uh-oh. Did Craig get a parking ticket he didn't pay for?'

'Craig?'

'Yeah. I lent him the car for a few days. But I had no idea he'd gone as far as Jarrett Creek with it.'

'What's his full name?'

'Craig Presley.'

'Any idea why he'd go to Jarrett Creek?'

He shrugs. 'None. Want me to call and ask him?'

'Not necessary. If you'll tell me where he lives, I'll ask him myself.'

His eyes shift away from me. 'I'm not sure where he is right now. He's been busy.'

'What do you mean?'

He grimaces. 'Craig lost his job. Got laid off and is worried about paying his rent, so he's frantic. I lent him my daddy's car because he said his wasn't running and he needed some way to get around for job interviews.' He shifts in his seat. 'Mind if I ask what this is about? Did he get in some kind of trouble?'

'He might have witnessed a crime, and I'd like to ask him some questions. I'd appreciate it if you'd give me his phone number.'

I sense his reluctance, but he jots down the number. 'You know, Craig is a good guy. I don't know what you think he's done, but he's always been straight up.'

'Then he won't mind if I ask him to help me with some inquiries.'

EIGHT

J oan Vincent has left a message to tell me she's back home and
I can come anytime. I was hoping to avoid rush-hour traffic, but
even at three o'clock it's already started.

Before I get out of the car, I get a return call from Craig Presley.
'In your message, you said Jason Schrage gave you my number?'

'That's right. I have a few questions for you.'

'About what?' He's curt.

'Is it possible for us to meet so I can explain?'

'Not unless you want to drive to Dallas.'

'Have you relocated there?'

'No, I'm only staying here a couple of days. I'm looking for a
job, and it depends on if they ask me back for a second interview.
Jason said you were a cop in Jarrett Creek. What's this about,
anyway?'

'It's possible you were a witness to a crime there, and I'd like
to find out what you might have seen.'

'Witness to a crime? Where?'

'In Jarrett Creek. When you're driving back from Dallas, you
can stop in Jarrett Creek and we can discuss it.'

'First of all, I'm not driving. I flew up here. My car's in the shop.
But I can't have been witness to anything in Jarrett Creek, because
I've never been there.'

I wish I could see his expression. Somebody is lying.

'Your friend Jason said you borrowed his car, and the car was
spotted in Jarrett Creek during the time you borrowed it.'

'Somebody must have gotten the wrong car. I promise you, I've
never been there.'

'Did you lend the car to someone else during the time you
borrowed it from Jason?'

There's the slightest hesitation, and then, 'No. I wouldn't do that.
It wasn't mine to lend.'

Why would he lie about that? 'How long have you been in
Dallas?'

'Got here yesterday morning for a ten o'clock interview. Like I said, I'm waiting to see if they call me back.' Which means he couldn't have been in Jarrett Creek to kill Maddy. Unless he's not really in Dallas.

'Where are you staying?'

'With a high school buddy.'

I get the name and phone number of his buddy so I can verify. 'And who is the interview with?' He readily gives me the name of a tech company and contact information for the man who interviewed him. Something is off. Either Craig Presley or Jason Schrage is lying.

Joan Vincent warms my heart when she offers coffee and blueberry muffins. The muffins aren't up to Loretta Singletary's standards, but I only ate a few bites of the sandwiches Carol Warren offered and I'm hungry. I down one of the muffins while she pours the coffee.

She's older than Maddy and Carol by several years. Sixtyish, with short gray hair and a wiry frame, she's got a hard look, as if she's had some difficulties in her life. Her house is tidy but rundown, the sofa and chairs in the living room shabby. Two cats are ensconced on one of the chairs and they eye me with suspicion, as cats are inclined to do.

Joan wants to know the particulars of Maddy Benson's death and I tell her the basic details. I follow up with the usual questions. Her kids were the same age as Maddy's and Carol's. 'I was an older mom and not all the parents were welcoming, partly I guess because I was a single mom. I decided if I was ever going to have kids, it had to be on my own. Some of the other parents were so young that I didn't have much in common with them.'

She reports the same thing about Maddy's move to Jarrett Creek that Carol did, that it was an attempt to work out things between Josh and Krista. But she's got a different take on the situation. 'I think Maddy was using it as an excuse to move.'

'Why would she do that?'

Joan eyes me, as if taking my measure. 'Carol and I thought Maddy had gotten in too deep with her women's rights activities and maybe she needed a change. I think she believed if she went to a small town, she could work behind the scenes without being hounded. Here, it's too out in the open.'

'Carol said she was harassed.'

'Yes, she was. We both were. I marched alongside her, but I had a full-time job and couldn't do as much for the cause as she did. She put herself out there, marching and writing articles. It threw her into the spotlight. So although we both got our share of being yelled at, spit at a time or two, I know she got threatening letters as well. She took it in her stride, but as I said, I was worried. I didn't want her to leave, but I hoped she would be safer.' She grimaces. 'So much for my hopes.'

'Tell me what Maddy was like as a person. Was she tough, funny, good-natured?'

'One of the reasons I liked her was that she had a wicked sense of humor – at least with people she was close to. And she was fierce about her belief in women's rights.' She looks haunted when she says that. 'Maybe it got her killed. There's so much hatred toward women believing they should be able to live their own lives.'

'Did she ever tell you she had a run-in with anybody in particular?'

'The only person she ever had an out-and-out argument with was one of the women in the PTA. A real piece of work, but not dangerous. Just a pain in the you-know-what. Thought Maddy should stay home and bake brownies, or whatever.'

'What's this woman's name?'

'Elizabeth Robinson.'

The name rings a bell. 'Goes by Libby?'

'That's right. How do you know that?'

'The name came up.' In fact, she wrote one of the hostile letters I found. 'Did Maddy get along well with her son and her daughter-in-law? I understand that Krista had an affair.'

'She was unhappy about that. But she confided to me that she understood that Josh wasn't the easiest person to live with.'

'Were there other problems?' I've already heard plenty on that score, but Joan is a chatty sort and might have more information.

'Maddy said Josh was unhappy that Krista is the breadwinner. Hurts his ego.'

'So her books are that profitable?'

'According to Maddy, she churns them out like candy, and they sell by the carload. But even if he didn't mind her making the money, Maddy said Krista thinks Josh doesn't respect her.' She smiles. 'I can understand that. Those romance novels can be awfully sappy. But he knew when he married her that she wasn't going to be an intellectual, at least not the way he is. Maddy was fairly sure Josh and Krista were going to call it quits. They just don't get along.

Between you and me, I think Josh is jealous of Krista's success. But what does he expect? He writes those dry histories, and she writes the things women eat up.'

'Maddy has a daughter. How is their relationship?' Josh said his sister lives in Los Angeles, but until I check on it, I'll follow the thread.

'She and Hannah got along great. Hannah was a bit of a prima donna, but Maddy didn't mind. She thought she'd get over herself eventually. The girl was actually a good actress. I saw her in a couple of plays in high school and she had talent. Not as much as she and Maddy thought, but solid. She went to Los Angeles to see if she could break into the movies. Last I heard, she was working in the costume department.'

'Her daughter-in-law said Maddy chose Jarrett Creek as a destination because she knew someone there. Do you know who it was?'

She cocks her head. 'I never heard that.'

'Then why did she choose Jarrett Creek?'

'I thought it was because she liked the idea of living near the lake. She told me it was a good place to walk. And she loved to walk.'

Makes more sense than anything I've heard so far.

Joan tells me she saw Maddy a few weeks ago. 'We met halfway in that big outlet mall near Cypress. We spent the day together shopping and catching up.'

'Did you get any sense that she was worried about anything?'

'No more than usual.'

'Did she mention that anything had changed in her life?'

She shakes her head. 'She was still getting over Luke's death. Even if he was hard to handle at the end, they'd been married a long time, and she missed the man he was before he got sick. She was sort of at loose ends. Trying to decide what she'd do if Josh and Krista split up, because they'd likely sell the house, and she didn't know if she was going to stay where she was or move back to Houston. Of course, you can imagine my opinion on the matter.'

There's nothing more she can add, so I head back to Jarrett Creek. I don't know that I've learned anything that will help me figure out who killed Maddy, but I have a fuller picture of the kind of person she was. She had people who were close to her, and she made the decision to leave them. I'm still not sure I understand why.

*   *   *

In the car, I call Maria to tell her I'm heading back. 'Anything new?'

'Maddy's daughter came by. She wanted to talk to you. I told her you'd gone to Houston, and she said to call her as soon as you get in.'

'It's been a long day, so I'll talk to her tomorrow. Do you have a phone number for her? I'll call her now.'

'I'll warn you. She's demanding.'

I sigh. 'Understood.'

She gives me the number. I sit for a minute, deciding whether I'd rather talk to her in person. But demanding or not, she deserves a hearing.

She answers on the first ring. She has a nice voice, musical.

I identify myself. 'I'm sorry I wasn't in when you dropped by headquarters. I'm still in Houston talking to some of your mamma's friends. Can we arrange to meet tomorrow morning?'

'If you're still questioning people, sounds like you don't know yet who killed my mother.' Peremptory.

'Not yet. It's early days.'

'I assume you've taken a good, hard look at my sister-in-law.'

'I'll be glad to hear what you have to say, so let's meet at head-quarters at nine in the morning.'

'Nine? You do realize I'm here from California. It's two hours earlier there.'

'You name the time, then.' I realize my voice is snappish. I've had a long day, and even though I'm trying to be understanding of her situation, my patience is nearly gone.

Apparently, she hears that in my voice, because she says she'll be there at ten thirty. Good. That gives me time to do another couple of things tomorrow morning.

Two hours later, after going through the traffic from hell, I pick up Dusty from Maria's apartment. He stayed with her while I was out of town. We agree to meet at eight tomorrow morning to parcel out the jobs that need to be done for the investigation.

I'm tired and not looking forward to cooking, or even heating up some food, and I sure don't feel like going out. But no sooner have I walked in than my phone rings. It's Jenny Sandstone from next door.

'I saw you come in. Will made some stew tonight and there are lots of leftovers. Would you care to have some? He can bring it over.'

'You'll have my eternal gratitude.'

'I thought I already had that.' She laughs, but she's right. A few years ago, when we were neighbors who didn't get along that well, she noticed a fire at my house before it got going strong enough to do any damage. She called the fire department and managed to come inside and save my art collection. I've been in her debt ever since, and we're pals.

'Even more,' I say.

Will comes over in five minutes. He hands me a covered bowl and says he won't come in. 'I've got an early trial tomorrow morning, so I need to get on home.' Jenny and Will have been a couple for a few years now. Both of them work in Bobtail as attorneys, Will as a public defender, and Jenny as a prosecutor. I don't know why they don't get married, but it's none of my business.

I demolish the stew in fifteen minutes, sip a beer, and watch TV for five minutes before I nod off. Dusty wakes me up with a sharp bark, telling me it's time to go out for his nightly constitutional. I groan, but he's right. Fresh air will do us both good.

NINE

'm up early, having tossed and turned a good bit. Despite everything I've heard about Maddy Benson, I feel like she's still an
unknown. There's something I haven't got a handle on yet.

I take Dusty with me down to the pasture where my cows are
fenced and spend more time than usual, because I find the cattle
soothing. They're big and calm and seem unruffled by much of
anything. Dusty goes off to chase some imaginary critter while I
go in the pen and check the cows' hides for any sign of skin disease
and their eyes for pinkeye.

Loretta is there with coffee cake when I get back. That's two
days in a row. She used to bake almost every day, but in the last
couple of years she's done it less.

'This is a surprise. Two days in a row. And my favorite. What
brought this on?' I know exactly what brought it on. She wants
information. But so do I.

'Where were you yesterday? Somebody saw you leave town.'

'Went off to Houston to talk to some of Maddy Benson's friends.'

'Did you find out anything more?'

'Not much. Did you ask around if anybody knew her?'

'I did, but everybody I asked said they didn't know her, hadn't
even met her. Mostly people were excited when I told them Oliva
Cartwright lives here.'

'Keep nosing around,' I say. 'I haven't found out as much as I
need to.'

'People you talked to in Houston weren't able to help?'

'Not much.' I get up. 'I'd better get going. A lot to do today.'

'I'm going to stay inside today. I was going to work in the garden,
but this humidity is going to kill me.' She grins. 'Might even read
one of those novels.'

When I get into the office, Maria is already there, poring through
the last of the folders. 'Well, this was a dead end.' She asks what
I found out in Houston.

'Slim pickings,' I say. 'But there was one thing. You remember the business card you found when you were going through Maddy's pockets?'

She gets up and goes to her desk and picks up the card. 'The Time Is Now. Isabella Lopez.'

'One of Maddy's friends mentioned Maddy was on a committee with Lopez, and they didn't get along well. See what you can find out – maybe talk to her and ask why Maddy had the card, if they worked together on The Time Is Now.'

'I'll be glad to do that, but first tell me about the guy with the car the neighbor saw near her house. Anything there?'

I tell her something seemed off. 'Both men swear they've never been here. And I asked if Presley lent the car to anyone, but he said no.'

Maria cocks her head. 'Is there some way to check out their stories?'

'Schrage said he has a sister. I suppose I could call her and see if she knows anything different. But if Schrage is lying, he'd probably warn her to cover for him.'

'It's also possible the guy wrote down the wrong license number.'

'Possible.'

'Do you know if the forensics team went back out to the Gainer place to search for cartridge fragments?'

'Did you get a number from the team? I'll call right now.'

She did get a number and I call them. No surprise that they've moved on. 'With all that rain, I expect we wouldn't find much.' Translation, it's a small-town matter and they don't have time for it.

Maria gets that gleam in her eye when I tell her. 'I'll go back out there myself,' she says. 'I can take a proper look.'

'Maria, that's a big area to cover.'

'I can narrow it down. Leave it to me.'

No way I can stop her. When she heads out, I have barely enough time before Maddy's daughter gets here to call Tom Gainer and find out when he's going to be in town. I've been wondering why Maddy went there when she left her house. I want to know if Tom knew her.

He lives down on the Gulf Coast, in Galveston, and has an auto rental business called Rent Any Old Heap. He buys up old cars and rents them cheaper than people can get from the big companies.

When I phone, Tom's wife, Bonnie, tells me he's on his way to Jarrett Creek. 'He heard that a woman was killed on our land, and he figured you'd want to talk to him. Not that he needs an excuse to go there,' she adds dryly. 'I don't know what he does out there in the place he built, but he loves to go there. Fishes. Has a few head of cattle. Never could figure out the appeal myself.'

It occurs to me that he may be up to more than she thinks. 'Bonnie, does he have Wi-Fi out there?'

'He does. He said he has to have it for business. You know the car rental business is twenty-four hours a day. Sometimes those kids he has working for him don't know squat, so they have to call him. Anyway,' she says, 'he should be there by noon. He has to stop to do a couple of errands in Bobtail on the way.'

I get his cell phone number from her. When I call, he doesn't answer, so I leave a message asking him to let me know when he arrives.

Hannah Benson shows up right on time at ten thirty, looking grim. Dusty immediately goes over to greet her.

Hannah yelps. 'Down, doggie!'

'Dusty, come!' I say.

He usually doesn't obey me, but for once he slinks back to me and dives under my desk.

'Sorry,' I say. 'You afraid of dogs?'

'No, I just don't like them to jump on me.' She's an attractive, willowy girl, wearing a sundress that is dressier than most women around here wear, and white sandals. 'I presume you're Chief Craddock?' She extends her arm fully, with a sort of flourish. 'I'm Hannah Benson.'

'Yes, I'm Chief Craddock. Can I offer you some coffee?'

'I don't drink coffee, so I have to refuse your kind offer.' It's a stuffy kind of comment and has a certain snobbish sound to it.

I indicate that she should sit on the chair next to my desk. She does so, but keeps a stiff posture. Her smile tightens. 'I have questions. I hope you can answer them.'

I remember her voice being melodious from when I talked to her on the phone. Her voice is her best feature.

From the queenly way she has presented herself, I know that I have to take control of the conversation or she'll run away with her own agenda. She's playing the benevolent ruler, and I have the feeling she's got a backbone of steel. 'Let me get some information from you first. When was the last time you saw your mamma?'

She looks startled, not used to being pre-empted. 'I guess it was last Christmas.' She opens her mouth to say something else, but I intervene.

'When was the last time you talked to her on the phone?'

Now she looks indignant, her chin raised in haughty disapproval of my question. 'What difference does it make?'

'Was it recent?' I can be really kind, really empathetic, but I can also be relentless if needed.

'I call her almost every Sunday.'

'So you spoke with her last weekend?'

She blinks. 'Well, maybe it was the Sunday before that.'

'Did she tell you anything alarming? Was she worried about anything? Scared? Any threats?'

Her shoulders sag as she realizes that my questions really are relevant. 'Not that I remember.' She frowns. 'I would have remembered that.'

'What did you discuss?'

She shrugs. 'The usual. She always wanted to know what I was doing. She was . . .' Her eyes suddenly tear up. 'She was my biggest champion. She wanted me to succeed.'

'Yes, her friend Joan told me that.'

'Pfft. Joan. She was not on my side, I can tell you that.'

'What were you aiming for that your mamma wanted you to succeed at?'

'I wanted to be . . . *want* to be . . . an actress. In movies or TV.'

'Any luck?'

She sighs. 'I had a walk-on in a movie you've never heard of. But nothing else. So far,' she adds, with gusto.

'What are you doing for a living?'

'I'm working in the costume department at one of the studios. And I've gotten a couple of jobs as a voiceover for TV ads. Money's not bad.'

'I'm not surprised. You have a nice voice.'

'Thank you.' She preens herself with a satisfied smile.

Maria comes in looking pleased with herself, so I presume she found something useful at the Gainer place. I nod to her. She takes in my visitor and goes to her desk.

I turn my attention back to Hannah. 'Let me ask you this. Do you have any idea who might have wanted to hurt your mamma?'

'I can tell you who has already hurt her, and that's Darling Krista.'

'In what way?'

'Did she tell you she was having an affair and that's why they moved here? That's why my poor mother was stuck here and got killed? It's Krista's fault!' There's some drama in her words, but some of it rings true as well. Her mother's death has hurt her.

'You think your mamma was stuck here? The story I get is that it was her idea to choose Jarrett Creek.'

'Maybe she chose the place, but she had to move away and leave her friends because Krista was having an affair. Did they tell you that?'

I nod. 'Krista told me. She also told me your mamma knew someone here in Jarrett Creek who suggested that she move here. Do you know who it was?'

'Krista told you that? I wouldn't believe anything she said.'

'You never heard your mamma mention knowing anyone here?'

'No. Who is it?'

'That's what I'd like to find out. No one seems to know.'

'Like I said, I wouldn't put a lot of stock in what Krista said.'

'Sounds like you don't get along with your sister-in-law.'

'She makes me mad, the way she treats my brother. I don't even know why she married Josh. He needs somebody to fuss over him. That isn't my sister-in-law.'

'You said you had questions for me,' I say. 'What can I tell you?'

She takes a deep breath. 'I want to know if you've called in the FBI or maybe the Texas Rangers. You seem like a nice enough man, but it's going to take experts to figure this out.'

'I have spoken with the head of the area Department of Public Safety. They'll be helping in the investigation with things I don't have the resources for. But for now, I'm going to be doing all I can to find out what happened. And you can help me by talking to your family. If anyone remembers any kind of hint that your mamma knew someone here in town, or if she was feeling scared, or anything seemed out of the ordinary with her, I need to know that.'

'But that's your job, isn't it?'

'Of course it is. But you'd be surprised at how often when family members start to talk among themselves, they remember things that can be useful. I'm asking you to keep your ears open.'

She nods. 'I understand. But you will do everything you can, right?'

'You have my word.'

Hannah goes out and gets into the car that I recognize as Josh's.

As soon as she's gone, I wheel my chair around to face Maria. 'What'd you find?'

She picks up an evidence bag from her desk. 'Casing. That means if we find the gun, we can get a match.'

'*If* we find the gun,' I say.

'We will,' she says firmly.

She tells me the approximate area where she found it, on the side of the road fifty feet east of Gainer's entrance, which means the gunman shot from at least thirty yards away. Definitely a sharpshooter.

'I'm going to the café to get some lunch. You want me to bring you a hamburger?'

'Yes, I'm starving. And while you're gone, I'm going to dig into that woman you mentioned – Isabella Lopez.'

TEN

I often bring my lunch back to the office to eat, but today I want to see what the scuttlebutt is about the murder. People say women gossip, but I've found I can often pick up bits of information from the men who come in here to congregate for lunch. I'm eating enchiladas and drinking iced tea with some of the usual crowd, answering their questions about the murder, when my phone rings. It's Gainer. He says he's out at his place.

'I can come in, or you can come out here,' he says.

I want to go back to where Maddy Benson was killed and to point out to him exactly where it happened. Maybe Tom has some idea of why she chose to go there. I tell him I'll be there in thirty minutes. 'I'm at Town Café. You want me to bring you something?'

He tells me he stopped at a grocery store in Bobtail and picked up a few things, including a sandwich for his lunch.

When I hang up, Harley Lunsford says, 'That Tom Gainer?'

'Yep, you know him?'

'Not well, but I've seen him at the rifle range in Bobtail a time or two. He's a hell of a marksman. Kind of man who talks softly and carries a big gun.' Lunsford is a staunch member of the NRA and is of a belief that everyone would be better off if they carried a gun. So he takes every opportunity to mention guns in any conversation. But his comment about Gainer is a surprise. Gainer is mild-mannered and doesn't strike me as being someone who'd be a big gun advocate like Lunsford.

'I have a question for you,' I say. 'How good a shot does somebody have to be to kill someone with a shotgun at long range?'

Lunsford gets serious. 'Depends on a few things. If they're a good shot, naturally. But also if they know their weapon, and if the conditions are right. No wind, good visibility.'

'Hmm, the wind was kicking up around the time she was killed. That could have thrown off the aim?'

'For your regular gunman, yes. But an expert would know to

take that into account. Somebody who practices a lot at the range. Or maybe a veteran.' He pauses and wipes his mouth. 'You asking if Tom Gainer could have killed her?'

I fling up my hands in exasperation. 'No. Gainer was not in town when it happened.'

Lunsford loves a good argument so he comes back with, 'Could have slipped out of town and gone home and no one would be the wiser.'

I tell him I suppose he's right. 'But until I have a good reason why Gainer would have attacked the woman, I'll be looking for somebody more likely.'

I take Maria her usual hamburger before I leave for the Gainer place.

'Any luck with the Lopez woman and The Time Is Now?'

'I reached their number. It's a women's rights group. The woman manning the phone didn't mind filling me in. She said there's been recent squabbling in the group because different factions want to focus on different women's issues. Most of them are concerned with abortion rights, but some are more interested in LBGTQ rights and racial issues.'

'The women's rights thing goes along with what Maddy's friends told me.'

'I asked if she knew Maddy Benson, and she said she wasn't at liberty to reveal the names of individual members. But when I told her that Maddy Benson had been killed, she said she'd have the organization's president call me.'

'Do you think she'll follow up?'

'No idea.'

'Did she happen to give you the name of the president?'

Maria smiles. 'Yes, she did. It's Isabella Lopez.'

'Interesting. According to Maddy's friends, Isabella and Maddy didn't get along well, but they certainly traveled in the same circles. So I'm anxious to hear from her.'

She tells me there was a call from someone out at the lake, saying there was rowdy behavior, so she's going off to handle it. 'Connor will be in this afternoon,' she says. 'Anything you want me to tell him?'

'I won't be gone long,' I say. 'I'll be back before he comes in.'

*   *   *

Despite the ensuing wind and rain, there are still remnants of yellow crime scene tape strung out across the barren landscape at the Gainer place, as if anyone needed a reminder of what happened here.

Tom is waiting for me nearby, hands on his narrow hips, hat tipped back. He's in his forties, a wiry man with prematurely graying hair and leathery skin. He spends most every weekend here, fishing and hunting. And I suppose going to the firing range, if Lunsford is to be believed.

I get out of my pickup and walk over to join him.

'Chief,' Gainer says, nodding. 'When can I tear this tape down?' I'd forgotten he's got a laconic way of talking as if nothing too much bothers him.

The wind and rain have already done most of the work of removing the tape. I don't think it actually detracts from what is already a desolate landscape, but I tell him we can tear it down now. 'I'll get a bag.'

It only takes a few minutes. During that time, a few of his cows have ambled over to see what the commotion is about. I notice one of them has a scruffy hide. 'You had him checked out?' I ask.

'Doc England is coming out this afternoon. I just noticed it today.' Doc England is the vet. I have a soft spot for him because he saddled me with Dusty. 'Grass is poor here. I've been supplementing the feed, but may not be enough.'

'Expensive,' I say.

'Ha.' A mirthless laugh. 'You got that right. I don't know why we even bother with cattle.'

'Tell me about it.'

He turns to me. 'Tell me what happened here. I was surprised to hear that some woman had been killed. What was she doing on my property?'

'I was hoping you could tell me. Her name was Maddy Benson. You know her?'

He screws up his face and shakes his head. 'Doesn't ring a bell. Somebody said she lives up in the new development.'

'She did. With her son and daughter-in-law.'

'I don't know anybody who lives up there. How did she get here?'

'That's the sixty-four-dollar question. And another thing. Do you usually keep your gate locked?'

'Always. Ever since I came out here one weekend and found a

bunch of teenagers had set up camp in the pasture and spooked my cows. They had a campfire and everything. I don't know what the attraction was, but I had to kick them out and they weren't happy. I've been careful to keep the gate locked ever since.'

'It wasn't locked when Maddy Benson was killed. It was open when my deputy and I came to look for her.'

He frowns and looks off. 'You know, my son was here last weekend with me, and he left after I did. He must have forgotten to lock it. I'll have to talk to him.'

'How old is your son? Dell – is that his name?'

'That's right, Dell. He's eighteen. We normally travel together, but he was staying a couple of extra days to go fishing with a kid he knows here.' He tells me it's the Baptist preacher's son, Aaron. 'Dell met him out at the lake, and they hit it off. They've gone fishing a few times.'

I tell Gainer I want to take one more look around his cabin in case I missed something. 'I found Maddy's cell phone in the back of your place.'

I whistle for Dusty, and he hops in the truck and we drive up to the cabin. Gainer says he'll walk. For a while, we both wander around. Eventually, Gainer calls out, 'Take a look at this.'

Over by the pond, there's a crushed bit of grass and a tire track in an area near the water that appears to stay damp from proximity. I examined this area when we found Maddy's body and didn't see it. Plus, it has rained since then.

'Somebody was here, but I don't think it was the shooter.'

'Right. Maybe Aaron and Dell were out here. I wouldn't be surprised if they heard about the killing and came out here to check out the site. You know kids. Nosy.'

'Before I go, let me ask you one more time. I need to press you on this. Are you sure you don't know Maddy Benson? Maybe rented a car to her?'

'It's possible she rented a car from my company, but I wouldn't know. I can certainly look into it, though.'

'I'd appreciate that.'

I'm just back at headquarters around one o'clock when I get a call from Hannah. 'Something odd has happened. Can you come over here?' She doesn't sound scared, but she's keeping her voice low.

'Be there in five minutes,' I say.

Instead of Hannah, it's Eileen who greets me at the door. 'Do you have news?'

'No, ma'am. Not yet.'

'Don't you think it's time to call in the Rangers?'

'I've been in touch with the Department of Public Safety. They're helping look into it.' Not exactly true, but I'm getting tired of this family assuming they know more about investigating a crime than I do.

'Well, I never heard of such nonsense, letting a small-town police chief run an investigation!' Eileen says. 'If this were San Antonio . . .'

Hannah has come behind Eileen. 'Eileen, leave it,' she says. 'This isn't San Antonio.' They glare at each other.

Of course, if Maddy had been killed in a city, like San Antonio where Eileen lives, there would have been a whole different set of considerations, but I don't say that. No sense in stirring the pot.

Josh comes down the stairs and sees us standing in the foyer. 'What's up? Why are you here?'

Hannah says, 'I called him. Let's everybody go in the living room.'

We sit down, but no one seems to be ready to speak so I ask if they've managed to get in touch with Maddy's folks.

'Yeah, this morning,' Hannah says. 'They finally called Josh back.'

'You'd think that if someone's grandkids called and left an urgent message, they'd get right back to them,' Eileen grumbles.

'They were in New Orleans,' Josh says.

'Like they don't have cell phone coverage in New Orleans,' Hannah says to her brother. To me, she says, 'They are the world's most self-absorbed people.'

'I'm sorry,' I say. 'Are they going to be coming for the funeral service?'

'They said to let them know when the funeral is going to be, so I guess they plan to be here,' Josh says.

'Oh, right,' Eileen spits out. 'As if they can't be bothered to come one minute earlier.'

She gets up and walks to the sliding glass door that leads to the outside, her back to us. Her shoulders are slumped. It occurs to me that this whole ordeal is hitting her harder than she wants to show, and that her caustic comments are a way of deflecting.

'Hannah, it's probably just as well,' Josh is saying. 'The last time you saw them, they pissed you off.'

'You're right. It's just, she's their daughter! And if you believe what Eileen says, she was the favorite. It makes me so mad.'

Hannah looks at her aunt, but Eileen doesn't turn around.

'Hannah, you called me,' I say. 'Do you need to speak with me privately?'

'No. I called because Krista's gone.'

'What do you mean "gone"?'

Neither Hannah nor Josh replies, so Eileen wheels around, strides back. 'Tell him!' she snaps.

'Tell me what?' I ask.

'The thing is . . .' Josh stutters to a halt.

'We don't know where she is,' Hannah says.

'How long has she been gone?'

'I got to bed late last night,' Josh says. 'And she was asleep. When I got up this morning, she was gone.'

I hadn't noticed whether her car was in the garage. 'Is her car gone?'

'Yes.'

'Did she leave a note?'

'OK, there was a note,' Josh says. 'But it didn't make any sense.' He's looking increasingly nervous.

'What did it say?'

'It said not to worry and that she wanted to get away for a couple of days. No explanation of where she went or when she'll be back.'

'Do you have the note?'

He goes upstairs and comes back with it. It's on a sticky note with Krista's name printed on it. It says exactly what he said it did.

'Is this her handwriting?'

Josh nods.

'Do you have reason to believe something has happened to her?'

'Not really,' Josh says.

'Has she done anything like this before?'

'Not since we've been living here.'

'But she did before that?'

He looks so stricken that I realize she must have done that when she was having an affair.

I turn to Hannah. 'Are you worried that something has happened to her?'

'I just think it's strange that she would go away right now, with Mom just being killed.' Hannah's voice is subdued. 'She was close to Mom.'

'Did either of you see her this morning?' I ask the women.

'I didn't,' Hannah says. 'But I didn't get up until almost ten and I had to rush out to meet with you.'

Eileen walks back to us. 'I got up early, but I went for a walk,' she says. 'When I got back and saw she wasn't here, I assumed she had gone on an errand.'

'Have any of you phoned her?'

'I did, but there was no answer,' Josh says. He looks very unhappy.

'Did any of you have an argument with her last night?'

Hannah sighs. 'We were sharp with each other.'

'About what?'

Eileen speaks up. 'Hannah thinks Krista should have been more protective of Maddy. And I agree.'

'That's ridiculous,' Josh says, in the biggest show of forcefulness I've heard from him. 'Mamma would have had a fit if Krista had hovered over her. She was independent.'

'You always take Krista's side,' Hannah says.

'Well, she is my wife,' he snaps.

'Did you check to see if she took anything with her?' I ask. 'A suitcase? Her computer?'

Josh looks blank. 'No, I didn't think to do that.'

'I'd like you to go check.'

He moves faster than I've seen him do before. He's glad to have a mission. He's back in five minutes. 'OK, that explains it. Yes, her small suitcase – the one she usually takes on weekends – is missing. And her laptop is gone, and her desk is bare. I think she took some notes with her. I'll bet she went somewhere to get some work done. She has a deadline, and I guess she decided she had to get away.' He's babbling, likely relieved to have some evidence that she's OK.

But I'm with Hannah. It still seems odd that she would leave under the circumstances. 'OK. I would like to locate her, though. Can you think of any friends she might have gone to?'

'The only friends she has are in Houston.'

'Could she have gone to visit one of them?' But why wouldn't she have told someone if that was what she intended? 'Is it possible she planned to do that and told you and you didn't remember?'

'Could be,' Josh says, hanging his head. 'I'm not good with those things. Krista is always complaining that I don't listen.'

Eileen scoffs.

He glares at her. 'It isn't that I don't listen; it's that I don't commit things to memory.'

'I bet if it was important to you, you would remember,' Eileen shoots back.

I'm getting tired of their sniping. 'Josh, do you know how to get in touch with any of her friends in Houston?'

'Yes!' he says eagerly. 'Tracy Gibbs. Tracy and her husband Mike came over every so often. And he and I went to a baseball game a couple of times. I have their number.' He digs his phone out of his back pocket and starts scrolling through.

'Here it is.' He hands me his phone with the number displayed.

'I'm going to go outside to call her.' I may have to get into subjects I'd rather not discuss in front of Josh.

'I'll put some coffee on,' Eileen says.

I go out through the sliding glass door onto the back patio. It's hot outside, but at least the patio is in the shade. I dial the number and it rings several times. Just as I'm ready to hang up, a woman answers, out of breath. 'Hi, who is this?'

'I'm Samuel Craddock, Chief of Police in Jarrett Creek.'

'We don't donate to the police,' she says crisply.

'Ma'am, this isn't a request for donations. This is about Krista Benson.'

A beat of silence. 'What about her?'

'I wondered if you had seen her or heard from her in the last couple of days.'

'Oh my God! Why are you asking that? Has something happened to her?'

'I hope not. I don't know if you are aware, but her mother-in-law died two days ago, and Krista has apparently gone off somewhere. She left her husband a note saying not to worry, but we want to be sure she's OK. I'm wondering if any of her friends have heard from her.'

She takes a noisy breath. 'No, not at all. Oh, God. She did call to tell me that Maddy had been shot, but she didn't say anything about going away. Should I call around and see if anybody has heard from her?'

'That sounds like a good idea. I'd appreciate it.' I give her my email address and tell her people can either call or email me. 'One more thing. When you talked to Krista, did she say how things were going between her and her husband?'

Another long silence. 'Not when she called about Maddy. It was a short conversation.'

'Before that?'

Tracy sighs. 'If you're asking that question, you know that things aren't great between them.'

'As I understand it, Maddy wanted to move here to try to help them give their marriage another chance.'

'That's what Krista said. But if you ask me, it was never going to work. She and Josh just aren't on the same wavelength. And then there's Loren.'

'Loren? Is he the man Krista was having an affair with?'

'So you knew about that?'

'Yes. But Krista said they weren't seeing each other anymore.'

'Not at the moment, they aren't, but I'd be surprised if they didn't get back together. There was a lot of chemistry there.'

'Do you have a number for him?'

'No. I don't even know his last name. Krista didn't say much about him, and what she did say didn't impress me.' She laughs, but it doesn't have much humor in it. 'I always thought because she wrote those romance novels, she had unrealistically romantic ideas and that she put rose-colored glasses on for Loren. Also, maybe she was looking for a reason to leave Josh.'

'When you ask people whether they've heard from Krista, if anyone knows more about Loren, I'd appreciate a call back.' I need to find out if she has gone off with him.

'I'll do whatever I can to help. And if you hear from her, will you get back to me?'

I tell her I will.

When I get back to the living room, Josh gets up from the sofa and asks eagerly, 'Had she heard from Krista?'

I tell him no but that she's going to ask around.

'Can I talk to you in private?' I ask Josh.

Eileen darts a frown at me, but Josh follows me into the foyer. 'I'm going to come right out and ask. Do you know the name of the man Krista was having an affair with?'

He jams his hands into his pockets, and I see his jaw tighten. 'All I know is his name was Loren. She didn't volunteer anything else, and I didn't ask. But she told me they weren't seeing each other anymore. Did Tracy say otherwise?'

'No, she didn't. Can you think of anyone else who might know where Krista has gone? Did she have siblings?'

Josh's face brightens. 'She has a brother, Tony. I forgot him. They aren't close. But it's possible if she was looking for someplace to go, she might have called him.' But his face darkens right away. 'Somehow I doubt it, though. He lives in Florida. And besides, Krista says he's an asshole.'

'So they don't get along?'

'That's right. It's politics. He and Krista are on the opposite ends of the spectrum. He's super-conservative – you know, one of those MAGA types.'

'Where is he in Florida?'

'Miami. He owns a nightclub, someplace popular. Can't remember what they call it. I've never been to Miami.'

'Has Krista ever been there?'

'Not that I know of.'

'Can you find the name of his club? Maybe a number?'

'I could if I had Krista's phone, but she probably took it with her.'

'Does she have an address book?' As soon as I ask and see the bemused look on Josh's face, I know the question is anachronistic. Young people keep everything digitally. 'Would she have the information on her computer?'

'Maybe. She has taken her laptop, but she has a big desktop computer, too.'

I follow him upstairs and into Krista's office. It's different from the other rooms – more cluttered, but not messy. It has a more lived-in feel to it than the public rooms. There is no file cabinet, but there are a lot of plastic containers stacked along one wall with labels of what I presume are the names of her books. There are bookcases against two walls, crammed with novels and personal items – ceramics and framed photos. Her desk is a big table with books stacked on it, yellow pads and notes spread out. Shoved to the back of the desk is a desktop computer with a keyboard and a big screen.

Josh sits down at the computer and switches it on.

'You know her password?' I ask.

'I think so.' He enters a password, and the computer springs into life with a mass of files scattered across the screen. Josh looks at the files and finally says, 'This should do it.' He opens a file called 'Names and addresses.' He scans and says, 'Here it is. Anthony Walker. His club is called South Beach Sands.' He jots down the information for me.

'I'll give him a call. Do you mind if I take a look at her emails from the last day or so? Krista might have been in touch with someone she planned to see.'

His hands hover over the keyboard. 'I've never checked up on her before. It feels invasive.'

'I understand.' I don't blame him for hesitating. No telling what he might find out. I wait him out, hoping he'll relent.

With a grunt, he gets up and waves toward the chair. 'Go ahead.'

A hasty look yields nothing personal in the last few days. It's mostly junk emails and reminders. Nothing to indicate where she might have gone.

I search for the name Loren, hoping there might be an email from him, but nothing shows up. He might not have used his name in his email address.

'I'd like you to print out that address file for me,' I say.

He does so and I fold the printout. 'And one last thing. I need to get the make and model of Krista's car and the license number.'

Once again, he looks challenged by the question.

'Which one of you keeps the car records – insurance and that kind of thing?' I ask.

'That's Krista.' His eyes travel around the room as if the folder containing the information might come strolling toward him.

'Could be in one of those containers.' I nod toward the stack of twenty or so containers.

He walks over and reads the labels, seizes one of them, and pulls it out of the stack. 'Household,' he says. He opens it. It's full of file folders. He grabs one. 'Here it is. Cars.'

He opens it on the desk and rifles through until he finds what he's looking for. He jots down the information.

In my pickup, I consider calling the DPS and putting out a BOLO for Krista's car, but it's early for that. They won't want to act until she's been gone twenty-four hours anyway.

ELEVEN

I intend to go straight to the office and call Krista's brother in Miami, but as I'm getting in my car, a call comes in from Junior Addison's office that he's done with Maddy's backpack and I can pick it up anytime. I head straight for Bobtail. It's mid-afternoon, and Addison isn't in his office, but his receptionist gives me a note he dashed off. 'No stray fingerprints. All belong to the victim.'

Back at headquarters, I take a look in the backpack. In addition to the laptop, she brought a wallet, a small notebook and a pen, a purse-size container of tissues, and a folded-up rain jacket. There's also a pamphlet for the organization called The Time Is Now. On the cover, there's a photo of a group of women of all ages reaching upwards. The inside front cover says the goal of the group is 'to seize the moment to move forward with women's rights. *The Time Is Now!*' Inside, there are other photos of women, and a section decrying the rights lost when the Supreme Court came to the Dobbs decision. There are quotes from female leaders in Texas politics. And, of course, the inevitable request for donations.

I wonder why she took the laptop with her. Was she going to show something to whoever she was riding with? And why was the pamphlet in her backpack? Was she meeting someone to ask for a donation? Or did whoever picked her up give the pamphlet to her?

Which brings me back to why she was out on the farm to market road in the first place. I wonder if whoever Krista said urged Maddy to move to Jarrett Creek might have a house on that road. But if so, since she was running from someone, why not go there to ask for help? Unless she had already been there and found them either not home or not willing to help. Or unless they were the ones chasing her, for whatever reason. I lay the pamphlet on Maria's desk to add to her information about the organization.

Maddy's wallet contains almost forty dollars, tucked alongside a few grocery coupons. She has a few credit cards and a library card from Houston. I turn to the notebook. It appears to mostly be used for grocery lists, but there's a note that says, 'Call Iz. Haven trouble?' followed by a phone number. Isabella Lopez. I wonder when she wrote that note to herself. And what is Haven?

I sit down and dial the number. Isabella Lopez has a husky voice, vibrant. Her voicemail tells me I've reached Haven and to leave a message, which I do. Isabella Lopez looks like my best lead at the moment.

Next, I call Tony Walker, Krista's brother, to find out if he's heard from her.

'This is Tony.' There's loud music and chatter in the background, and I remember that it's an hour later in Miami, getting on for five o'clock there. So the club is open.

I introduce myself and tell him I'm calling to ask him a question about his sister.

'My sister? Krista?' As if he has a collection of sisters.

'That's right.'

The noise shuts off abruptly as if he's shut a door. 'Is she OK?' His voice manages to be aggressive rather than worried.

I ask if he was aware that her mother-in-law was killed a couple of days ago.

'Yeah, Krista called and left a message. I didn't know the woman, but Krista called because she thought I ought to be told what happened.' He snorts. 'I guess that self-righteous bitch got crossways with somebody.'

'What makes you say that? Did Krista have trouble with her?'

'Oh, hell no. Krista loved her. Of course she did. They were both liberals. Thought they knew everything. But from the way Krista talked, it sounded like Maddy stuck her nose in places it didn't belong.'

'What do you mean "stuck her nose in places it didn't belong"?' I wonder if she was complaining that Maddy wanted to move so Krista would break up with her lover.

'Krista wasn't getting along with her husband, and she said her mother-in-law interfered.'

'And she was angry about that?'

'She didn't say so, but if it was me, I'd be aggravated. So what are you calling about exactly? I need to get back to work.'

'The thing is your sister seems to have gone missing.'

'What?' He spits out the word. 'Why didn't you say so?'

'Don't get excited; she hasn't been gone long, but she didn't let anybody know where she was going. I'm calling to see if you've spoken with her.'

'Not since she called to tell me about her mother-in-law getting shot. She didn't tell her husband where she was going?'

'No, but like I said, it's early to be worried. Anybody you can think of who might be in touch with your sister?'

'Not a clue.'

'One more question. I don't know if you were aware, but Krista was seeing another man for a while. Do you happen to know his name?'

He grunts a half-laugh. 'She never said. The only reason she told me is when I asked why they were moving to some hick town. I have no idea who the guy was. You think she's gone off with him?'

'I'm just trying to follow up on every possibility. If she does get in touch, will you give me a call?'

'Depends on if she wants to lie low.'

'If that turns out to be the case, I'd appreciate it if you'd at least ask her to call me to let me know we don't need to be spending resources trying to find her.'

'Will do.' The noise cranks up again and he abruptly ends the call.

'Nice family,' I say to nobody.

Maria comes back in, looking flustered and smelling fishy. She has Dusty with her, and he's obviously had himself a fine time. His tongue is lolling out and I swear he's grinning. Maria goes into the restroom and comes out wiping her hands.

'Who knew fishing could get people into such arguments?' she says. 'I thought they fished so they could relax.'

'What happened?'

'A half-dozen guys were out at the lake, here for the weekend, and I guess they started drinking early and went out in a couple of boats, and when they got back, they started arguing over who caught what fish. They were at Dooley's, and he didn't like the way things were going, so he called me to come out and settle them down.'

I laugh. 'How did you handle it?'

'I told them if they didn't cut it out, they'd be spending the weekend staring at the bars of our jail from the inside rather than out on the water. Then I offered to hand the fish out to them at random, since they couldn't decide who caught what.' She rolls her eyes. 'You won't believe this, but they said that would be OK. But that meant I had to handle the fish. I don't know if I've ever told you, but I don't like fish. And I don't like the smell of it.'

By now I'm laughing outright. 'I'll remember not to ask you to go fishing with me.'

She starts to laugh too. 'By the way,' she says, 'Dooley asked me to tell you whoever has been sneaking one of his boats out at night is still at it. He wants you to come by and talk to him.'

'I'll take care of it.' I've been putting off calling Dooley, but I ought to at least let him know I haven't forgotten him and his trouble. He called me last week to tell me that somebody had been breaking into his boathouse and taking a boat out at night.

Connor walks in as my phone rings. I wave at Connor and answer my phone. It's Josh Benson.

'I heard from Krista. She's fine. She said she needed to get away to get some work done.'

I'm caught off-guard. Somehow, I hadn't expected her to show up so quickly. I'm glad, but also wary. 'That's good to hear. Did she say where she is?'

'She . . . well, no.'

Anybody else, I wouldn't ask, but this family is so odd that I feel I have to. 'Did you ask her where she was?'

'Yes, but she didn't want to tell me.' He sounds decidedly unhappy now.

'When did she call?'

'Ten minutes ago.'

'How did she sound? Relaxed? Upset?'

There's a long pause. I realize that I'm asking him to do something he wouldn't normally do – analyze his wife's mood. 'I wouldn't say relaxed. Tense.'

I'll have to feed him every question with care. 'What makes you think that?'

'I don't know. She . . . she stuttered. You know, like she was nervous.'

'You're sure it was Krista?'

'Uh . . . I think so. Who else would it be?' That's the question, isn't it?

'And did she say when she might come back?'

'No. She didn't talk long. She said she wasn't where she could talk easily.'

'Was there noise in the background?'

He takes a few seconds to answer. 'Not really. It sounded like she was walking around. Like she was pacing.'

'I'd like you to call her back. Think of some good reason you'd need to call her. Like tell her you forgot that you need to ask her about the funeral arrangements or something.'

'I suppose I could, but . . .'

'But what?'

'She told me not to.'

'She said not to call her back? Did she say why?'

'No, that's all she said.'

'Josh, did she sound angry?'

'I don't think so.'

'Then call her back. If she answers, say you called by accident. And then phone me.'

'OK.'

Maria is frowning. 'What's going on?'

I tell her Krista is missing. 'That was Josh saying that she'd called and said she was OK.'

'But from the way you were talking to him, I have a hunch you're not convinced. Do you think he's lying?'

'I hadn't thought of that. Of course, it's possible, but I was more wondering if she has been taken against her will.'

'But you said she took her car.'

I nod. 'So it's probably OK. I want to make sure.'

My phone rings again. 'Chief Craddock? Krista didn't answer her phone.'

'Josh, I'm coming out there. I'll be there in ten minutes.'

I tell Connor and Maria that I'll be right back. 'I may call you to do something for me,' I tell Maria.

'Before you go,' Maria says, 'what's this?' She's holding the pamphlet I left on her desk.

'I got Maddy's backpack. That brochure was in it. I'll tell you about it when I get back.'

When I ring the doorbell, it's late in the afternoon and Josh answers the door, but instead of asking me inside, he steps out on to the front porch. 'Eileen and Hannah are driving me crazy. I'd rather talk out here.'

There's no shade on the porch, and it's hot and so muggy you can practically drink the air, so I get right to the point. 'I'm glad you've heard from Krista,' I say, 'but it troubles me that she wouldn't say where she was. Mind if I take a look at your phone?'

He looks puzzled, but hands it over. I ask him for his password and when he gives it to me, I go right to the list of recent calls. Sure enough, there's a call from Krista's number. At least he wasn't lying about that. Unless someone has killed her and taken her phone and dialed Josh's number to make it look like he got a call from her. That's a far-fetched scenario, but I have to check it out. In front of him, I call Maria and tell her I'd like her to contact Krista's phone provider and get a line on where she made the call from.

'I didn't know you could do that,' Josh says after I hang up.

'We won't be able to know exactly where she is, but we'll get a general area. Meanwhile . . .' I take out my phone and dial her number. It rings several times before the message clicks on.

'Krista,' I say. 'This is Chief Craddock. It's important that you get in touch with me as soon as you get this message.'

When I hang up, I say, 'I got your mamma's backpack back from the coroner's office. Have you ever heard of Isabella Lopez?'

'Sure,' Josh says. 'Mamma knew her back in Houston and did some work with her. She's kind of a crazy lady. She and Mamma didn't get along at all.'

'Crazy in what way?'

'You couldn't talk sense to her. At least, that's what Mamma said.' He frowns. 'Why are you asking?'

'In the backpack, I found a note she wrote to herself to call Ms Lopez. Do you know if they've stayed in touch since you moved here?'

'She didn't say one way or another, but she never mentioned her.'

It's frustrating not to be able to ask Krista the same thing. And I doubt Eileen would know.

'How long before the phone company will know where Krista was calling from?' he asks.

'It could take a couple of hours. Given how late it is now, probably not until in the morning.'

'Can you tell me where she is when you find out?'

'Yes.' But I probably won't.

TWELVE

When I get back, Connor and Maria are arguing over who should go out on a call about a dog 'acting funny.'

'Connor, that'll be you,' I say, even though I know he's not comfortable around dogs. He needs to get over it. 'Maria is off tomorrow and she's heading out for San Antonio. She needs to leave before the traffic gets too bad.'

He sighs and says OK.

'You don't need any heroics. Just decide whether you need to call Doc England to come and pick up the dog to check it for rabies.'

'How will I know that?' His voice is alarmed.

'Let me show you.' I open my computer and find a website that shows photos of rabid dogs.'

He still looks doubtful. 'Seems lot a lot of dogs are snappish,' he says.

'True, but a rabid dog will hang its head and maybe stagger.'

After Connor leaves, I bring out Maddy's backpack. 'I got this back from Addison. Maddy's laptop is here and there's a note.' I show it to her. 'I called the number for Haven and left a message.'

'Did you google it?' she asks.

'Haven't had time.'

She opens her computer and keys it in.

'Here we go.' She turns the computer for me to read it.

Haven has a very minimal website of one page that says it's 'A place where women can find a safe and caring community. We have staff members who can listen, give advice, and help you determine the care you need to obtain a healthy and productive life.' The text is also written in Spanish. There is no telephone number, just a form for a woman to complete and send off by email. It asks for first name only, 'the safest way to contact you – your own telephone number or email, or that of a trusted friend or relative.' The final line on the page says, 'We will contact you within twenty-four hours.'

I look up from the page. 'Simple and direct.'

'But what does it mean?' she asks. 'The Time Is Now seems to be focused on political campaigning around women's rights, whereas Haven feels vague. I'll write them and give them my phone number. Maybe I can get a conversation going.'

'And here's her computer.' I take Maddy's laptop out of the backpack.

Maria groans. 'I wish I didn't have to go to San Antonio. I want to look through this computer right away.'

'I thought it was your mamma's birthday.'

Maria makes a hissing noise through her teeth. 'Right. But that's tomorrow, and I can be back Sunday morning. This can't wait.'

'I might take a run at it myself,' I say.

She glares at me. 'Don't mess with anything.'

I give her my innocent look. 'You think I'm a complete idiot?'

She narrows her eyes. 'No, but I think you don't know your way around a strange computer.'

I promise to approach it carefully, and she scoots out the door.

It's almost five, and I wonder what's keeping Connor. Maybe the dog really was rabid.

I'm still waiting for the phone company to notify me where Krista's phone call originated from. I'm supposed to go over to take Wendy out to dinner, but I call and ask if she can come to Jarrett Creek instead. She says of course she'll come over. 'We haven't been to that new barbecue place on the way to Bobtail.'

Like magic, as soon as I hang up from talking to her, the phone company calls with a surprise piece of information. Krista called from the east side of Bobtail. She may have wanted to get away, but she didn't go all that far. I know there are several motels in that area, near the junior college. I'm tempted to go to Bobtail and cruise around to see if I could spot her car at one of the motels in the vicinity, but that will have to wait until tomorrow.

Since Connor still isn't back from checking on the reported dog problem, I put in a call to his cell phone, but he doesn't reply. Unusual. I call the vet's office, It's closing time, and they say they haven't heard from him. I'm annoyed because I didn't pay attention to who the rabid dog call came from. I call Maria's cell, and she tells me it was Mrs Dawkins. 'The Baptist preacher's wife. I wouldn't worry. She thinks every dog she sees is rabid. Connor probably just went on home.'

Not without calling he wouldn't.

The Dawkinses' place is on the way to my house, so I roust

Dusty from under my desk where he's sound asleep, lock up the station, and head out. The Dawkinses live in a house that's large but without distinction, the sort of utilitarian architecture that defines most of the older houses in Jarrett Creek. It's next door to the Baptist church, where Dawkins is the pastor. Connor's car isn't here. Phyllis Dawkins answers the door. She's a prim-looking woman, with a rigid posture. The few times I've seen her, her mouth is always set in a firm line.

I tip my hat to her. 'I wanted to make sure Deputy Loving came by to check out the dog you were worried about,' I say.

'He was here, but the dog had run on down the street, and I think your deputy was going to look for him. That dog needs to be put down.'

'I'll look into it.'

She steps out on to the porch, and it seems to me her posture is even more rigid than usual. 'While I've got you here, I have something to talk to you about. It's important.'

'Of course. What can I do for you?'

She crosses her arms, which if anything brings her even more upright. 'That woman. The one who was killed. I want to know what she was doing here in Jarrett Creek.'

An odd question. I take my hat off and run my hand through my hair. 'What do you mean, "what she was doing here"?'

'Don't tell me you don't know what she was up to.'

I don't know exactly what she means, but her expression is so angry I think I need to tread carefully. 'I know that she was politically active when she lived in Houston.'

Her eyes narrow. 'I've heard that she was breaking the law and asking for trouble.'

I'm momentarily speechless. Finally, I say, 'Mrs Dawkins, whatever law you think she was breaking, it's my job to find out who killed her.'

'Were her people working with her to carry out her dastardly work? Her son? Her daughter-in-law?'

I'm more and more puzzled. 'Exactly what is it you're talking about? What dastardly work?'

'If you don't know, you aren't doing a proper job and you ought to be ashamed of yourself.'

'It would help if you'd spell out what you mean.'

'All right, I will. She was helping women kill their unborn babies.

And if she's been murdered because she was killing babies, I see no reason for you to pursue her killer, because they did it in the cause of righteousness.'

Her words stun me.

'You think she deserved to be murdered?'

She blinks. 'I'm not saying that. But if you'd arrested her, she might not have gotten herself killed. We have a righteous community here in Jarrett Creek, and people won't put up with her kind of mischief. Leading young girls astray.' She's worked herself into a state and is practically spitting.

I feel like I've been slapped. Was Maddy Benson performing abortions? 'And you know this how?'

'Never mind how I know. It doesn't seem to me like you're trying very hard to find out, either. And what about her son and daughter-in-law? Were they involved, too? I think you should arrest them until you find out what was going on in that house.'

'It might help me sort this out if I could talk to the person who gave you this information.' A rumor like this is bound to stir people up.

'That's for me to know.'

'If I can't check out your information at its source, I can't do much. You can be sure if I find evidence of a law being broken, though, I'll take the appropriate measures. Now, I'm sorry to say I can't stay and chat with you. I need to go find my deputy.' I set my hat back on my head and trot down the steps.

'Well, I never!' she says, and she slams the door behind her. Something tells me I haven't heard the last of this.

In the car, I sit and collect my thoughts. Could it be true, what the preacher's wife said? Or is this some vicious rumor because the woman was a stranger? Could this be why Maddy Benson's family is so peculiar? Do they know more than they're admitting? I start the car up. I've got some digging to do.

I've only gone a block when I see Connor's old heap of a car parked askew, with the door open, in front of a small house set back from the street.

Connor is an orderly person in many ways, and it isn't like him to leave his car that way. I screech to a halt behind it and jump out, on the alert, leaving Dusty in the cab. The last thing I need is for him to get bitten by a rabid dog. I hear yelling from behind the house, between Connor and a woman, who sounds hysterical.

I reach into my pickup and retrieve my Colt from the glove box and strap it on. In the front seat, Dusty is sitting at attention, ears pricked, straining forward.

As I walk around the side of the house, I hear a strange kind of sound, like a cross between a howl and a snarl. I call out, 'Hello!'

'Chief, I'm back here.' Connor sounds panicky.

Whoever the woman is cries out, 'No, don't shoot him.'

Around the back of the house, I'm greeted with the sight of Connor with his gun drawn and a young woman cowering in front of him, sobbing. Connor is focused on a big, scruffy black dog who's backed against the fence with his teeth bared. This has to be the dog that Mrs Dawkins claimed was rabid. Like I told Connor, rabid dogs have a certain look that's unmistakable – cringing and terrified, but at the same time hostile. They're confused and hunched as if they're in pain. This dog is not like that. He's snarling, but there's no sign of confusion.

'That your dog?' I ask the woman.

'Yes, he's just scared. Please don't shoot him.'

'We need to get him penned up.' I tell Connor to lower his weapon.

The woman calls out to the dog to be a good boy, and he relaxes his mouth, although he still looks wary. 'He'll be OK in a minute,' she says. 'And then I'll pen him up.'

I introduce myself and the woman says, 'Oh, you're Chief Craddock. I'm Becky Peltier.' She glances at the dog and back at me, still worried.

To set her at ease, I say, 'You lived here long?'

'A couple of years, but we both worked in Bobtail until recently, so we weren't around much.'

'You work here in Jarrett Creek now?'

'My husband does. He's a mechanic. He's gone to work for Skippy Ryland at the service station downtown. I haven't gotten a job yet.'

The dog has settled down on its haunches, tongue lolling. 'Ms Peltier, let's get your dog in his pen.'

'Come on, Duke, you're a good boy,' she says. She leads the dog to a pen in the back of the property. He goes in willingly and she latches the gate.

When she comes back, I say, 'Why was the dog out if he's dangerous?'

'He isn't dangerous,' she wails. 'Or, at least, he never has been. We usually keep him in the yard, but I guess somebody forgot to close the gate, and he got out. I was out front and I saw him run down the street so I ran after him. And then this woman came screaming out of her house and chased him with a broom. I tried to stop her, and she yelled at me and that's when he started barking at her.'

'Well, try to keep him penned up.'

'I will, but that woman shouldn't have gone after him like that. She was swatting at him with her broom, trying to hit him. That's not right.'

'Ms Peltier, has your dog ever bitten anyone?'

'No! Duke is a really sweet dog. He's six years old and we've never had a bit of trouble with him.'

'Is he up to date on his shots?'

She looks embarrassed. 'Probably not. We've had some money problems and I think we didn't keep them up.'

'I'll tell you what. Go to Doc England – he's the vet – and tell him you need the shots but you can't pay him all at once. He'll give you a payment plan. It's important that you get those shots.'

'Thank you. I'll do that.'

I tell her where the vet's office is, and she says she'll call him right away.

Connor walks back with me to our cars. When we reach his car, he says, 'Chief, I don't think she was completely honest. That dog was crazy when I got here. She had him on a leash, and he broke away. I thought he was going to go after me, but she chased him into the back yard so he wouldn't attack. I really was afraid he had rabies.'

'I'm glad you didn't have to shoot him,' I say. 'I'd like you to call Doc England and tell him what happened. He may want to come out and take a look at the dog.'

By the time I get home, I barely have time to change clothes before Wendy gets here.

But the day isn't finished messing with me yet. The new barbecue place is a sham – somebody who thought they could get away with cooking meat and slathering ketchup on it and calling it barbecue. So neither of us is satisfied with our meal.

Meanwhile, my mind is stuck on the events of today. I'm still uneasy that Krista Benson might be in some sort of trouble, and I wonder if she actually left of her own accord. I'm also curious why Maddy's folks haven't been in touch. And I keep going back to the nasty attitude of the preacher's wife. I can't get over her sniping vengeance. I'd like to know how she found out what Maddy was doing, and if it's true.

'Samuel!'

I realize Wendy has been saying my name, trying to break into my reverie.

'I'm sorry, it's been a troubling day.'

'You could have told me if you didn't want to see me tonight.'

Wendy is usually forgiving when she knows my job is taking my attention, and her sharp tone surprises me.

I reach across the table, where she has pushed aside her plate, the food half eaten, and take her hand. 'I do want to see you. It's been a troubling couple of days. You know, this woman who got killed, I can't seem to find out much about her.' I tell her the things that are bothering me. What catches her interest is Phyllis Dawkins's diatribe against Maddy.

'Ugh, this Dawkins woman sounds hateful. Do you think what she said is true?'

'That's a good question, and not one we're likely to find the answer to tonight.' I smile. 'I appreciate you letting me vent. I promise I'll put everything aside now.'

She sighs. 'You know, I always understand when you've got things on your mind with a case. It's just that I had something in particular to talk to you about.'

'What's up?'

'I've decided to take a trip with a couple of friends. We're going to San Francisco for a few days.'

'Good. I know how much you love to travel. And you haven't been anywhere in a while.'

She sighs again. I've said the wrong thing. 'What's the trouble?'

'I was hoping you'd say you'd come with me.'

'When are you going?'

'Sheila wants to go now. Like, Sunday. She was supposed to go with her husband, but he's been sick and doesn't feel up to it, so she wants me to use his ticket. I hoped you could come along.'

'Wendy, you know I can't get away that soon, but I'll be glad to make a plan for us to go as soon as this case gets wrapped up.' I read stubbornness on her face. 'But look, why don't you go with her, and while you're out there, you can scout it out. That way, when you and I go, you'll know your way around.'

We end up with her deciding I'm right, that she should go to San Francisco with her friends.

'If some miracle happens and this gets wound up in a couple of days, I'll come and join you.'

When I get home, I take Dusty for a walk before bed. We're only gone for fifteen minutes, but when I get back, I spy a package on my front steps. It wasn't here when I left. What's it doing here? It's approximately ten inches by twelve, the size of a shoebox, wrapped in plain brown paper and taped shut. I shine my flashlight on it and see no visible markings. I stand with my hands on my hips, staring down at it, trying to decide if I need to be concerned about it. Dusty has been out trolling the yard for critters, and he comes back and charges up the steps toward the package. 'No!' I yell. I guess my voice is sharp enough, because he backs up and crouches on to his haunches, dividing his attention between me and the package. I pick him up, which surprises him so much that he doesn't try to wriggle free. I open the front door, tuck him inside, and shut the door.

I scan the area to see if anybody is lurking nearby. I see no one. Jarrett Creek is a quiet town – most of the time, anyway – and by now it's after nine, and everyone is hunkered down. I walk out to the street and peruse the cars parked out there, but I only see familiar vehicles.

I don't go back up the steps, but stand out in the yard, thinking. Is this package dangerous? A bomb? That seems unlikely. Why would someone put a bomb on my porch?

I'll feel like an idiot if it's a gift from someone I know, and I overreact. But who would wrap a gift up so securely and not leave a name on it?

Still standing outside, I phone Maria, Jenny, and Loretta to ask if they've left anything on my porch, but they all say no. I ask Jenny if she noticed anybody hanging around who shouldn't be here, but she says she's been inside all evening. 'I'll call Will and ask him,' she says. 'He just left.' She calls back in a few minutes and says he didn't notice anybody. 'But he said he was intent on getting home, so he wasn't paying attention.'

'I don't like the sound of that,' Maria says, when I tell her someone has left an anonymous package. 'Maybe you should call Sheriff Hedges.'

'I have half a mind to leave it out here, but if it's a bomb, I may wake up in the middle of the night with my house flattened around me.'

'Boss, this isn't a laughing matter. You know as well as I do that it could be serious. Too many crazy people around these days. I'm coming over there.'

She's right. We're investigating the murder of a woman we don't know much about. She seems to have drawn some anger from people because she was outspoken politically, and then there's that charge from Phyllis Dawkins, but I don't know if any of that is enough for someone to send me a bomb.

'It's not necessary for you to come over. What are you going to do that I won't do?'

But she's hung up. She knew I'd protest, and she didn't want to hear it.

There are several possibilities for dealing with this. Starting with the low end of the spectrum, I can notify Sheriff Hedges. He'd most likely get someone out here from one of the larger cities – Austin, Houston, or San Antonio – to come out and take a look. Or I could call the Department of Public Safety headquarters in Bryan/College Station. I suppose they have people who deal with bombs, or they'd call the FBI. All that seems excessive. It could take hours, and I'm tired and don't want to spend half the night waiting. I find it hard to imagine somebody around here having the wherewithal to put together a serious bomb. But what if I'm wrong?

Five minutes later, Maria comes wheeling up. And Jenny Sandstone from next door comes striding up, dressed in a flowered dressing robe. It isn't a garment I would have imagined she'd own. She sees me looking at it. 'Don't say a word,' she says. 'Will got it for me as a present. Men!'

We all focus on the package. 'I'm trying to decide if I should call somebody,' I say and I lay out the possibilities.

'DPS is more likely to have the resources to look into this,' Maria says.

Jenny concurs. 'I'm nervous that there could be a timer on it or a remote control. It could go off before anybody gets here. You two come on over to my place and we'll wait for them there. This little bundle is big enough to blow up your house if it has an explosive like C-4 in it.'

I wonder how she knows anything about C-4, but Jenny is always full of random information.

The two of them start walking toward Jenny's, but I walk around the side of the house, where I know a rake is leaning up against the side. I come back around carrying the rake and call out, 'Look, you two go on. I'm going to at least see how heavy it is.' Before they can protest, I gently nudge the package with the rake. It moves freely, which means it isn't heavy.

'Don't!' Maria says.

I nudge it harder. 'If there's anything in it, it's light,' I say.

They come back closer. 'Could be some kind of toxic material,' Jenny says.

But why? I'm thinking this is some kind of practical joke, or a warning. 'You two stay back,' I say. I lean down and pull the tape off one end. I pull out my pocket knife and cut away the paper. It is a shoebox. I step back and loosen the top with the tines of the rake. Nothing happens, so I go back closer, shining the flashlight on it in case there's powder.

'The box is full of tissue paper,' I tell them.

'Wait,' Maria says. 'Use gloves to look inside.'

She's right. I go inside and grab some gloves. With gloves on, I gingerly take out the top tissue, the kind shoes are wrapped in. It's crinkled, but there are only a couple of pieces. I shake them each gently, and out of one falls a piece of paper with typewritten words. I shine the light on it. It reads, *Stop your investigation! Benson was helping girls to commit murder. She deserved to die.*

I let out a breath I didn't know I was holding.

'This is the message.' I show it to Maria and Jenny.

'Somebody went to a lot of trouble to send you that message,' Maria says.

'And made you think it was a bomb,' Jenny says. 'Scare tactic.'

'Mission accomplished with the scare,' I say. 'But if whoever did this thinks it's going to stop the investigation, they're wrong.'

I drop the note back into the shoebox.

'I assume you're going to bring that in tomorrow morning so I can dust it,' Maria says.

'You can take it now,' I say. I hand it over and Maria takes it to her car and drives away.

Jenny heads back to her place and I go inside mine. As tired as I was after my trip to Houston, I'm too wired to go straight to bed. So I pour myself a couple of fingers of bourbon and watch some kind of nonsense on TV until I'm nodding off again, and I head off to bed.

THIRTEEN

Saturday morning

I don't sleep well and am up early. First thing, I patrol the front area in case anyone dropped a clue when they left the package last night. No such luck. Whoever left it must have been watching for me to leave. There's an overgrown hedge on the property next door, which someone could have been standing in, but Dusty would have alerted me to someone there. So whoever it was most likely was in a car, watching, and dashed on to my porch when they saw me leave. But how would they have known I was going to leave unless they knew I take my dog out every evening? Or maybe they were waiting for me to turn out my lights before they put the package on the porch, thinking I'd find it in the morning, and when they saw me leave, they decided it was their chance. I hadn't noticed any unusual cars out front, but it had been a long day, and I was impatient to get the walk over with. I won't make that mistake again.

I go down and take a cursory look at my cows. I'm eager to get to work. But when I get back to the house, I've just gone inside when Loretta knocks on my screen door and calls out.

I tell her to come in.

She's brought me coffee cake. 'I can't stay,' she says, 'I just wanted to know who that was coming to your door last night so late.'

I come alert. Could Loretta have seen whoever left the package? 'Late?'

'Well, it was after nine. That's late for me.'

'What were you doing out?'

'I was over at Jolene's for a committee meeting, and it ran late. So who was it?'

'I don't know. I wasn't home. I was out walking Dusty. Did you recognize the person coming to my door?'

'No. I was just passing by and noticed him walking up to your house.'

Him. 'Did you see a car?'

'Why are you asking these questions? Who was it?'

'I don't know. Somebody left me a package, and I wondered who it was.' I'm making light of it. I don't need Loretta to start worrying about possible bombs.

'What kind of package?'

'Nothing important, but whoever it was didn't leave a name. So I'm curious: did you see a car or just a person walking up to my porch?'

She peers at me, frowning. 'I didn't see a car, just a man. I only saw him from the back. He was shorter than you, had on dark pants and T-shirt.'

'Did he move like a young man, older man?'

'I'd say young. He was moving fast, not running, but moving right along. What do you mean, the package wasn't important?'

I laugh. 'There was just a note inside.'

'That sounds strange. They didn't sign the note?'

'Loretta, you're going to have to let this go. It's something to do with the case I'm working on.'

I can tell she's ready to press me farther, so I tell her I've got to get to the office. I decide to leave Dusty at home, inside. It's hot, and there's no telling what I'll get up to today.

When I arrive at work, I'm surprised to find Connor Loving there before me. I came early so I could get started looking through Maddy Benson's laptop.

'I thought Brick was on this morning,' I say.

'He is. But I need to talk to you, so I came in early.' He looks decidedly unhappy.

'Let me get some coffee and we'll chat.'

When we're settled, he fidgets in his chair until I say, 'Just come out with it. It can't be that bad.'

'I don't know if I'm cut out to be a police officer,' he blurts out.

'What brought this on? The dog?'

'Partly.' He pauses. His face is getting red, as it tends to do when he's upset. 'But it's that woman chasing him with a broom. You know I'm not a big fan of dogs.' A guilty look appears on his face. He doesn't get along with Dusty. 'But I would never go after one like that. And I don't understand somebody being so mean.'

'You know, she's a fearful person.'

He swallows. 'There's more. She said something. I don't know what it meant.'

'About Maddy Benson?'

'Yeah. She asked me if I knew Maddy Benson was murdering innocent babies. What did she mean? I mean I know what she's saying, but . . .' He grinds to a halt.

'She's heard some kind of rumor. I'm chasing it down. What did you say when she told you that?'

'I told her I didn't know anything about that, and that I needed to find that dog. And I left.'

Good for him.

'Connor, I'm sorry Mrs Dawkins upset you. No doubt she's got something on her mind. Whether there's any truth to it, I don't know. But either way, I'd hate for her to force you out of your job.'

'It's not just that.' He shakes his head, his expression sad. 'I feel like every time I go out on a call, I worry that I won't be able to take care of business the way I should. Like Maria would.'

'You and Maria are different. No question. But each of you has something you're good at that the other one doesn't have.' I remind him of the times I've asked him to help older people when they're troubled by neighbors or hearing noises. 'That's your strong point, helping people. How do you think Maria would handle that?'

He thinks for a minute. 'She doesn't have as much patience as I do. She'd tell them to buck up.'

I wouldn't put it quite that bluntly, but he's right: she wouldn't have much patience. 'I trust you to listen to their concerns and soothe them. And let's face it, that's half our job, settling people down. Now let me ask you this: what do you like about being a police officer?'

His face is bright red by now. 'I always wanted to be a cop. I liked the idea of helping people, but now I think I might have gotten most of my ideas from TV shows.'

'OK. So the job isn't what you thought it would be.'

He nods.

'What would you rather do instead?'

He looks off into the distance. His hands are knotted together in his lap. 'You know what I think I'd like? I'd like to be a social worker.'

'Have you talked to a social worker?'

'No, but I've looked it up online, and some of the work they do really appeals to me. I know it means I'd have to go back to school, but I have two years of college, so it's only two more years.'

'You think your folks will help you with your college expenses?'

'No, sir, they don't have the money, but I've been saving and I can get a loan.'

'What would you think of working part-time here and going to school part-time at Texas A&M?'

'If I can get enrolled there. That's a hard school to get into.'

'You won't know until you apply. You could consider taking a couple of classes this fall to see how you like it. I know you went to Bobtail Junior College. How were your grades?'

'Not bad.' He says it with some pride, so my guess is the grades were good.

'Then go for it! I'll give you a good recommendation if it will help. That's where I went to school.'

He seems relieved and says he's going to apply right away.

After he leaves, I sit thinking for a few minutes. He's right; he might be better as a social worker than a cop. But meanwhile, I'll try to make him feel like he's contributing.

As much as I hate to, I have to notify Leeland Reagan about the package. Even though it turned out not to be much of anything, the Department of Public Safety needs to know.

Reagan keeps the same early hours I do, and he answers right away. I tell him what happened.

'Well, your little old town does get some excitement,' he says dryly. 'Why would anybody threaten you like that?'

'You got me. All I can figure is somebody had a grudge against Maddy Benson.' I tell him that we found some threatening notes in her desk drawer and that her friends said she was active in women's rights politics when she lived in Houston. I decide not to tell him about Phyllis Dawkins's comments.

'She sure made somebody mad,' he says. 'You going to send them to forensics to get fingerprints?'

'My deputy can do that. She's good at it.'

He grunts. 'Look, with that package being left, you think it might be better to pass the investigation off to the DPS?'

'You could be right, but I'm stubborn. I don't like being warned off. I want to find out who killed this woman. And I don't want to jump to the conclusion that she was killed because of her political activities. Could be some other reason entirely.'

'Hmm, could be, but . . . well, either way, let me know if you need resources. And Craddock?'

'Yeah?'

'Next time you get a suspicious package, dispense with the hero act and call us. The DPS has a perfectly good bomb squad we can call on.'

'Got it.'

'And you mentioned that she got threatening letters. I want you to turn those over to me. I'll pass them on to the FBI. They have a section that deals with that kind of thing. They may be able to get some idea of who shot the woman. At least they can see if the threats she got match others on file.'

'I'll be glad to turn them over. There's one to pay particular attention to.' I tell him that Elizabeth Robinson was a member of the PTA who had a particular animosity toward Maddy when their kids were in school together.

'Sounds like a lead.'

'Maybe. I talked to a couple of people who knew Maddy, and they said Elizabeth Robinson was an annoyance, but they didn't think she would be dangerous.'

'Won't hurt to check.'

We arrange for a highway patrol team to pick up the file sometime when they're in the area today.

When I hang up, I consider what I should do. I need to know who has been spreading rumors about Maddy Benson. The longer the rumors fly, the more outrageous they're likely to get.

The grapevine is a tortuous vine with a lot of hidden tendrils. It's almost impossible to know who grabs hold of a bit of information and passes it on. I didn't have time to go into it when I saw Loretta this morning, but if anybody knows, she will. I'll call her when I have time.

But first I phone Josh Benson to see if Krista has returned. He doesn't answer, so I leave a message and then call his Aunt Eileen.

'No, she isn't back,' Eileen says, 'and as far as I know, Josh hasn't heard any more from her, although I don't know that he would bother to tell me anyway.'

I ask her to let me know if Krista shows up.

I've no sooner hung up than my phone rings again, and this time it's someone I want to talk to. Maddy Benson's father, Andrew Dillard.

'You've been trying to reach my wife and me? I assume it's about our daughter's murder.'

'Yes, Mr Dillard. I'm sorry for your loss. I need to ask you a few questions. Is this a good time?'

'What kind of questions?'

'I want to get a clearer picture of your daughter and maybe get some sense of why she was the target of a shooter.'

He snorts. 'Well, first of all, we live in a gun-happy state, and it hardly takes a genius to figure out that with all these guns, people are bound to be random targets.'

'Maybe it was random, but maybe not. I need to explore all possible motives.'

I hear a woman's voice in the background, indignant.

'Why is it up to you? Isn't her death important enough to turn over to the Texas Rangers, or the FBI?'

Another member of the family who wants to take this out of my hands. 'The Department of Public Safety is involved in the investigation. Law enforcement would appreciate your cooperation.' That ought to be vague enough.

'Well, we don't know anything. We've never been to visit her in that town, and she's only been to see us once since she moved.'

'I see. When was the last time you spoke with her?'

He says something to his wife. 'My wife says she talked to her a month ago.'

'Did your daughter indicate that anything was worrying her? Anybody she'd had problems with?'

'Hold on a minute. I'm going to let you speak with my wife, Helen.'

I ask her the same question.

'I don't remember her being troubled by anything. Seemed like a normal conversation, just catching up. I regret that I didn't spend more time talking with her. Maybe she would have opened up to me.'

Does she regret it? From what I've heard, she and her husband didn't focus much on their daughters. And they didn't bother to call Josh back until a couple of days had passed, even though he told them the call was urgent.

'Did your daughter ever indicate that she had problems with anyone?'

'Not really, although I did wonder if she was making a mistake getting so caught up in politics. My husband and I try to keep away from that kind of thing. It's upsetting, and there's nothing you can do about it anyway. Do you think her politics made her a target?'

'I'm looking into it.'

Neither of them is able to give me any more information than I already have. I thank them for their time and tell them to call if they think of anything to add.

Another call comes in, this one from Dooley. I should talk to him, if only to assure him that I'll look into his problem as soon as I get a minute.

'I know you're busy,' he says, 'and I don't want to bug you, but I need you to put a stop to whoever has been sneaking my boats out. No harm has been done so far, but I'm afraid at some point somebody will have an accident and I'll be liable because it's an attractive nuisance.'

'You've got a lock on the door to the boathouse?'

'Hell, yes. But either somebody stole a key or one of my workers is letting people in.'

He wants me to come out and talk to him. I tell him I'll come by as soon as I get a minute. Whenever that is.

While I was talking to Dooley, I got a call from Tom Gainer. I phone back and he says he's back home in Galveston. 'What did you call about?' he asks.

'Is your son there?'

'No, he's staying one more week in Jarrett Creek.'

'Who's he staying with?'

'The kid I mentioned before.'

'Right, the Baptist preacher's son.'

I ask for the boy's cell phone number. Tom had told me his son probably left the gate open out at his place and that's how Maddy got in. I want to check with the boy to make sure it was him, and find out if there's a reason he left it open or if it was carelessness. Not that I suspect him of anything, but maybe he had some reason to leave the gate open for somebody he knew. Stray bits of information like that don't always lead to anything, but it's the kind of thing you have to follow through on.

I call Dell Gainer's phone and he picks up. He tells me he and his friend have just gotten back to Dooley's Marina after a morning of fishing. 'We're grabbing some lunch and then going back out for more,' he says.

'You catch anything?'

'Not this morning, but we will.'

I like his optimism. 'I'd like to ask you a few questions. I'd appreciate it if you'd stick around at Dooley's until I get there.'

'What kind of questions?' He suddenly sounds younger.

'About the woman who was killed out at your daddy's place.'

'Oh, that. I don't know anything about that.'

I wonder what he thought I was going to ask him. 'I'd like you to hang around until I get there.'

'I guess we can stick around.'

FOURTEEN

I head right out in my pickup. Since it's noon on Saturday, traffic is light going out to the lake and I'm at Dooley's Marina in fifteen minutes. I walk in and Dooley is behind the counter. 'You coming to check out my complaint?'

I was so intent on questioning Dell Gainer that I'd forgotten I needed to address his complaint. 'I wasn't here for that, but when I get done talking to the boys I came here to talk to, I'll get back to you.'

Two older teenage boys that I presume are the ones I'm looking for are sitting out on the deck. Dooley has recently put a couple of picnic tables out there with umbrellas. Place is getting downright fancy. Whatever they ate, they haven't left a morsel. Teenage boys are never full.

'Which one of you is Dell Gainer?'

One of them stands up. 'That's me.' I should have known. He looks like his daddy, spare and lithe, with sandy hair and blue eyes.

I introduce myself. 'And you are?' I ask the other one, although I think I know who he is. He's heavier than Dell, stocky. Although he's not overweight, he has a bit of flab around the middle, like his daddy. And he has his daddy's look of self-assurance.

'Aaron.'

'Aaron Dawkins?'

'That's right. You know my folks?'

'I do.'

I nod to Dell. 'Let's sit. This won't take long.'

Aaron says, 'I hope it doesn't. We need to get back out there.' There's an undercurrent to his words that I can't quite grasp. It's like he has an ulterior meaning that Dell will catch.

'You boys in college?'

They both nod.

'Going back to school soon, I expect. Where are you enrolled?'

Dell says he's at Texas A&M in Galveston, studying marine biology, and Aaron is at Dallas Baptist University studying liberal arts. They're due back in school in a couple of weeks.

'That's why we don't want to waste a minute. We want to get out on the lake,' Aaron says.

'Dell, it's you I want to talk to. I am interested in how the woman who was killed out at your place got on to the property. Your daddy said he usually keeps the gate locked and he suggested you might have left it unlocked.'

Dell squirms. 'I probably did. I might have been in a hurry to get out to the road because Aaron was picking me up. Look, I'm sorry if that means the woman got killed.'

I hold up my hand. 'No, whoever killed her had her in their sights no matter where she went. I just wanted to check out how she got on to your property. Do you sleep at your dad's place when you stay over during the week?'

'No, I stay at Aaron's.'

'Did you ever meet Maddy Benson?'

Dell's eyes widen. 'Heck, no. Why would I meet her?'

'No reason. Have you ever heard her name before? Either of you?'

Dell shakes his head, but Aaron just stares at me.

All this seems straightforward, and yet it isn't sitting right with me. The boys seem on edge. Aaron, in particular. His leg is jiggling up and down. He's either impatient or nervous, and I'm betting on the latter.

Aaron's mamma had a lot to say about Maddy Benson. I expect he's already heard an earful about her, but I doubt he's met her.

The man who works for Dooley's as a jack-of-all-trades, Red Russell, comes out on the deck to collect the boys' paper plates and plastic forks. I'm surprised. Seems like the boys could have thrown them away themselves.

He avoids looking at me. 'Everything OK out here?' he asks the boys.

'Fine with us,' Aaron says.

'You need anything?' he says to me.

'No, I'm good.'

'If you do, let me know.' Something is definitely going on here. Red has a shifty manner at the best of times, as if he's got secrets. Now he seems to be reluctant to leave. I wonder what these three are up to.

'That's all I wanted to ask.' I move to get up, and they exchange relieved glances. It suddenly comes to me what might be going on. I settle back down. 'You boys have your own boat?'

'No, sir,' Dell says. 'My daddy lets me have some money to rent a boat.'

'I see. You always bring it in at the end of the day?'

'Yes, sir, we have to have it in by dark.'

'Ever do any night fishing?'

'No,' Aaron says. His reply is quick and loud. The boys exchange guilty looks. I know I'm on the right path. I may be able to get rid of two annoying birds with one stone.

'I'd think night fishing would be hard. Can't really see what you're doing. Dooley told me somebody has been sneaking one of his boats out at night, maybe for some night fishing. But I expect it isn't about fishing at all; maybe it's about joyriding in the boat.'

Both of them are staring at me, but for some reason, they can't seem to come up with a reply.

I stretch my legs out, tip my hat back, and fold my hands over my belly. Getting comfortable. At least, I hope it looks that way. 'You boys wouldn't know anything about that, would you?'

'No, why would we know?' the preacher's son says. His tone is belligerent. Reminding me again of his daddy.

'Like if I were to get some DNA readings from the handle of the motor or maybe from the boat itself? You wouldn't mind if I asked your folks if I could get a sample of DNA from you for a match, would you?'

This is preposterous, as anybody with any sense would know, but I'm talking to what I think are guilty teenage boys, and I suspect they're too nervous that they'll be found out to pay attention to details. They probably don't know how DNA works anyway, not to mention that fingerprints would be more likely than DNA to be accessible. But somehow DNA sounds more formidable. Of course, if it's the same boat they rent during the day, their fingerprints and DNA would be all over it anyway, but I'm betting they won't think of that.

'I don't think my daddy would agree to that,' the preacher's son says.

'I could at least ask him. Even if he didn't say yes, he might be inclined to ask why I'd think you might do something like that. I mean, as a parent.'

While he considers my words, looking like he swallowed a frog, I turn my attention to Dell. 'How about you? I have a feeling your daddy would be glad to comply with my request.'

'Wait a minute,' Aaron says. 'Can Dooley prove somebody took the boat out?'

'Absolutely,' I say. Again, I'm fudging. 'He wouldn't have bothered to ask me to investigate if he wasn't sure. That would be a waste of everybody's time.'

Dell clears his throat, and Aaron shoots him a warning look.

'Here's the thing, boys. I don't think Dooley would want to prosecute, although he'd be within his rights. But I think he'd want to know two things. One, who has been sneaking a key to the people who took the boat out. And two, he'd want to make sure it didn't happen again.'

'We don't know anything about it,' Aaron says, but Dell won't look at me. One of these boys has gotten good parental guidance on being honest. The other one not so much.

'I'm going to be talking to Red, the man who was out here collecting your trash. I expect if he has been slipping somebody a key in exchange for a few bucks, he'll be happy to own up to it if he thinks he might lose his job. And I imagine he won't mind turning in whoever he gave the key to.'

'Hold on,' Aaron says. 'The boat wasn't damaged, so why does Dooley care?'

'He's worried that if something happened while the boat was out without a contract, he'd be liable. He's done the right thing by locking the boats up at night, but it's what's called in legal terms an "attractive nuisance" which means he could be prosecuted if anything happened. Like if boys were drinking a few beers and someone fell overboard and drowned, or if they hit something in the dark and the boat got damaged. So it's important that the joyrides stop. Do I make myself clear?'

'Yes, sir,' Dell says.

Aaron shoots him a furious look.

'To make sure, I'm going to ask Dooley if he has any work that needs doing around here. You could help clean some boats up, that sort of thing. I think maybe ten hours of service from each of you would stand you in good stead with him.'

'Wait a minute,' Aaron says. 'We don't have that kind of time to spare.'

'In that case, I better find out what Dooley has in mind for you. He may decide he wants to have you arrested after all. At the very least, he probably doesn't want to rent a boat anymore to someone he can't trust.'

'There are other marinas we can rent from,' Aaron says. I notice it's him doing the talking here. Dell is looking down at the table, not saying a word.

'Not if Dooley puts out the word that you can't be trusted. It's too bad. Could have been an easy fix.' I stand up. 'Seems like ten hours of your time over a couple of weeks would have been worth it.' I settle my hat back on my head.

Aaron stands. 'Now look here,' he says. 'We're talking a hypothetical here. Suppose we agree to this? Not admitting to anything you understand, but as a neighborly thing to do to help Dooley out.'

I look off, as if I'm considering the question. 'I think I can persuade Dooley not to make a fuss. He might need an assurance that it won't happen again.'

'Chief Craddock, it won't happen again,' Dell says. 'And I'd appreciate it if you don't say anything to my daddy about this.'

I take my time answering, giving them a chance to worry. 'I see no reason to drag him into it. He'd be disappointed, but as long as the problem is solved, I think we're done.'

Dell looks relieved, but Aaron is frowning. 'What's to keep you from going back on your word?'

That tells me all I need to know about this young man. 'Do you ask that because you might go back on *your* word if you tell me you won't take the boat out again at night?'

There's that frog again. He swallows. 'No, I won't do that.'

He doesn't call me sir. 'Dell tells me it won't happen again, but you haven't made that promise yet. Let's hear it, and then we're done. I'll take the agreement to Dooley, and we can move on.'

'All right, I guess I can say it won't happen again.' But then his expression gets hard. 'But that doesn't mean I'm admitting anything.'

'As long as it stops.'

I go back inside. Red tells me Dooley isn't in at the moment and I tell him to ask Dooley to give me a call. 'And by the way, Red, I wouldn't use your position of trust here to make a few extra bucks if I were you.'

'I don't know what you're talking about.' He glares at me.

'I think you do. Do I need to discuss it with Dooley?'

'What did those boys tell you? They're liars.'

'Whoa! What makes you say that?'

'Nothing in particular. It's just their reputation.'

'Interesting. One of them is the preacher's son. The preacher would be disappointed to hear that. So if you can give me particulars, I'd follow through.'

He grumbles some but eventually says he doesn't know anything except rumors. I tell him it's probably best not to spread such gossip. 'And by the way, if I hear that you've harassed those boys, I'll be back for another visit, and this time I'll have more to say to Dooley.'

It's twelve thirty, and I go straight from the marina to Loretta's place.

'Samuel, what are you doing here?' Her face is flushed and there's perspiration dotting her forehead.

'Came to ask you if you'd like to go to Bobtail and get some lunch.' It's a spur-of-the-moment decision. I can accomplish a few things at the same time. Get Loretta out of the sun, do something nice for her in return for all those baked goods she brings in the mornings. And grab the chance to do some investigating.

'You know I don't eat much lunch. I already had a salad.'

'If you don't mind sitting with me while I eat lunch, afterwards we can get ice cream.'

'Ice cream? Well, you know I do love ice cream.'

'Then let's do it.'

She looks at the pile of lopped-off greenery and up at the sky. 'I guess I'm ready to finish for the day. And I wouldn't mind having a glass of iced tea while you eat.'

While she gets ready, I call Dooley. 'I'm happy to tell you, your problem is handled.'

'What? Hold on a minute.' There's noise in the background. 'I'm going in my office.' He shuts a door and says, 'So who is it? Did you arrest them?'

I give him the rundown. 'I hope you think that's a fair punishment.'

'Seems good to me. I can use somebody to do work around here.'

'And I hope you don't mind keeping their names to yourself. I told them that if they followed through and did the work, and swore they wouldn't get in any more trouble, I wouldn't tell their folks.'

'I can do that.'

'Good. But if you have any more problems, let me know. And

be sure to get the whole ten hours from both of them.' I hesitate before I continue. 'You might have more trouble with Aaron Dawkins than with Dell Gainer. Let me know if he slacks off.'

'I appreciate this. It's been on my mind.'

'One more thing, Dooley. I'd keep my eye on Red if I were you.'

He sighs. 'I know it. He's not always on the up and up. Did he have something to do with it?'

'I'm just telling you to pay attention.'

On our way to Bobtail, I keep the conversation light with Loretta, but I tell her I have an ulterior motive for going to Bobtail. 'I'm looking for somebody's car.'

'Whose car? And where are they?'

'I can't tell you whose, because it's confidential. But I can tell you the make and model of the car, and I know the general area where it might be located. You can help me by keeping your eyes peeled for it when we drive around,' I say. 'But first we'll get ice cream.'

We stop at the Bobtail Grill and Steakhouse. I get a steak sandwich and Loretta picks at a chicken salad. We both get jumbo glasses of iced tea. 'It's been too long since we had a meal together,' I say.

'I know it. But you've got Wendy, and I've got . . . well, I *had* my friend Dave.'

'What happened? I thought you two were getting along well.'

She sighs. 'He wanted to get married, and, Samuel, that's the last thing in the world I want. I've known a couple of women who married late and ended up being a nursemaid to their husbands. Dave is several years older than me and not in the best of health. I don't want to be hard-hearted, but I'm not in a mood to marry someone who might be bedridden.'

'Well, suppose he kicked off and left you a bundle of money?'

'Samuel!' She sees that I'm joking and flaps her hand at me. 'He doesn't have a bundle of money. I like him. I do. But I also like my life the way it is. I have my friends, my church work, my baking, my books, my garden. Who has time to get married?'

'When you put it that way, I understand.'

'What about you? Are you and Wendy going to get married?'

This isn't the first time she's asked me that, and I still don't have an answer. 'I don't know. But there's something else I need to discuss with you.'

'You always change the subject when I bring up you marrying Wendy. But anyway, what do you want to talk about? I kind of figured you didn't ask me here out of the goodness of your heart.'

'Maybe you'll change your tune when I treat you to a hot fudge sundae.'

Her eyes light up. 'Maybe. So what's up?'

'I want to know if you've heard any rumors about Maddy Benson. Some troubling accusations.'

She sits back and crosses her arms, her eyes narrowed. 'I might have.'

'What does that mean?'

'If we're talking about the same thing, people say she was involved with, you know, stuff with girls.' Loretta has always been a prude concerning bodily issues of any kind. Her cheeks have pinked up.

'You mean abortions?'

'Well, yes. If you want to be blunt.'

'Involved how? Was she providing abortions illegally?'

'Samuel, I don't know. I heard a rumor, but I didn't hear the particulars, and I don't really want to.'

'Do you know how the rumor got started?'

'Is it true?'

'I'm not going to confirm or deny.' Because I don't know, but I'm not going into that with her. 'Do you know what started people talking?'

She takes a sip of iced tea and dabs at her mouth, stalling. 'Why do you want to know?'

'Because it's my business to find out what has people stirred up. I ran into Phyllis Dawkins, the preacher's wife, and she gave me an earful.'

Loretta raises her eyebrows. 'I can imagine. She's not the kindest person I've ever met.'

'Her attitude was harsh.'

'How some people can call themselves Christians and be so uncompassionate, I don't understand. I'm not saying I condone what the Benson woman was doing, but it's not my place to judge. That's in the hands of the Lord.'

'So how did the information get around?'

'I'll tell you what I know, but it isn't much. I know that Phyllis told somebody that the Baptist church got a phone call. An anonymous call, telling them that Madelyn Benson was wicked and didn't deserve any compassion. You know how those people talk, saying words like "wicked" and "the devil." Like they have the last word in what's evil. Anyway, the person who called said Madelyn was murdering babies. And that's the information Phyllis Dawkins was spreading.'

'And people believe it?'

'Some do. You know how that goes. Some people believe it and condemn her, and some keep their opinions to themselves. I see no benefit in spreading the rumor personally.'

I wonder how Loretta feels about the matter of abortion. It's not a subject we've ever been close to discussing. Before I can think how to ask, she scoots closer and looks around furtively. 'I wouldn't ever have done that myself, you know. I don't think it's right. But I've known a couple of women in my time who had a hard choice to make. It might not be the choice I would make, but how can I tell them what to do? People like Phyllis Dawkins think they know exactly how things ought to be, and they believe they should be able to make the rules for others. But I know it isn't that easy.' She sits back, looking stunned by her admission.

I've never known her to make a passionate speech like that. She's usually mild-mannered and leaves the ranting to others. 'It's a hard subject, especially these days,' I say.

'If you ask me, it shouldn't be the business of men, anyway.' She looks to see if I'm offended.

'There's something to that,' I say. 'But look, you told me what I need to know. Let's go get some ice cream.'

I don't have to say that twice. She hops up and clutches her purse to her stomach as if she thinks somebody might snatch it away. The conversation has rattled her.

We go to the Bluebell Ice Cream Parlor, and I insist on buying her a hot fudge sundae. 'You don't have to eat it all, but I know that's what you like.'

She ends up eating more of it than she meant to. And I finish off mine, which has whipped cream on it, too.

'Now we go to work,' I say, as we get into my car.

'If I can stay awake,' she says. 'I never eat much lunch because it makes me sleepy.'

She's right. She nods off as soon as I head out to the motel area where the phone company pinpointed that Krista Benson's call came from. That's all right with me. I drive slowly, taking note of the cars in the parking lots. This time of day, there aren't many.

Eventually, I hit pay dirt. I spot Krista's car in the parking lot of the Texas Trail Motel, one of the higher-end motels in the line-up. I pull into the lot and stop to think what I should do. I could go in and ask what room she's in, but she's done nothing wrong, so I really have no reason to bother her. Finding her car confirms she's here in Bobtail, and that's enough for now. Somehow, I think if someone was holding her captive, they wouldn't choose a nice motel like this one.

I head back to Jarrett Creek, and only when we pull up in front of Loretta's place does she wake up, blinking. 'I thought we were going to scout out some cars.'

'You were sleeping so peacefully, I did it myself.'

She shakes herself. 'Did you find what you were looking for?'

'I did.'

'I'm going inside to finish my nap.'

I go around to open the door for her and she eases out. I realize that she's moving more slowly than usual. Aging. Getting to all of us.

After I leave Loretta, I have some time left to check in with Maddy Benson's neighbors who weren't around when I first canvased the neighborhood. They might be in since it's the weekend. I still haven't heard from Isabella Lopez, which is starting to annoy me. I don't like the idea of having to go back to Houston to hunt her down, but it may come to that.

I call Wendy to see how her packing is going. She sounds upbeat, if a little manic. 'I'm excited to go, it's just that there's so much to do. And, of course, my sister called to see if I could take care of Tammy next week. I had to tell her it wasn't going to work out. She was mad. I think she believes I ought to be at her beck and call for that girl.'

Tammy is Wendy's niece, who is a teenaged hellion, always on the outs with her mother. She spends half her time at Wendy's. I've gotten the impression that Wendy's sister can't be bothered with the girl. She's a real estate agent and tears around all over the country selling houses and property. I don't know why she thinks Wendy ought to be on call all the time. Maybe a dose of reality will help her. Not that it will be good for Tammy.

'I know you'll have a good time. Don't let your sister do a guilt-trip on you.'

I ask her if she wants me to come over tonight, but she says she can't because she promised to go to her sister's for dinner. 'At least telling her I have to pack gives me an excuse to come home early.'

The people who live to the north of the Bensons are home, but they tell me they both leave early for work in College Station every day. 'We work at Texas A&M, and we leave before most people are up.' They're in their forties.

They tell me they don't know the Bensons. 'We've seen the older woman out walking a few times early in the morning when we're getting on our way. We wave, that's all.'

'Ever see her with anybody?'

They haven't.

In fact, no one I talk to has seen anything or knows the Bensons. As one woman explains, 'This isn't that kind of neighborhood. The houses are far apart, and we like it that way, keeping to ourselves. At least, I do. I don't want to know my neighbors. I moved here from Bobtail, and in the area I lived in, everyone knew everyone else's business. I got tired of it. I keep to myself, and I'm fine if others are the same way.' She tells me she's got a business where she buys and sells vintage jewelry. 'I go all over visiting garage sales and secondhand shops looking for jewelry that I think will bring a price. And I've got an online business. People contact me if they have goods they want to sell, although usually they want more for it than it's worth to me. I've got a good eye for what people are looking for and it has made me enough money to be comfortable.'

There's something chilling about the standoffish attitude of most of the people who live out here. I'm used to neighbors keeping an eye on each other. And with that in mind, I head back to my house to canvas my own neighbors to see if they observed anything suspicious around the time the package containing the warning note was left on my steps.

It takes a while to question them because they all want to chat and some of them want an update on the woman who was killed. After being in Maddy Benson's neighborhood, I don't mind taking my time.

But it turns out that although we may look out for each other, after eight thirty at night, most people are snug up in their houses. It was only because Loretta had gone out for a couple of hours that she happened to see the mysterious man who left the package. No one else saw a thing.

FIFTEEN

I t's threatening to rain again. The sky is gloomy and, along with the heat, we have humidity so high that it's like walking through mist. After I check on my cows, I pop over to Town Café for breakfast. I usually eat some baked goods that Loretta has brought, but being Sunday, she won't be baking today. It's early when I get to the café, and I'm alone for the first half hour. A few people straggle in, but no one is in the mood for gabbing, so I have a chance to think.

I feel like I'm in suspended time. I haven't heard that Krista is back home, haven't heard from Isabella Lopez, and until Maria gets back from San Antonio, I don't want to tackle Maddy's laptop. I have a few people I want to talk to right away, but with it being Sunday, they won't be available until this afternoon, after church.

When I walk into the office, Maria is sitting at her desk, hunched over Maddy's laptop.

'What are you doing here?' I ask.

'I couldn't get this computer out of my mind, so I left San Antonio at seven. I just got here.'

'Before you get too far, there's something we should discuss.'

I've been trying to think how to talk to Maria about what the Baptist preacher's wife is claiming. Maria is Catholic, so how will the news affect her? She was angry when the US Supreme Court handed down the Dobbs decision, basically giving the State of Texas free rein to make a criminal out of any woman who terminated a pregnancy for any reason. And to criminalize their doctors or anyone who helped them. I was surprised to hear Loretta's take on the subject. She's as religious as anyone I know, and yet she said she refuses to judge women who have to make complicated health decisions. So I'm prepared for whatever re-action Maria has.

Maria pushes the laptop away from her. 'OK, tell me.'

I ease into the subject, reminding her that when she left for San

Antonio on Friday, Connor was going out to investigate a report of a rabid dog.

She rolls her eyes. 'Oh, right, Mrs Dawkins. She never met a dog she didn't think was rabid. Was there a problem?'

'Not with the dog.' I draw a deep breath and tell her that Phyllis Dawkins accused Maddy Benson of providing abortions. 'She wants me to investigate if members of Maddy's family were complicit in what she was doing, and to prosecute them.'

'Whoa! Where did that information come from? Did you check it out?'

'Loretta said the Baptist church got an anonymous phone call.'

'Oh, that explains everything. Some creep making an anonymous call. What do you think? Is there any substance to it, or just somebody stirring up trouble?'

'No idea. I need to find out more information. I haven't spoken with Reverend Dawkins yet.'

She's quiet for a moment, contemplating. 'Performing abortions? That makes no sense. She's not a medical professional. I mean, maybe she was providing "morning after" pills or some other drugs? Maybe we can get the answer from her computer. You know those groups she was involved with, The Time Is Now and Haven, might have some connection to that. Let me dig into it.'

'Maria, are you sure you want to do that?'

'What do you mean?'

I hesitate, and it gives her time to understand what might be a problem. 'Are you telling me that if it's true, you're going to step away?' she asks. Her tone is angry. 'You're going to let whoever killed her get a free ride?'

'No! Not at all. I just . . . I have no idea what your thoughts are on the subject of abortion, and I don't plan to pry. But if you feel like you can't participate in the investigation, I'll do it myself, so you don't have to compromise your beliefs.'

Her eyes are steely, but then they often are. She's a serious person. 'Boss, you don't have to worry about that. First of all, I will always set aside my personal feelings when we're on a case. It's a professional matter, and my opinions have no bearing on it.'

'This is a radical subject, though. People have strong feelings. If you said you were uncomfortable, I'd understand.'

She pauses for a minute, as if she's searching for the right words. 'I suppose you think because I'm Catholic that it would be a hot button for me. And the Church certainly has a strong stance. But I have personal reasons for thinking women should have the kind of healthcare they need and that it's none of my business what they decide. It's . . .' She hesitates. 'My abuela, my grandmother, had a sister who died under "certain circumstances." But we all knew what that meant. That kind of thing influences a family's lives. My grandmother never stopped mourning her.'

I nod. 'Just so we're clear.'

She's quiet for a second. But then she clears her throat. 'Would you arrest her son and daughter-in-law if they were involved? Like the law says?' She bites her lower lip, a sure sign this is a big deal to her.

There's no backing away from the question. 'No, I wouldn't.'

Her shoulders relax. 'Why not?'

'I have my reasons.' Strong reasons, but I'm not prepared to spill them. 'Now, let's get busy.'

She nods and turns back to Maddy's laptop.

I shut off the part of my mind that could easily dwell on our conversation, but I can't settle my thoughts that easily. So I watch Maria work, hoping she comes up with something useful.

After ten minutes, she says, 'Chief, why don't you go get us some kolaches? You're making me nervous watching me.'

I'm glad to have an errand, especially if it means getting pastries I'm fond of. When I get back, as soon as I walk in, Maria pounces.

'What do you think of this?'

She moves the laptop around so I can sit at her desk and read it. On the computer, she has opened a folder entitled, 'Haven.' The folder contains four files entitled CA, CO, NM, NV.

'Looks like initial of states,' I say. 'California, Colorado. New Mexico, Nevada.'

'Yes, and look at this.' She opens the first file, CA. It has ten lines of print, all in some kind of code. Letters and numbers that look like dates. She opens each of the others and they have all the same data. California has ten entries, Nevada has twenty, Colorado twenty-five, and New Mexico has thirty-five.

'Boss, you know what these are, don't you?' Her expression is unreadable.

I think for a minute before I realize what they are. 'States that allow abortion.'

'She wasn't performing abortions herself; she was helping girls go to other states where it isn't illegal.' She folds her arms tight across her chest, her gaze penetrating. 'And somebody killed her for it.'

'Possibly,' I say. 'Let's not jump to conclusions. Even if she was working with a group helping girls get abortions, her death might not have anything to do with that.'

'Maybe, but I'd be surprised if it wasn't connected. I was thinking, these files are discreet, and that might account for why her family seems to know so little about her. Maybe she was keeping her activities secret from them.'

'Why would she do that?' I ask.

'You remember the statue outside – St Francis?'

I nod.

'Suppose Krista is Catholic and opposed to abortion,' Maria says. 'Maddy wouldn't want her daughter-in-law to know that she's helping girls in trouble.'

'This is going to be tricky. If Krista is opposed and found out what Maddy was up to . . .'

Maria sighs. 'Yeah, that could make her a suspect. Her claiming she didn't know where Maddy went the morning she was killed and then going to the grocery store could just be a cover-up.'

I remind her about the phone call I made that was abruptly terminated. 'If it's true that Maddy was helping women go out of state, that could account for why the woman hung up. My guess is there's a network of people involved who have to be very careful.'

'If anyone found out, they could go to prison,' Maria says.

'Or be fined thousands of dollars, or both,' I say.

'Shouldn't we start by talking to Krista Benson again?'

I remind her that she's missing. 'I mean, theoretically.'

'What do you mean by that?'

I tell her that I found Krista's car at a motel in Bobtail.

'Should we go there and question her?' she says.

'First, let's go talk to Josh and his sister.'

Hannah answers the door and invites Maria and me inside. I ask her to get Josh. 'Something has come up and we'd like to talk to the two of you.'

'You have a suspect?'

'Not yet. Just some information we need to check out.'

She starts to speak but changes her mind and hollers upstairs for Josh.

When he arrives, we sit in our usual spots in the living room. I sit forward, hands between my knees. 'Question for you, Josh. Krista said she, you and your mother all had the same political leanings – is that right?'

He shrugs. 'Vaguely. I'm probably more conservative economically than they are, but in the traditional sense, not depending too much on big government. But socially for sure, we were all more liberal.' He takes a moment. 'Why are you asking this?'

'We have the sense that your mamma might have been involved in some political activities that were dangerous.'

I see that Hannah has gone absolutely still.

'Are you kidding?' Josh asks. 'Like what?'

'We found evidence that she might have been helping women go out of state to get abortions. Do you know anything about that?'

His face flushes deep red. 'No! Not that I'd be surprised. She was really into women's rights. But what a stupid thing to do in this political environment. You think that's what got her killed?' He glances at his sister, who has gone rigid.

'It's too early to draw that conclusion, but it's certainly a possibility.'

'Hannah?' Maria asks. 'Did you know?'

Her expression is full of horror, and she flushes. 'No! She never said a word. Are you sure? Who told you that?'

'She had files that looked like that's what she was doing.'

'So you're blaming her for being killed?' Her beautiful voice is gone, replaced by harsh outrage.

'Not at all,' I say.

'Then why these questions?'

'We're trying to piece together who might have worked with her and what kind of threats they got.'

Hannah has gone pale, and her breathing is shaky. She moans and puts her head into her hands. 'Oh, Mommy, what have you done?' she whispers.

Maria stands up. 'Josh, we need to talk to Hannah alone.'

He looks at his sister and then at me. I nod and tell him I'll let him know if we have follow-up questions, and I ask him to call Krista again and tell her it's urgent that we speak with her.

Once he's gone, Maria says, 'I'm asking again if you knew that your mother was helping girls who were in trouble.'

Hannah nods. Her face crumples, and she leans forward and covers her face while she sobs. 'She told me a couple of months ago. I told her I thought she ought to stay out of it, but she said she couldn't. Because of me.'

'How old were you?' Maria asks when she stops crying.

'Fourteen.' She's practically whispering. 'I was raped after cheerleader practice. They were never able to figure out who did it. But of course . . .' Her lips twist bitterly. 'Of course I got pregnant, and it was . . . taken care of. And when the Supreme Court made that ruling, Mamma went nuts. She called me and she was hysterical. She said she couldn't stop thinking about all those poor girls who had their lives blighted by men having their way. And she didn't mean the rapist; she meant men who make laws. And now they've killed her!' The last part is said in a shriek.

Maria goes to Hannah's side and puts her arm around her. 'Can I get you anything? Some water?'

Hannah puts her hand across her mouth and shakes her head. 'It's all my fault,' she whispers.

'No,' Maria says, her voice strong. 'It's not your fault. You didn't ask to be assaulted. And Maddy made her choice to help other girls in need. Period.'

'Oh . . .' Hannah moans. 'If only she'd never moved here.'

I have no response for that. Maddy would have dedicated herself to helping girls and women wherever she moved, and whoever killed her would have found her just as easily anywhere else. I hope Hannah will figure that out once she has a chance to think things through. Blaming herself does no good.

SIXTEEN

Maria heaves a big sigh. 'This case. Seems to keep getting worse instead of better.' We're back in the office. Maria looks as drained as I feel, and it isn't even noon.

'They all do, early on.'

'I suppose. But this is different.' She sounds haunted.

And I feel the same. Talking with Hannah has left me feeling somber. At least I've gotten more of Maddy Benson's motivations fleshed out. Before I talked to Hannah, I saw Maddy as a busy, engaged woman who moved here to try to rehabilitate her son's marriage. Now I understand how very important her kids are to her, and that she made sacrifices for both of them. Her daughter's experience led Maddy to become engaged in the battle for women's rights, and then in illegal activities. That doesn't bring me any closer to finding out who killed her, but sometimes it's necessary to get a full picture of a victim before you can successfully investigate their murder.

'Maria, I'm going over to go talk to Father Sanchez. Meanwhile, I want you to dig deeper into the Haven group. See if there's more on Maddy's laptop about them. Names of members, anything.'

She nods. 'Maybe I can call them and pretend to be someone who needs help?' she asks.

'What do you think?'

'I don't like the idea of lying, but I'm afraid if I identify myself as law enforcement, they won't talk to me.'

If anybody will have an idea of what goes on in the anti-abortion contingent in this area, it's the Catholic priest. He holds Sunday morning mass early, and it should be over by now. Father Sanchez answers on the first ring and says I should come right over.

The Catholic church in Jarrett Creek is a wonder. It's tiny, reflecting its small congregation, a stucco and wood structure that looks as if it could have been a mission at one time. But it never was; it was put up by members of the Mexican community who came here to work in the 1920s when Jarrett Creek had a larger population because it was a railroad stop with a Harvey House. And it's beautiful. The men who built it put graceful architectural touches on the doors and around the two small stained-glass windows that reflect their care and love for it.

Sanchez is waiting at the front door of the church when I arrive. I've brought Dusty with me, because the priest always seems to enjoy him. Sure enough, he crouches down and gives Dusty a good scratching. 'Glad you brought this mutt. I should get another dog, I suppose, but I'm out a lot, and not everyone appreciates a dog.'

He stands up and shakes my hand.

Father Sanchez is a good friend. He knows I'm not a churchgoer, but he periodically checks in with my decision not to join his church, to make sure I'm not harboring a change of heart.

A wiry, short man in his fifties, his hair has gone almost completely gray. He looks cheerful, as always. I know he has had a chance to move on to larger churches, but he told me a few years ago that he has no interest in changing and has resisted efforts to replace him.

He has brewed coffee and offers buñuelos made by his house-keeper. We sit in the yard of his small apartment at the back of the church, in two small wooden folding chairs at a wooden table. He has a garden teeming with vegetables and a wild assortment of flowers, which I remark on because I know he's proud of it.

Dusty flops down in the shade as if he belongs here, while Sanchez and I catch up with each other before settling into why I've come. I know that he had to have a knee replacement a couple of months ago, and I want details on his recovery, since I suspect the same surgery is in my future. He says he's completely recovered. 'Medicine is a miracle these days,' he says. 'I'm so grateful.' He smiles and sticks his legs out in front of him, crossing them at the ankles. 'But you didn't come to talk about my knee. What's on your mind?'

'It's a delicate subject. I'm sure you've heard about the woman who was killed on Wednesday.'

He nods and crosses himself. 'How can I help with that? Is she Catholic?'

'No, in fact, I think you'll find the opposite.'

'Oh?'

'This will, of course, be in strict confidence.'

'Always.'

'We believe she was working to help provide transport to out-of-state clinics for women who needed certain healthcare.' I say the last two words carefully.

His expression undergoes a subtle change. 'If you mean what I think you do, I'm afraid I can't help you. I'm sure you can appreciate that this is a difficult subject for me.'

'Of course. I'm asking you if you are aware of anyone in your congregation who may be so zealous on the subject they would be tempted to take the law into their hands if they found out what she was up to.'

'I see.' He folds his hands under his chin and props his elbows on the table. 'You know, Samuel, I have a very small congregation. On Christmas and Easter, as many as fifty people show up, but it's usually half that. And most of them are not young. Abortion is not a subject that comes up.'

'So you haven't heard any strong talk from anyone on the subject?'

'Oh, I wouldn't say that. After the administration put together those draconian laws, we had discussions on the subject. Contrary to what you might think, even though most Catholics know that abortion means the taking of a life, many of us also have a deep sorrow for those who feel they have to make such a terrible decision. And for the government to pass a cruel law turning neighbor against neighbor . . .' He sighs. 'That isn't what I think of as an approach that helps anyone. How much more useful it would be if they figured out generous ways of helping people who feel they can't afford to raise a child, or who have no one to turn to in their despair.'

I nod. I know Sanchez to be a generous and caring priest, so I'm not surprised he has a conflicted view of the subject. I can't help noting the contrast between Sanchez and the Baptist preacher. 'If you could keep an ear open for conversations that suggests someone has stronger feelings, I'd appreciate your keeping me informed.'

By now the Baptist church services will be over, and it's time to have a serious conversation with Reverend Dawkins. I want to know more about the anonymous phone call that came into the church office. I've hardly had any contact with Dawkins. The Baptist church circulates ministers through here like it's a pipeline. He's the third in as many years.

I catch Phyllis and John Dawkins, just arriving from church.

They're dressed up, Dawkins in a suit and tie and Phyllis in a prim navy-blue suit with a white blouse with a bow at the neck.

'What brings you around here?' Dawkins asks with a firm handshake.

Phyllis nods, but doesn't offer her hand. I suspect she knows exactly why I'm here.

'I have a couple of questions to ask. But if you're in a hurry to get to your dinner, I'll come back.' Part of me wishes he'd send me on my way.

'No, no, we had a beautiful spread at the church after the service,' Dawkins says. His manner is expansive. 'Celebrating the new deacons being sworn in. Come on in.'

Inside, he takes off his jacket and loosens his tie. 'It's too hot for this monkey suit,' he says. 'Phyll, you think you can rustle up some iced tea?'

'Certainly.'

She disappears into the kitchen, and Dawkins sits us down in the living room. It's nice and cool, the air conditioning on full blast. Despite Phyllis Dawkins's rigid disposition, the room is cheerful, with comfortable chairs and pleasant decorations – throw pillows and some nice pictures on the walls. Not great art, but good landscapes.

'Now, what can I do for you?' Dawkins says, his voice amiable.

'Well, it may be Phyllis I need to talk to. It's about an anonymous phone call that came into your office.'

I've never seen anyone's demeanor change so quickly. His expression hardens, and suddenly he looks like the fire-and-brimstone preacher he's reputed to be. 'I know what you're here to ask. You don't have to talk to my wife, you can ask me what you want to know.'

'I need some particulars. When the call came in and who took it.'

He sits back, folding his hands across his belly, his face stern. 'What right do you claim to obtain that information? It was a private phone call.'

'I'm sure you're aware that I'm looking into the death of a woman here in town, Madelyn Benson. She was shot and killed on Wednesday. The phone call that came to your church may have a bearing on the case.'

'What kind of bearing?'

'I won't know exactly until I hear more about the call. When did the call come in?'

He licks his lips. He's stalling, deciding whether to cooperate. 'Thursday.'

The day after Maddy was murdered. 'Did you talk to the caller?'

He stares at me, his eyes icy. 'I wasn't there.'

'Who took the call?'

'That would be the church secretary, Mary Mayhew. And I won't have her harassed by you.'

'I don't know why you'd think I want to harass her. I'm just trying to find out the facts of the case. Was the caller a man or a woman?'

'Man.'

'Did Mary tell you what he said?'

He folds his arms across his chest and for a minute I think he's going to stonewall me. 'I'm a big supporter of law and order,' he says, 'and on that condition, I'll tell you what you asked. The words are burned into my brain. He told Mary that the woman who had been killed was in league with the devil, and putting young girls' souls in jeopardy by arranging for their babies to be murdered.'

This is the kind of talk Loretta warned me about. 'Did he explain what he meant?'

'He said Madelyn Benson was part of a group that helps pregnant people evade the law by going out of state to have their babies aborted. If it's true, and I believe it was, she was asking for trouble. I'm not surprised someone decided to take action. Furthermore, it stands to reason that if she was circumventing the law, so was her family. So you may be aiding and abetting an illegal operation here in town by not arresting them.'

I'm determined not to lose my temper, but it's fraying. 'It's my job to investigate her murder, not go looking for imaginary crimes.'

'You're also charged with upholding the laws of the great State of Texas, which means catching people in criminal pursuits. Am I wrong about that?'

'Reverend Dawkins, I'm one man with a small police force here in town. I have to take my crimes as they come. Crimes I know have been committed, rather than those that someone worries might be committed.'

'Well, I know what my secretary reported.'

Phyllis Dawkins comes in bearing two glasses of tea.

Dawkins stands. 'Chief Craddock, I assume you're a God-fearing man. Will you pray with me about this?'

I stand up, too. I'm ready to get out of here. 'That's between me and my conscience. I came here to get answers to questions that might help solve a murder. And I've gotten my answers.'

Phyllis stands rooted.

'Give the man a glass of tea,' Dawkins snarls at her.

She shoves the glass toward me, and I take it automatically. 'Thank you,' I say and turn my attention back to Dawkins.

He's working his mouth as if he's chewing something nasty. His wife hands him a glass, and he takes a long swig. He wipes his mouth.

'I have one last question,' I say. 'Did the caller give his name?'

'No, he did not. And Mary was right not to ask. I don't need to know who made the call. Someone righteous – that's all I need to know.'

'Suppose they were lying? Maybe it was the person who killed her, and they wanted to start a rumor.'

He blinks. 'Why would somebody do that?'

'To deflect attention from themselves.'

'Well, I've asked around, and the Benson woman was standoffish, didn't seem to want to be friendly with anybody. The kind of way somebody would act if they had something to hide. And I've prayed about it, and I have a strong feeling the caller was telling the truth. Now, if you find out information to the contrary, I'll hear it. But until then, I'll be looking into this woman and her kin.'

I put the glass of tea down on a side table. 'As long as you don't interfere with law enforcement, you can do as you please. Thank you for your cooperation. I'll be on my way.'

As I reach the door, I hear Dawkins come up behind me. 'Craddock.' His voice is like a whip.

I turn, and he says, 'You haven't heard the last of this. I'm calling an emergency city council meeting. I expect after that you'll be out of job, and maybe even turned over to the DPS for prosecution.'

'Do what you need to. Until then, I'll be doing my job as I see fit,' I say.

As I get into my car, I'm glad Maria wasn't with me. Despite my stoic reply to Dawkins, I was shaken by the fury in his voice. I know that the preacher's information is correct, but he doesn't know that, and the idea that he's willing to damn Maddy Benson

on the word of an anonymous caller is chilling. And I'm also horri-
fied by the thought that I may actually lose my position as chief
over this. The city council has every right to fire me, but I have no
idea if they would actually do it. I expect they are as divided as
everyone else on the subject of women's rights.

Not that leaving the job is the worst thing I can imagine. I sometimes think it might be good to retire, especially since Wendy has
been pressing me. But if I go, I want to go on my own terms, not
because I've lost the regard of the citizens.

I know that across the country the issue of abortion rights is
controversial, but it's hard for me to think that my town could be
torn apart by the two opposing stances on the subject. And then I
think of Loretta's strong words. She's conflicted, but her opinion
comes down on the side of compassion, as does Father Sanchez's.
It's a matter I never thought I'd have to be involved in. Even though
it had a deep meaning in my own life and that of my late wife.

SEVENTEEN

It's late afternoon, but I have time left to do something I've been trying to get to for two days. I call to check up on whether Maria wants to go with me, but she's checking on a report of vandalism out at the construction site of the new motel that's being built north of town, so I'm off to knock on doors alone. It's just as well. I may get nothing for my efforts.

I stop by my place and change into my uniform. Wearing it at least makes me recognizable and I can hope for a polite reception.

Dwellings out on the farm-to-market road where Maddy Benson was shot are few and far between, and a lot of people who live there tend to be reclusive, which is why they moved there in the first place. The lots out here are big and lonely, the opposite of a neighborhood.

I drive a couple of miles past Tom Gainer's place where Maddy was killed and turn into the long gravel driveway of a sprawling collection of buildings that have been here for as long as I can remember. I've never actually been inside and have no idea who lives here. There are four structures, all of them weathered to gray boards. The main house is a utilitarian place that looks to be no more than a thousand square feet. Its roof is sagging in places. The other buildings are a barn and a couple of sheds. The yard is littered with cast-off goods – a washing machine, an abandoned tractor, rusty farm implements, a wash tub and, various household goods, most of them unidentifiable.

There's the inevitable dog, an old hound, barking hoarsely and straining at its leash. When I get out of my squad car, I tell Dusty to stay put. The door to the house opens and an old man steps out onto the porch. He's heavy, wearing overalls and a T-shirt under it. 'Daisy, be quiet!' he hollers. I can't imagine a more unlikely name for this dog.

The dog sits down and the two of them watch my approach. I'm sure that Maddy Benson didn't come here, but I have to follow through.

'What can I do for you?' he says.

I introduce myself. 'I don't believe we've met.'

'Jeb Russell,' he says. He doesn't seem hostile, just reserved.

I tell him I'm investigating the murder of a woman and want to know if he might have seen anything unusual last Wednesday when she was killed.

'I mostly stay inside,' he says. 'My old woman is poorly, and she needs me to take care of her.' He tells me his wife has lung problems and is on oxygen.

I tell him I'm sorry to hear it, and ask if he needs help. 'There are church groups could help if you need somebody to run errands or whatnot.'

'We haven't been to church in while, but our minister comes by. Our son lives over in Burton, and he comes over and brings groceries, so we do OK.'

The next house is a quarter-mile up the road. It's a small, tidy place, with a thriving vegetable garden on the side. The woman who answers the door says she only comes to town on the weekends, and wasn't around the day Maddy was killed.

The next two houses are the same.

A mile from where Maddy was killed, I run into an odd situation. Like all the other houses, it's small, set back one hundred feet or so from the road. It's painted gray with white trim. The yard is scrub brush and bare ground, but not weedy.

When I knock on the door, I hear someone moving around and low-pitched voices, but no one comes to the door until I knock again and call out who I am.

The other houses along here are inhabited by older people who seem cordial. But here, the door opens a few inches and all I can see of the girl standing there is one side of her face, ghostly pale with a pale blue eye, and a swath of long, brown hair. She's young. 'What do you want?' she asks. Although the question is blunt, the tone is neutral.

'Who am I speaking to?'

She glances back into the room, and when she turns to face me again, says, 'My name is April.'

'April, I'm Samuel Craddock, Chief of Police here in Jarrett Creek. A woman was killed near here a few days ago and I'm asking people who live in the area if they saw anything suspicious.'

'No, we didn't.'

There's something unnerving in her reluctance to be seen, as if she's been held hostage by someone threatening her. 'I'd like you to open the door for me.'

She opens it a few more inches.

'Is someone here with you?'

Suddenly, a woman steps up and gently moves April aside. She has that same vulnerable look as the girl, and her voice shakes as she says, 'I'm April's mother, Pat Willis. We only got here yesterday, so we know nothing about anyone being killed. Are we in danger?'

'I don't think so. But I'd keep my door locked if I were you, and report anything that bothers you.'

'We will.' The two women are as wary as cats. It puts me on alert.

'We haven't met before,' I say. 'Have you lived here long?'

'We, uh, we don't actually live here. We're visiting. The owner will be here tomorrow.'

'And who might that be?'

'Madelyn Benson.'

I blink. Why would Maddy Benson have a second house? Did she rent it to people? Why didn't Josh and Krista mention this to me? Did she buy it because she thought they were going to kick her out?

'You know Maddy Benson?'

She looks panicky. 'Not exactly.'

So she doesn't know Maddy is dead. I need to find out more. 'Do you mind if I come in? I'd like to ask you a few questions.'

She looks like a deer ready to bolt. 'Um . . .'

'It won't take but a minute.'

'I guess . . . April, please go to your bedroom.'

The girl complies without a word of protest, walking swiftly from the room.

'I'd rather you not come in,' Pat Wills says. 'Can you ask me out here?' She's a pretty woman, with her daughter's brown hair and light blue eyes. Her hair is pulled back into a ponytail at her neck, carelessly, as if she couldn't be bothered. Her clothing is wrinkled, again as if she can't be bothered. Her hands are clenched at her sides, and I get the impression she's barely holding it together.

'I don't mean you any harm. But I do need to get some information.'

'We haven't done anything wrong.' Desperation in her voice.

'Please . . .' I gesture toward the interior.

With a sound of distress, she steps back, and I walk in. 'Let's sit down,' I say.

'I'll stand,' she says. I'm put in mind of a mother bear, ready to defend her cub. And that's when I realize what's going on here. This is a safe house, and the girl is waiting with her mother for transportation to out of state for an abortion.

This brings a whole new level of problems. What am I going to do, knowing these women might be set to break the law? If they are. I could be imagining what they're doing here. But it's better that I don't know for sure, so I don't have to make the decision whether to let them break the law. I do need to find out if they know more than they're saying about Maddy Benson. 'Here's what I want you to know. I don't care why you and your daughter are here. In fact, I'd rather not know. But I need to ask you when you last saw Maddy Benson.'

Her shoulders slump and she looks as if she might faint. She walks over and sits at the edge of an armchair. I sit nearby on the loveseat sofa. The room is small and doesn't hold much furniture – the love seat, two armchairs, a coffee table and a couple of random tables with lamps. There are no signs of comfortable habitation here – no pictures on the walls, no books or magazines, not even a rug on the floor.

'I've never met her,' Pat says. 'She just offered to let us stay here.'

'I understand. Did you talk to her by phone?'

She sighs. 'I've actually never talked to her. Our, uh, stay here was arranged by a mutual friend.'

'I'll need the name of the friend.'

She shows some of her previous spunk. 'I don't want to give it to you.'

'Then let me guess. Isabella Lopez, also known as Izzy.'

Her eyes open wide. I've hit the mark.

'Like I said, I don't want to know your situation. But I need to tell you that Maddy Benson was the victim of a shooting on Wednesday. All I want to do is find out what happened to her.'

Her face, already pale, has blanched with the news. 'Oh my God,' she whispers. 'What . . .'

I'm sure she's wondering what she's going to do now.

'You said you arrived yesterday. Has anyone approached you since then?'

Her mouth is quivering and tears pooling in her eyes. 'What I said wasn't exactly true. We got here Tuesday night. We've been waiting . . .'

I hold up my hand to stop her. 'So Maddy was supposed to come here?'

She nods.

'And you swear she never showed up.'

'No. I kept hoping . . .'

I'm surprised that Isabella Lopez hasn't gotten in touch with her. Maybe she has. 'Have you spoken with Ms Lopez?'

She wrings her hands. 'She came to us Wednesday early and made sure we were OK. That's when she said we should expect a call from Madelyn Benson. If Mrs Benson was killed, wouldn't Ms Lopez know that, and contact us?'

'I'm sure she will.' I hesitate. 'You said she came early? What time was it?'

'I don't know the exact time. Before eight.'

That's when Maddy Benson was shot. Could Isabella Lopez be involved in the shooting? It seems unlikely, since they appeared to be working together, but why hasn't she been in touch with Pat and April Willis?

'You should be safe here. Are you worried that someone might find you?'

She presses her lips together and nods.

'I want you to call Ms Lopez and tell her that.' I hand her my card. 'If you feel at all threatened, notify me. That's my cell phone. We need you to be safe.'

She stares at the card and then lifts her eyes to meet mine. I think she has finally understood that I don't intend to meddle in her daughter's situation. 'Thank you.'

I go back to my car, wondering if Maddy Benson was headed here when she was killed. I believe Pat Wills when she says she didn't meet Maddy, but it's a strange coincidence that Isabella Lopez was here the same day Maddy was shot. Was Maddy on her way here when she saw someone she recognized, and ran to the Gainer place instead, to lure whoever it was away from the safe house?

Before I tackle the other houses on the way to Gainer's place, I drive down the road, pull over, and call Isabella Lopez's number again. This time when I leave a message, it's to tell her my call is urgent and that if I don't hear from her by five p.m. today, I'll put out a warrant for her to be brought in for questioning at her local police station. I don't know what more to do.

There are five more houses between where I am and Tom Gainer's place. Only two of them are full-time residents, and the others are closed up tight. The two I speak with can offer no new information about Maddy Benson's death, except that both of them are concerned for their own safety. I reassure them that the shooting was targeted and that they need have no fear. I hope I'm right. I've focused so much on Maddy Benson's abortion-related activities that I've put aside the idea that something else entirely may be in play.

I go back to headquarters. Maria is back, and I tell her about the two women.

'You think they ought to be moved? If anybody like the Dawkinses gets wind of them being here, they'll be harassed at the least, and probably turned over to the DPS.'

'I think they're OK for now. I told them to call me if they had any problems.'

I ask her how she got on with the vandalism, and she says it was clearly a stunt. 'I told the foreman if it happens again, we'll take it more seriously. He said he might keep a guy at the site for a couple of nights just in case.'

EIGHTEEN

've just set Dusty's dinner down when my phone rings with a number I don't recognize.

'Chief Craddock? This is Isabella Lopez. You called me and said it was urgent.' She sounds impatient.

'I appreciate you calling back. I have a few questions to ask pertaining to the death of a woman here in town, Madelyn Benson.'

'Yes?'

'May I ask where you're calling from?'

'I'm in a motel.'

'Where?'

She hesitates and then sighs. 'I'm in Jarrett Creek.'

'I'd like to come talk to you in person.'

'Why? Can't this be handled on the phone? I need to get some rest. I've had a long day.'

'I sympathize, but talking to you in person would be better. I'm willing to come to you rather than asking you to come to police headquarters.'

She tells me she's at the Best Value Motel, the more modern of the two in town, and I tell her I'll meet her in the lobby in ten minutes.

She's already there when I arrive. She's a short, chunky woman wearing black slacks and a colorful oversized top. Her dark, gray-streaked hair is in a bun at the nape of her neck. She stands up and shakes my hand firmly.

I ask the clerk at the front desk if there's a room where we can talk without being disturbed. 'We have a meeting room,' he says with pride.

He takes us there. The room has a big table and eight business chairs. It's freezing cold.

'I need to go get a sweater,' Isabella says. While she's gone, I get us coffee from the lobby. She's back in a minute wearing a long, warm sweater. 'I swear I don't understand why places have to keep these rooms so cold,' she says. 'Oh, good, I can use a hot drink.'

We settle in and I start by telling her I'll try not to keep her long.

'I'm investigating Maddy Benson's death and several people have mentioned you in connection with her.'

She nods.

'What was your relationship with her?'

'Maddy and I were . . . not exactly friends, but we worked together on various projects over the years.'

'I'd like to know when you last saw Ms Benson.'

She takes a sip of coffee and grimaces. 'God, that's awful.' She sighs. 'I was with Maddy Wednesday, the day she was killed. I didn't see what happened,' she adds hastily, 'but we were together earlier that day.'

'Where was this?'

'I picked her up at her house at seven. She and I were going to talk to . . . some people.'

'Did you talk to them?'

'No, we didn't get there.'

'So what happened?'

'It was odd. We were driving toward our meeting, and suddenly she said she needed to get out of the car and that I should go on without her.'

'Did she say why?'

'No, and to be honest, I was annoyed. We'd been arguing, and I thought she was angry. So when she told me she wanted me to stop the car, I thought she was being obtuse. I told her she was acting foolish. She shouted at me that she needed to get out. So I pulled over and she got out.'

'Where was this?'

'It was . . . I'm not sure exactly. Some desolate road.'

She's hedging. She doesn't know that I know about the safe house. 'Was it on the farm-to-market road where she was killed?'

'I think so.'

'Why didn't you call with this information when you heard she'd been murdered?'

She knits her hands together on the table. 'Look, Chief Craddock, I felt terrible when I heard what happened. I know I should have called, but I didn't really know anything useful. I was driving, and Maddy asked to get out of my car. So I let her. I looked in the rearview mirror and saw her walking along the road. That's the last I saw of her, so I can't tell you more than that. I didn't think it could be helpful.'

'Was she just walking, not running?'

'That's right.'

'Did she continue to walk in the direction you'd been driving?'

'Yes. Like I said, I thought she was being stubborn. We'd argued. It was nothing really. So stupid. I should never have let her out.'

'So you continued on your way to your errand. Did you ever go back and try to find her?'

'I went ahead and saw the people I intended to see, and I drove back the way I came, but I didn't see her.'

I can't help feeling frustrated. 'Ms Lopez, I need to be frank with you. I know about the two women you've got hidden, the woman and her daughter.'

She gasps. 'Oh, no. Please don't punish them. If anyone has to answer for them, it will be me.' Her voice is determined but scared.

'My investigation has nothing to do with those women. I'm looking into Ms Benson's death, period.' I pause to let that sink in. 'I assume you and Ms Benson were on your way to see them. How far away were you when she asked to be let out?'

'I'm a terrible judge of distance. Maybe a half mile? Less?' Her voice is tight. Now that she knows I'm aware of her activities, she's bound to be nervous.

'Do you know if Maddy knew anyone else who lived out there nearby?'

'If she did, she never said.'

'And you have no idea what caused her to get out of the car when she did? Is it possible she was afraid of leading someone to where the women were hidden?'

'I've gone over that in mind again and again. You may be right. She said something just before she asked to get out. She said, "God, what is he doing here?" I didn't know who she meant.'

'Could she have seen someone in a car? Did you meet any cars on the road?'

'We didn't meet anyone. I looked in the rearview mirror and saw that someone was following us closely, but I didn't think anything of it, because I was driving slowly. I just thought they were impatient to get around me. Maybe she recognized them.'

'Do you remember anything about the car or the driver?'

She whimpers. 'It was a man, but I couldn't describe him. And the car was nothing special. Not light, not dark. Medium-sized. I'm sorry, I just wasn't paying much attention. I was focused on the way Maddy was acting.' She rubs a tear away. 'Maddy and I didn't always get along. I'm practical. I'm down-to-earth. And she could be unrealistic. She'd see problems where I didn't see them. Now I wish I hadn't let her out of the car. I wish I had asked her what was wrong.'

'So when you slowed to let her out of the car, did the other car pass you?'

'It must have, because I didn't see it after she got out. I was so intent on Maddy's behavior that I didn't pay any attention to the other car. I'm sorry. I wish I had.'

'You did clear up one thing, and that's how she got to where she was killed.'

'Oh, I wish I hadn't picked her up. She wanted to meet April. I should have told her it wasn't necessary. It really wasn't. But she liked the personal touch.'

'Do you know if she had received any threats, anybody who might have borne a grudge?'

'Mr Craddock, we get threats all the time. We can't take them seriously, or we'd fold, and I know Maddy would rather have died doing good work than live being a coward.' Her voice is shaking. I suspect she thinks the same thing about herself. It's frightening.

'I found a file that she kept on threats, but I'd like to know if you can think of anyone in particular I ought to look into.'

'I suppose I can send you a couple of names.'

'Send them to me.' I give her my card. 'That has my email address on it.'

'As for grudges,' she says, 'I'd think, for starters, any man whose wife or daughter decided she needed our services without his know-ledge, and he found out, would be angry, and we'd be targeted.'

'Anyone in particular who fits that description?'

'Not right off. And if you're thinking of asking me for a list of names of women we've helped, you can forget it. That's not going to happen.' She lifts her chin in defiance.

'I understand. If you would be so kind as to look over the list, though, and see if anyone pops out whose relatives – male or female – you might suspect, I'd appreciate it if you'd let me know.'

'I don't know if I can do that. It might lead you to the girl or woman, and then she'd be in danger from the law.'

'Not from me, she wouldn't, but I get that you have to be cautious.

But if you have a strong suspicion about someone, consider passing it on to me. I do want to find the person who killed Maddy.'

'I'll think about that.' Her tone doesn't encourage me.

'Now, I want to clear up one thing. Those two women in the cabin, Pat and April Wills, are scared. You need to contact them.'

'I was waiting until I could . . . well, waiting. But I'll call and set their minds at ease.'

'Are you sure they're safe there?'

'We mostly worry about the law. It sounds like you're not going to give them any trouble, but can I trust you? Do I need to move them somewhere?'

'They'll be safe from me,' I say, 'but I have to tell you that someone called a local church and informed them that Maddy Benson was active in helping girls, and I have no way of knowing how much information the caller actually had. I hope they don't know about that cabin, but I thought I'd better tell you that someone is talking.'

'Damn it,' she says. 'It sounds like it's best if I move them.'

I don't have my notes in front of me, and I'd almost forgotten the note I found jotted in Maddy's backpack. 'I need to ask you something else. You're connected with a group called Haven?'

'Yes.'

'There was a note in Maddy's backpack that said she was concerned that there were problems with the group. She intended to contact you about that. Did she?'

'Yes. That's what we were discussing on the way to the safe house. She thought an anti-choice advocate might have infiltrated the group.'

'What made her think that?'

'Like I said, Maddy could be a little paranoid, so I didn't really take it seriously. She said one of the girls who contacted the group for help said the woman who answered the phone tried to talk her into bearing the child and finding an adoptive home. Not that I think that's a bad solution, you understand. In fact, I wish every girl who found herself in that situation could do that, but it isn't for everyone, and it's not up to us to push them.'

'Did she have the name of the person she talked to?'

'The girl said it was someone named Tina. The problem is we don't have anyone by that name working in the group.'

'Which means someone was using a fake name.'

'If that's true, it's going to be a devil of a problem finding out who it is.' She sighs. I can tell she's flagging.

'I imagine you'd worry about the safety of the other women in Haven.'

'And men. We have a few men who help as well. But mostly, I'd worry about the safety of the girls we help. All it takes is one person reporting to the authorities, and we'd all be in big trouble, at the very least financially. Not to mention that if someone blabbed to a girl's parents or a guy who didn't want her to have an abortion, her life might be in danger.' She rubs her hand across her face. 'It's such a nightmare. How much longer do you need me? I really need to get some rest.'

'One more question. This one is just for my curiosity. Planned Parenthood supposedly is available to help girls who need to go out of state. Why don't girls go to them? Why come to some small group like yours?'

'Oh, we aren't trying to replace Planned Parenthood. They're doing solid work. We're providing another avenue. In case there isn't a PP close by, or they're worried that someone will see them go into a PP facility.'

'How are you going to try to find out who Tina is?'

'Ha. I have no idea. If you have suggestions, I'm open. We investigate the background of anyone who says they want to work with us, so somebody lied.'

'Or maybe changed their mind. The only thing I can think of is to update the background check.'

'That's expensive and time-consuming. But we're alert to the problem now, so there are ways we can look into it. Figuring out who was on duty at specific times, being aware of anyone who seems to have fewer positive interactions. It's such a worry.'

When I get home, I change into a T-shirt and jeans, and sit down in front of the TV with a beer and a couple of warmed-up tamales. The TV doesn't hold my interest. I've got too much on my mind. I'm worried that 'Tina' might be part of an organization of a different kind – one that would think nothing of hunting down key members of the Haven group and killing them. I hesitate to think they would be a vigilante group that would murder people, but now that I've heard the Dawkinses' line of thinking, I realize I may be naïve to think that. I have a duty to notify Leeland Reagan.

When I take Dusty out for his evening constitutional, it's still hot and muggy. Could be raining again tomorrow. I wish it would. Might cool things down.

By the time I get back, I know I'm too keyed up to get to bed right away. And there's one thing I can do that will set my mind at ease. After Dusty gets settled into his bed, I get in my pickup and head back out to the cabin where Pat Wills and her daughter are holed up. I don't know how anyone would find out they were there, but that anonymous phone call to the church has me worried. I drive by slowly and see a couple of lights on, but there's only one car outside, the same one that was there this afternoon. It's ten o'clock. A few yards east of the cabin, across the road there's a pullout with a locked gate to someone's property. I park in the pullout and sit to wait and see if anything happens, even if it means I'm there all night.

I tune into a country-and-western music station, on low. I'm not all that interested in music, but it will keep me company.

Thoughts I've been resisting crowd into my mind and my spirits sink. I remember holding my wife Jeanne while she cried when she told me we could never have children, and why. When she was in high school, she got pregnant with her boyfriend. She was only sixteen. Terrified to tell her parents, she had a back-alley abortion and she almost died. The ordeal left her unable to bear a child. We discussed adoption, but although neither of us was entirely against it, we also didn't have much enthusiasm. But the desire to have a child sometimes overwhelmed Jeanne. She would be in low spirits for days, and all I could do was hold her and tell her I loved her no matter what.

We were lucky, in a hard way. Our nephew Tom came to live with us when he was six years old because my brother and his wife sank into drugs and couldn't care for him. We adopted him, and he gave us a lot of joy. But I know Jeanne regretted to the day she died not being able to have a houseful of kids.

I've wondered in the past few days if I should tell people why I refuse to comply with investigating a woman who defied the abortion laws that Texas lawmen have seen fit to impose on them. I could tell Maria or even Isabella Lopez. But it's my wife's story to tell, and I've held the secret so long that it feels embedded. And what good would it do for anyone to know? All they need to know is that I'm standing back.

A car startles me out of my revere, careening back and forth down the road, going too fast. A young boy sticks his head out the window and is hollering, most likely drunk. Probably happens a lot out here on this deserted road. I would usually pursue them, but I have a mission and I stay put.

An hour later, a car comes along, driving slowly, and pulls in next to Pat Wills's vehicle. A woman gets out – Isabella Lopez – and hurries to the house. It's too dark for me to see much, but in a few seconds the door opens, Isabella steps inside, and the door closes again. After a half hour, she comes back out, followed by Pat and April. They're carrying bags, which they stash in their car. Pat goes back in, the house goes dark, and she comes back out and gets into the driver's seat.

Lopez pulls out, heading away from me, and the other follows. Good. Looks like Lopez has decided not to keep the two women here. I wait until they are out of sight before I head home.

I wonder if the cabin is compromised and will have to be sold. What a hell of a thing for people to have to go to these lengths for their safety.

NINETEEN

Monday morning

First thing the next morning, I call Wendy to wish her a good trip. She answers right away. 'I was just going to call you. Nancy is picking me up in twenty minutes.'

'You all packed?'

'Finished last night. I hate to rush around at the last second. So this morning, all I have to do is leave a note for Tammy. She's coming over to water the plants.'

'You trust her to do that?'

She sighs. 'Not exactly. But I keep thinking if I act like I trust her, maybe she'll become trustworthy. Am I being foolish?'

'It's an admirable thought. Do you want me to go over to make sure she's done it?'

'No, I'll call her. I'm still holding out hope that you'll finish up and come join us.'

She gives me the information about where she'll be staying, and their approximate schedule. 'I know it's silly. I've been there a few times, but I'm excited. It will be beautiful this time of year.'

I hang up, feeling wistful, not so much that I'm left behind, but that I'd like to go with her. I haven't been back to San Francisco since my wife Jeanne died. It would be nice to reconnect with the city, and to explore it with Wendy.

When Maria comes in, I fill her in on the interview with Isabella Lopez last night, and I tell her I went back to the safe house to keep an eye on the women until I saw Lopez take them away.

She's quiet for a minute, looking stricken. 'You're sure Isabella Lopez didn't have a hand in Maddy's death?'

'Of course, I can't be sure, but I thought she was telling the truth. She said a car was following them and that Maddy apparently recognized the driver. I just wish she had paid more attention to the car. I'm betting that's who killed Maddy Benson.'

'But why would Maddy get out of the car?'

'I suspect it was so they wouldn't lead the driver to the safe house. And she might not have been aware that he intended to hurt her.'

'Kill her,' Maria says. 'So here's a question. If he was going to kill Maddy for her hand in helping girls get out of state, why didn't he kill Isabella, too?'

'We'll only know the answer to that when we find out who did it.'

Maria shakes her head. 'I can't believe these women are so brave, helping those poor girls who need to get out of state.'

'I want to go over and talk to Josh Benson first thing, to ask him if he knew his mamma had bought that cabin to use as a safe house.'

'You want me to check with city records to find out if it actually belongs to her?' Maria asks.

'That would be good.' I give her the address. 'If it isn't in her name, find out who owns it.'

Hannah opens the door with a resigned expression. 'Come on in. Josh said you called.'

'You may as well be in on the conversation.'

'And Eileen?' she whispers.

'Not necessary.'

'Good. I don't know how long she plans to stay, but she's getting on my nerves.'

'Does Eileen have kids?'

'Sort of. She married a man with two kids, and she raised them, but as far as I know, they hardly ever talk to her.'

'That's too bad.' I don't find her a particularly easy person to be around, but I imagine it was hard to raise kids and then have them turn their backs on you. Also, her husband seemed arrogant and disinterested in his wife when I talked to him. That may have had something to do with her situation. Poor woman.

'I suppose.'

Josh is waiting for me in the living room. Gloom seems to hang around his shoulders like a cloud.

'Any new word from Krista?' I ask.

'I talked to her last night. She said she'll be home tonight. What did you need to talk to us about?'

'Let's sit down. This won't take long,' I say.

When we're seated, I tell them that I found out Maddy had bought a small house out near where she was killed.

'Mamma did?' Josh asks. 'Where did she get the money?'

'I could ask you that. Did your dad leave her anything?'

The light dawns. 'He did. But it wasn't much.' The two siblings exchange glances.

'I thought that's what she lived on,' Hannah says.

'Did she pay rent here?' I ask.

'Oh, no,' Josh says. 'We wouldn't ask that.'

'Maybe someone else bought it in her name,' I say.

'Who?'

'I was going to ask you that. You know anyone? Are her folks in a position to do that?'

'They might have the money, but I doubt they would have spent it on a place for her when they knew she could live with Josh and Krista,' Hannah says.

'Would your aunt have helped?'

'Eileen seems to have plenty of money,' Josh says. 'Maybe she bought the house. But why?'

'Look, it was a place being used for a safe house,' I say. 'For girls who needed a place to stay while they waited for someone to take them out of state.'

'Really?' Josh says. 'They needed a place like that? Seems kind of extreme. I mean, couldn't girls just travel from where they were and be picked up somewhere?'

'Josh, don't be naïve,' Hannah says. 'It isn't always that easy for women to get away. Some of them have husbands or boyfriends who keep close tabs on them.'

'OK, I get it. Maybe one of those organizations she worked with paid for it and put it in her name.'

I had thought the same thing but needed to check it out with her kids before I jumped to conclusions.

'Anything else we can help with?' Josh asks. 'I mean . . . it's been almost a week. Have you made any progress?'

'I wish I could say I had, but with no witnesses, it's a tough case. But I'm working on it.'

Hannah laughs bitterly. 'I thought in small towns everybody knew everybody else's business. It seems like nobody knew hers.'

'Hannah, that's not fair,' Josh says. 'She kept to herself. We haven't lived here that long. There's no way people would know much about her.'

'You're right,' she says. 'I'm sorry. I'm just impatient. I can't stay here forever. I have a job to get back to.'

'Has the medical examiner released her body? Have you made funeral arrangements?'

'He said he'd release her body sometime tomorrow. We called the funeral director, a man named Ernest Landau, and he said he could do a funeral on Wednesday afternoon.'

'Landau and the woman who works for him are good people.'

He nods. 'I don't know what we would have done without Belle. She took us through everything and made it easy. Well, as easy as it could be.' Not the first time I've heard that about Belle.

'And Krista wasn't involved in the decisions?'

'Well, she's not here, is she?' His voice is testy. 'I left a message asking if she wanted to have a say in the way the funeral went, and she texted me that whatever we did was fine.'

He tells me the funeral is set for four p.m. on Wednesday and I tell him I'll be there. 'I want you to call me as soon as Krista gets home.'

Over the weekend, we got a couple of messages that I need to return. Becky Peltier, the woman whose dog was harassed by Phyllis Dawkins, called to say that she had made an appointment for this morning to have the dog's vaccinations updated. I call her back to confirm.

'You were right,' she says. 'Doc England gave me a payment plan. He said it was more important to him that Duke be vaccinated than that he make a quick buck.' Her laugh is a delight. I need to take Doc England out for a meal to thank him for more than just this. I've never properly thanked him for urging me to take Dusty. I look down at the mutt, who seems to sense what I'm thinking and thumps his tail on the floor.

After we hang up, I sit back to consider where the investigation stands. I only have strands of oddities, none of which lead to a real suspect. There are persons of interest and areas of interest, but no actual evidence pointing to anyone. I'm old-fashioned. Maria makes notes on her computer, but I like a pen and paper. I pull a yellow pad and start to jot down the stray points in the investigation.

Going back from the beginning, I review the notes I've taken with an eye to catching loose ends and making a plan to go forward.

At least now I understand why Maddy ended up at Tom Gainer's place. And after talking to Gainer's son, I know why the gate was unlocked. And I have an idea Maddy got out of Izzy's car because she didn't want to lead the driver to the safe house. But I have no clue who the driver was.

Regarding Maddy's activities, I need to know more about the particulars. In some cases, travel arrangements had to be made. How was it done? Did they rent cars? Did people volunteer to use their own cars?

I had also planned to call a few of the clinics in other states to find out if they knew of Maddy, had met her, or had any threats that they took seriously. And along with that thought of threats, I needed to ask Reagan if the FBI has gotten back to him about the threats to Maddy.

Continuing through my notes, I run across the fizzled lead with the car Jason Schrage lent to Craig Presley. Maddy Benson's neighbors, the Russells, saw that car sitting off the road near the Benson house. Although Craig Presley said he wasn't in Jarrett Creek and didn't lend the car to anyone, I have a question in my notes: *Lying?* I sit back and ponder that. It's possible the man who jotted down the license number got it wrong. But the make and model of the car were the same. I checked Presley's claim that he was in Dallas at a job interview. And he said he flew there. So where was the car during that time? Had he given it back to Jason? Something doesn't feel right, but what?

There are more loose ends: was the person who was in the car sitting outside Maddy's house the morning she was killed the same one who left the suspicious package on my doorstep? I get a mental image of someone lurking around town, someone guilty. But this is a small town, and people keep a sharp eye on strangers. Surely by now, someone would have reported seeing a stranger lurking. I think about the run-in I had with the Dawkinses yesterday afternoon. I have no doubt they've aired their opinions. Could it be that a member of their congregation took it upon himself to get rid of the 'demon' Maddy?

Then there's the matter of the organizations Maddy was associated with: Haven and The Time Is Now. It's a stretch to think that someone from either organization would have killed Maddy. But there's that possible mole in the Haven organization. I have no way to follow up on that myself, but I need to check in with Isabella Lopez at some point to see if she has ferreted out who 'Tina' is.

Finally, there's the matter of Krista's disappearance. It nags at me. If she really is back tonight, I need to have a stern talk with her, and to find out why she so carelessly worried everyone.

In the end, I have these threads to follow up on:

1. Call Jason Schrag to find out where his car was when Craig was in Dallas.
2. Organizations: Find out how travel arrangements were made to transport girls. How did the organizations work?
3. Threats: Call clinics to find out their knowledge of Maddy and any threats that may have involved her.
4. Contact Reagan re threatening letters. Any info? Stay on 'Tina' and the Haven group and the possible vigilante activity.
5. Church involvement: Who called the church? Same person who left the suspicious package? Who sat in the car near Maddy's house? Member of the congregation?
6. Krista's disappearance. Still seems strange. Maybe nothing.
7. As an afterthought, I add that I still haven't found out who Maddy was supposed to have known in Jarrett Creek.

It's getting on toward noon. I call Craig Presley, the man who borrowed Jason Schrage's car to find out if he's back from Dallas. When he doesn't answer, I call Jason, and in a small miracle he actually answers the phone.

I tell him that I'm curious to know where the car he lent to Craig Presley was kept when Craig was in Dallas. 'Did he give it back to you while he was gone?'

'No, I said he could borrow it until his was repaired. I don't need it. I'm just going to sell it.'

'Where was the car while Craig was in Dallas?'

'I assume he left it at his place. Or maybe he left it at my daddy's. I didn't check on it.'

'Craig said he didn't lend it to anyone. Is it possible someone borrowed it without his knowledge? Who has keys to the car? Your sister?'

'Yes, she has a set.'

'And you gave Craig your keys?'

'Yes.' He sounds impatient now. 'What is this about?'

'I told you the car had been spotted here in Jarrett Creek, and I want to know who might have driven it here. Could it have been your sister?'

'I told you, she's in Seattle . . .' He stops abruptly. 'Wait. She was in town for a couple of days to sign some papers and get some things out of Daddy's house. We're putting it up for sale. But she was busy the whole time. I can't imagine her driving to some town in the middle of nowhere.'

Not to mention that the Russells said the driver was a man. Still, it's worth pursuing. 'I'd like to talk to her.'

'Whatever.' He gives me the number. 'Don't be surprised if she doesn't answer, though. She's working on some tech project, and she's swamped.'

I strike out when I call and ask her to get back to me. Why doesn't anyone ever answer their phone anymore?

Maria comes back from city hall and says the safe house was in Maddy's name, but the loan on it was in the name of the Haven group. 'They bought it six months ago.' That explains where the money came from.

I tell her I'm going over to the café to get some lunch, but the phone rings before I can get out the door.

'Chief Craddock? It's Krista. Josh said I should call you.'

'You back home?'

'Yes, sir.'

'I'd like to stop by and have a chat.'

'I'll be here.'

I ask Maria if she'd like to come along to interview Krista, and she's all in.

When we leave, it's almost eleven o'clock. It feels suddenly cooler and the sun has disappeared. Dark clouds are massing to the north. We're in for another round of weather. Maria goes back in for a jacket.

Krista opens the door. She looks haunted. There are dark circles under her eyes, and her cheeks are pale. She leads me into the living room, where there's a glass of white wine on the table. No one else is in evidence. 'I'm having a glass of wine,' she says. 'Can I tempt you?'

It seems too early for wine. Maria and I decline.

'I suppose I'm in the doghouse,' she says with a wan smile.

'You are. Surely you realize that to disappear right after there has been a murder is alarming.'

'I know, I know. I just couldn't face everything. I don't know if Josh told you, but I have a deadline, and I felt like everything was crowding in. The house seemed full of everyone moping around and the whole atmosphere was too much. I needed space to work.'

'Surely, under the circumstances, your deadline could have been extended.'

She stares at me, and I see a glimpse of resentment. 'I suppose so, but I didn't want to do that. I pride myself on meeting my deadlines.'

'I see. Still, you could have let me know where you were.'

'You're right. And I apologize for that.'

There's not much else to be said. 'Did you get the work done?'

A short huff of laughter. 'That's the stupid part. I found it almost impossible to work. I couldn't get Maddy out of my mind, picturing her running from someone and being shot. It must have been terrifying.' She picks up her glass and takes a sip of wine. Her hand is shaking.

'Krista, is there anything you aren't telling me?'

She sets the glass down. 'Like what?'

'You tell me. Was there another reason you left here? Were you alone?'

The question was a stab in the dark, but her response tells me it was a good instinct. She chews her lower lip, her eyes downcast. 'Not the whole time.'

'Who was with you?'

'An old friend.'

'The man you were seeing before you moved here?'

She nods. 'I needed to talk to someone that I knew understood me.'

'How long was he with you?'

Fire sparks in her eyes. 'Oh, please, is this important? I feel guilty enough as it is.'

'Have you told your husband?'

She glances toward the stairs. 'God, no. It would really hurt him, and I don't want to do that.'

'Krista, we've come across new information since the last time we talked. About your mother-in-law's activities helping women.'

'Helping women?'

'Helping women go out of state to get abortions,' Maria says. She's impatient with my tentative approach. 'Did you know she was involved with that?'

Krista grimaces. I notice that her hands are tightly knit together. 'I knew she was involved with a group that formed after the Dobbs decision, but I didn't know any details. When I asked her, she said she didn't want me to get involved.'

'Why is that?'

'She thought it was dangerous.' Her face is grim. 'And at this point, I think you'd agree she was right.' As if to emphasize her words, there's a clap of thunder. She shudders.

'Did Maddy ever travel out of state?' Maria asks.

Krista narrows her eyes. 'You're not suggesting you would prosecute these people, are you?'

'No,' Maria says firmly. 'We're just trying to find out who killed her. So did she travel with these girls?'

'Not that I know of. I mean, I would have known if she went out of state. She would have been gone overnight. And I don't remember her going anywhere overnight.'

'Have you ever heard of a group called Haven?'

'No. What is that?'

'It's a group she was working with.'

'You have to understand, Maddy was tight-lipped. As I said, she didn't want us to know details.'

'And you don't know the names of anyone else she worked with?'

'I know some of her friends in Houston went on marches with her, but I don't know the extent of their involvement.'

'How did Josh feel about Maddy's work?' I've asked him, but I want to know her take on it.

'Maybe he knew she was doing something, but not what it was in particular.'

'Do you think he would have disapproved if he knew?'

'Disapproved? No, not of the activity itself, but maybe he would have thought it was dangerous and he would have been worried.'

We leave it at that. I tell Krista I'll be at the funeral on Wednesday.

When we get back to headquarters, Maria says before she leaves that she's going to dust the package that was left on my porch for fingerprints. 'We'll have them on file for when we catch the guy.' She sounds energized. She loves forensics.

TWENTY

Tuesday morning

When I get back to my house from seeing to my cows the next morning, Loretta is sitting at my kitchen table, and I can tell by her solemn look that she's got something on her mind. And I suspect I know exactly what it is.

I grab a cup of coffee and take a cinnamon roll from the stack she's brought me. 'You're out early,' I say.

'No earlier than usual. But I need to talk to you.'

'I imagine you do.'

She ignores my wry tone. 'You've stirred up quite a hornet's nest.'

'Reverend Dawkins?' I take a bite of the roll.

'And that wife of his, Phyllis. I don't know which is worse.'

'They told me they were going to have me fired.'

'They're gathering up a crowd.'

I take another bite and then a sip of coffee. 'They going to lynch me?'

'Samuel, be serious. They're looking to have you thrown out of office.'

'I guess if that's the worst thing that's going to happen, I'll have to accept it.'

'Not without a fight, I hope! They're the kind of people who think they ought to be able to tell everyone how to live. Even if he is the Baptist preacher, some things should be left to a person's own conscience.'

Loretta has been a Baptist her whole life, but she has had a hand in firing more than one preacher who she thought got above himself.

'Loretta, I appreciate your support, but I don't want to be the cause of getting between you and your preacher. I can take care of myself.'

'Anyway, they've called a meeting at the church tonight. You'll have supporters there, but it could get ugly. I don't want to see you thrown out of your job. We depend on you. Everybody trusts you.'

'Not everybody,' I say dryly. I pick up the last of the roll. 'If enough people decide they don't want me in the job, I'll call it quits. I've been at it a while, and I think Wendy would be glad if I was available more often to travel with her. It might be time for me to go anyway.' I feel more strongly about the matter than I'm letting on, but I don't want to upset Loretta or have her make enemies on my behalf.

She props her elbow on the table and drops her head on to her hand, kneading her forehead. 'You can't mean that. Who's going to take your place? Maria? She's not ready. Brick is brand new, and Connor, well . . . Connor.'

'If you remember, Loretta, when I took the job on the first time around, when I was thirty, I didn't have any experience at all. I was thrown into the job. Maria has a lot more experience than I did. And she's good. She's smart. As far as I know, people like her and think she's competent.'

'I hate to see you railroaded, that's all. And if that preacher thinks he can get away with having you fired, there's no telling what he'll do next. That kind of person gets power-hungry, and next thing you know, they'll be teaching the Bible in school.'

'Well, that's illegal,' I say.

'That wouldn't stop him.'

'So he thinks I'm doing something illegal, and I ought to be punished for it, but if he wants to do something illegal, that's OK?'

She blinks a few times before she replies. 'I don't think the contradiction would occur to him. Or to those people who think he hung the moon.'

'How bad is it? How many people do you think will follow him into the town council meeting?'

'I don't know, but I'd hate for it to get to that.'

'What do you suggest I do? Stop investigating Maddy Benson's murder?'

'No, of course not.'

'The preacher practically admitted he thinks I shouldn't be investigating Maddy's death, that she deserved what she got. And that I ought to arrest Maddy's family.'

Her mouth falls open. 'Why?'

'He says they probably were helping her. I've seen no proof of that, but that doesn't seem to stop him.'

Loretta's cheeks have gotten redder than I've ever seen them. 'That's not Christian.'

'I can't speak to that.'

She jumps up from the table. 'I've got some people I need to talk to. I'll see you later.'

'Wait. Do you think I ought to attend the meeting?'

She hesitates. 'Let me ask Ida Ruth. She's more political than I am. She'll have more of an idea.'

Ida Ruth Dillard has good sense. I hope she's on my side.

I stand. 'Loretta, don't upset yourself. The worst that can happen is that I get to retire. I might even like it.'

'You know you wouldn't.' She marches out the door. Reverend Dawkins may have gotten himself in over his head.

More than ever, with Dawkins's threats, I'm hesitant to involve Maria further in investigating Maddy Benson's case. Regardless of what Loretta said, I know Maria is capable of taking over as chief if they run me out of office. But it wouldn't do for her to be tainted by association with the case. I know she wouldn't take kindly to me pushing her off the case, but maybe I can keep her out of the spotlight.

When I get to the office, I have a call to make, hopefully before Maria gets in. I had previously decided not to tell Leeland Reagan, the district DPS manager, about Maddy Benson's activities, but I have to. If there is a vigilante group killing people, it needs to be ferreted out, regardless of the politics. I can't expect Reagan to be pro-choice, but I hope he at least won't be in the Dawkins camp.

When I reach him, I give him the details of what I've found out about Maddy Benson, being as discreet as I can.

'By "medical care," I presume you mean abortions,' he says, when I tell him. His voice is neutral.

'Affirmative,' I say.

He sighs. 'Well, that's a can of worms I hate to see opened.'

'It's already opened.' I describe the phone call someone made to the church, and the preacher's vitriolic reaction.

'You think somebody in that church could have had something to do with her murder?' he asks.

'According to the preacher, the call came in after the Benson woman was killed.'

'And you say the call was anonymous?'

'That's right.' I hadn't planned on mentioning Dawkins's threats, but I decide to lay it out that the preacher is trying to have me fired.

He takes his before time commenting. 'That won't stand,' he says, with surprising heat. 'This business of private citizens threatening officers of the law has gotten out of hand. I understand the reverend's point of view, I do, but I fail to understand how he hopes to convert people to his opinion by being so confrontational.'

'I don't think he has an interest in arguing his side. I'd understand it better if he just laid out his beliefs. But he insists I should drop the investigation of the murder because of his beliefs.'

'Over the top. What are you going to do? You might think of pre-empting him. You could take it to the city council and explain that you're doing your job.'

'I could. I'll take that under advisement.' I think it's gone beyond that.

'But if it comes down to you being booted, let me ask you this. You ever thought about coming to work for the DPS?'

I can't help chuckling to myself. This is a far cry from his tune when he first met me. 'It might be tempting, but I believe I'm more in the line of retiring than I am taking on a new job.'

'Well, there's that,' he says. 'Anyway, let me know if the good reverend steps too far out of line. Like I said, we can't have private citizens telling lawmen how to do our jobs. If they want to be cops, let them get the training and see how it works.'

I've decided not to bring up the safe house. I don't know what good it would do, and I don't want to risk Reagan deciding he has to go after Isabella Lopez and Haven. 'Has the FBI gotten back to you about the threatening letters?'

'Not yet, but I didn't expect them to. They take their sweet time. But I know they're keeping close tabs on the situation. We got a system-wide notification that there's been an uptick in threats against people working with Planned Parenthood and similar organizations, and the Feds are forming a task force to deal with it.'

'How long do you think it will be before the FBI gets back to you?'

'I wouldn't hold my breath. In my experience, which I admit is limited, the words "forming a task force" don't bode well.'

'Does this task force have the blessing of the State of Texas?'

'I didn't ask. Not my rodeo. But the FBI will want to know what you told me. And they may want to take over the investigation.'

'I hope you can hold them off. I'm not eager to have them swarming all over town, stirring up trouble.'

'Their wheels move slowly, you know that. So you have breathing room.'

If anyone had asked me, I would have bet that Reagan was eager to prosecute anyone helping women get abortions out of state, but if he is, he's keeping his opinions quiet.

'What kind of leads are you looking at?' he asks.

'Leads would put too much strength into it. Open-ended questions is more like it. A few things that are nagging at me. I'll follow up and see where it takes me.'

'Let me know if I can send you any help.'

I hang up, bemused by how much a few months in office has changed Reagan. He came in sure that he was going to personally oversee every investigation in every small town in his jurisdiction. He's learned how impossible that would be.

Maria has come in while I was talking and gone straight to her computer. When I get off the phone, she says, 'I got a reply from Haven.'

I put on a pot of coffee and sit down in the chair next to her desk. 'What did they say?'

'I filled in the form, and they got right back to me. They gave me a number to call.'

I immediately think of Isabella's problem with the possible mole in the organization. I tell Maria what Maddy was worried about. 'What would you think of calling and telling them that you know someone who was counseled by a woman named Tina and you wonder if you could talk to her.'

Maria considers. 'First of all, if she was using an assumed name, if I don't reach the person pretending to be Tina, she won't know who I am asking for. And then, even if manage to talk to her, how would I find out who she really is?'

'I wondered the same thing. I know it's a longshot, but I'd like you to try. I'm worried that whoever Tina is might be connected with whoever killed Maddy.'

Maria nods. 'In that case, it's worth a shot.'

'There's another issue we need to discuss. That business with the Baptist preacher? I spoke with Loretta this morning and there's a meeting tonight at city hall. The Dawkinses are going to try to have me ousted.'

'What? Are you serious? You really think people would go along with him?'

'A certain number would, but even if it wasn't very many, the city council tends to be averse to controversy. They might decide it's better to ask me to bow out.'

'You have to fight them. You ought to go to the meeting so you can confront them head-on.'

'I'm considering it.' I don't like the idea.

'Who do they think they're going to find to do the job? It's not like people are begging to be on the force.'

'You'd be the natural choice.'

'Oh, no, boss, I don't have enough experience.'

I remind her that when I was first slotted into the job, I had exactly no experience. 'You'd be great at the job. And it's not like I would disappear off the face of the earth. You could come to me for advice.'

She brightens. 'Or I could hire you as my deputy. That would be a change.' Maria doesn't always have a big sense of humor, and for her this is funny. I laugh along with her.

'The problem is if the preacher follows through with this and I get fired, I don't want you to be tarred with the same brush they're using on me.'

Her smile disappears. 'You mean you think I should not work this case with you.'

I nod. 'I need to be able to tell the city council that I was working it on my own, so that any fallout comes to me alone.'

'You could turn it over to Reagan.'

'I could.' But I don't want to. There's that old pride flaring up in me. I want to get this job done. I always thought I was determined to solve cases because I felt a sense of responsibility to the town, wanted to keep the citizens of Jarrett Creek safe, wanted to ferret out whoever had crossed the line and committed a crime, needed to see justice done and order restored. But in this case, I want to solve it because it's my pride on the line. Handing it over to Reagan would make me feel like a failure.

We stare at each other, at a standoff. 'Look, go ahead and make the call to Haven. And depending on what you find out, we'll think how to proceed. There are things you can do behind the scenes. We'll just make sure to keep you on the down-low.'

I pour myself another cup of coffee and get back to two loose ends I want to tackle right away.

The first is to call the out-of-state clinics Maddy was working with to ask if they had any threats or if they had any reason to worry that Maddy was in danger. It's such a long shot that it's most likely a waste of time, but it has to be done.

An hour later, I've confirmed that it's a waste of time. All the clinics I contacted in the four states – New Mexico, Colorado, California and Nevada – knew of Maddy and her work and praised her for her diligence. But none of them had ever met her, nor did they have any idea who might have been after her.

Maria has hung up the phone and is looking discouraged. 'That was a dead end,' she says. 'The woman said she never heard of Tina, and once I started asking questions, she knew right away that I was not someone in trouble. She was polite, but she said she didn't have anything to say about the organization and that I should contact the president.'

'Isabella Lopez?'

'Yes.'

'So what we've got here is two organizations that are doing the same work as Planned Parenthood, but much smaller in scale. They are dedicated to helping women, they have been targeted by threats, but as far as we know, Maddy is the only person who has been killed. Plus, Isabella Lopez is involved in both organizations.'

'Wait. Do we know that Maddy Benson was the only person killed?' Maria asks. 'Have we looked into whether there have been other murders like this one?'

'No, you're right, we haven't. You want to tackle that?'

'I'm on it. All we'd need to make this a bigger deal is to find another suspicious death.' She cocks her head. 'And what are you going to be doing while I look into it?'

'Some loose ends.' I'm going to run out of them soon, and then I don't know what I'm going to do.

I call Isabella Lopez. No surprise she doesn't pick up. I leave a message. 'When you get this, I'd appreciate a call. It's one quick question.'

Then I put in another call to Jason Schrage's sister, urging her to call me back. It's two hours earlier on the west coast, so I add, 'I know there's a time differential, but call me no matter what time it is.'

TWENTY-ONE

M aria is on hold with the DPS, calling to ask if there have been other murders associated with either Haven or The Time Is Now. 'I've been on hold for twenty minutes,' she says.

'I'll go over and pick up some lunch. You want the usual?'

She rolls her eyes. Of course she does. She's the hamburger queen.

I head over to Town Café. Maybe it's because Wendy is out of town, but I suddenly feel dissatisfied with eating at the same old place every day. Am I in a rut? Seems so. Too late to change it today, though, so I order Maria's hamburger, and I decide to get the same for myself instead of my usual enchiladas. Now I won't hear the end of her gloating that I've finally come to my senses.

I'm sitting waiting for the order when Gabe LoPresto and the high school football coach, the newly hired Donny Winslow, amble in. I signal for them to sit down with me. 'Plotting the football season?' I ask.

Donny is a big man in his forties with almost white blond hair in a crewcut and a perpetually sunburned face. He puts out a meaty paw. 'Yeah, we're discussing some fundraising strategy.'

'Uh-oh,' I say. 'I'll hold on to my checkbook.'

'The hell you will,' LoPresto says. He knows I'll donate a hefty sum, but nobody will match him. Even though his kids have graduated and left home, he's still the biggest booster.

'And what about you?' LoPresto says. 'You figured out what happened to that woman who got shot?'

Coach Winslow coughs. 'I heard some rumors about that lady.'

'What did you hear?' I ask.

He and LoPresto lean close. Winslow looks to the tables close by to make sure we aren't overheard. 'Is it true she was doing abortions in the back room?'

'Oh, for heaven's sake. Of course she wasn't. Where did a rumor like that come from?'

Winslow raises an eyebrow. 'Sounds like I hit a nerve.'

'It's absolutely preposterous. An unfounded allegation like that could blow back on her family,' I say. 'The woman was helping women find healthcare they needed, nothing more.'

'If you say so,' Winslow says. He doesn't seem particularly concerned that he was spreading a rumor. 'I understand the woman's daughter-in-law writes those steamy novels. My wife reads them, and she was excited when she found out the woman is living here in town. I expect any day now you'll have to put out a restraining order on my wife because she'll be staking out her house to get a look at her.' He guffaws.

The waitress comes and they order. LoPresto hasn't said much.

'What are you up to?' I ask.

'Same old, same old. Working on that new motel out north of town. Construction starts next week. I guess you heard we had a spot of vandalism. Probably kids.'

'Let me know if there's a repeat,' I say. 'Let me ask the two of you, since you've heard rumors about the woman who was killed. You know of anybody in town who knew her before she came here? Somebody said it was a young woman.' Both of them are out in public a lot and could very well have heard somebody say they knew her.

'Did you ask Loretta Singletary?' LoPresto asks. 'She knows every damn thing that happens here in town. At least, that's what Sandy says.' His wife Sandy forgave him for an embarrassingly public affair a few years ago, and he has deferred to her ever since.

'I did ask Loretta, but she didn't know. Her friends are older ladies, and they may not necessarily know some of the younger connections.'

'Tell you what, I'll ask Sandy,' LoPresto says. She keeps up with some of the women in their thirties because she teaches exercise classes.'

'That's right, I'd forgotten that.' That gives me another idea. I'll talk to Ellen Forester, who owns the art studio and gallery. She knows a completely different demographic.

My food comes and I hustle back to sit with Maria at our desks. As I expected, she ribs me for ordering a hamburger.

'Did you reach the FBI? Any luck with the question of other murders?'

'It took a while, but I got a woman on the phone who was interested in the question, and she got back to me. She says they don't have any record of anything that looks similar. There have been a couple of deaths associated with abortion access, but in both cases the perp was caught. She said she'd do more research and call me if she found anything.'

'I hate to say this, but she could have been targeted by somebody from out of town who came here for the express purpose of killing her.' I tell her that Reagan said the FBI is likely going to get involved. 'If they do, they might have better luck than me, although it could take a while.'

I tell her Winslow said his wife reads Krista's novels and that he joked she might stalk Krista, and that triggers me thinking about the suspicious person who Maddy's neighbors saw in a car near the house. Because Maddy was killed soon after, I assumed the person in the car was there to watch Maddy, but maybe it was someone interested in Krista.

The phone rings, and Maria takes the call. When she hangs up, she says she needs to go out for a while. She rolls her eyes. 'I have to hold Lola Gerson's hand. She thinks a neighbor has been spying on her. Why on earth somebody would do that . . .' She heads out the door.

Just as she leaves, Brick comes in, as usual looking fresh-faced and alert.

'What's doing around here, boss?' he says. He's taken up Maria's habit of calling me boss, which kind of tickles me.

'Not too much. You know, a few days ago, somebody asked us to go out and check on an abandoned car. I'd like you to go check it out.' I fish out the address I jotted down and the name of the person who called it in.

'What's going on with the investigation into the woman who got shot?'

'Working on it.'

'Anything I can do to help?'

Having been burned by the preacher's anger, I hesitate to say much to Brick. By now, I'm sure he's heard what Maddy was up to, but I don't know Brick's position. 'Brick, it's a complicated homicide – you know that, right?'

He scrunches up his face. 'I had dinner with my folks in Bobtail last night, and they told me what they'd been hearing.'

'There are citizens who seem to think that Maddy deserved what she got.'

'You're kidding. The woman was shot to death. You mean . . . oh, I see.'

'Let me put it this way. Nobody needs to work on a case they aren't comfortable with.'

'You're worried I don't want to find out who killed her because of who she was?' His voice is incredulous. 'No. That's not the way it works. At least not in my mind. You can't have people going around killing somebody because they think they were doing the wrong thing. That's why we have the law.'

I'm not used to hearing Brick talk philosophically. He's industrious, but he's young, and I suspect his ideas haven't been tested. 'I'm glad to hear you say that. If I need your help, I'll let you know. Right now, leads are slim.'

He heads out to check on the abandoned car, and I go over to talk to Ellen Forester. I want to get there before she closes up for the day. She keeps irregular hours and often closes up in the mid-afternoon.

When Ellen first moved to town a few years ago, we dated for a while. I liked her, but she was coming out of a divorce and hadn't quite let go of her ex-husband. Things got rocky between us. Plus, she was a vegetarian and I'm a confirmed meat eater. Not that we couldn't have worked that out, but along with the other issues, it was too much to deal with.

Still, we've remained friendly. I head over to the art gallery and workshop that she started when she moved here. One of the things that drew us together was our interest in art. I have a valuable collection of contemporary art, and Ellen was thrilled to find someone in town who appreciated art. At the time she opened the store, most everybody thought it would be a financial disaster. But it turned out that half the town seemed to think they had hidden talent as an artist and eagerly signed up for her classes. One of the surprises for me was when my friend Loretta started painting, and Ellen told me she had some talent. I knew she was always the one people called on for decorating the church, but it never occurred to me that she had artistic talent beyond that.

Ellen's shop, Art 36, is in the middle of town on Highway 36, which is also the main street, which is why she named it that. It's in what for many years was a mercantile store. The store's big display windows make for a great place to exhibit her students' work, some of which is more successful than others. She says 'success' is not the point; enjoyment is.

I've caught her at the end of a class. She has a few pieces of art on a table along with framing supplies. She looks up when she hears my footsteps.

'Samuel, what a treat. What are you doing here?' She wipes her hands on her apron and comes over to give me a peck on the cheek.

We make small talk for a few minutes, catching up. Turns out her daughter is pregnant, and Ellen is thrilled. 'I don't know how I feel about being old enough to be a grandmother, but I'm glad anyway. So what brings you here?'

'I'm sure you've heard about the woman who was killed last week.'

She shudders. 'That was awful. It's all anybody talked about for the rest of the week.'

'There's a rumor that she knew someone here in town before she moved here, and I'm having a hard time finding out who it is.'

'If you're asking if I knew her, then no.'

'You get a lot of people through here; I wondered if anybody had mentioned knowing her.'

She thinks for a minute. 'No, but I do know there was some controversy. A couple of my students got into a heated discussion over it.'

'I can imagine.'

'One of the women said that Maddy – is that her name? – was asking for trouble. And the other one said nobody asks to be killed. And the other one said, well, maybe she *was* asking to be killed, that there are a lot of people who have extreme positions on the abortion issue.'

'The same thing I've been hearing. I guess I'm surprised at how hard-hearted some people can be.'

She raises her eyebrows. 'Surprised? I know you've run into some bad people.'

'That's true, but they're usually the criminals. This is different.'

She tells me she'll keep her ears tuned if anyone mentions knowing Maddy.

I'm back at headquarters when my phone rings and I see that it's Wendy calling.

'Hey, are you having a good time?' I ask.

'It's so beautiful here, and I am having a good time, but it would be a lot better if you were here. Any chance of you getting away?'

'It's not looking good,' I say. 'I haven't gotten much farther along investigating the Benson woman's death.'

'Samuel, how long do you work on a case before you decide you aren't going to solve the crime?'

'Good question. I don't think I ever thought about it.'

'That's because you've always been successful. Maybe this is that one time when you aren't going to figure it out. I mean, this woman came from Houston and hasn't lived in the area that long. It could be that someone from out of town killed her.'

'Look, it's only been a week. Less than.'

'What's Maria doing?'

'She's pursuing some leads.' I don't want to get into the details with Wendy – threats to my job and not wanting to get Maria too involved in case she has to take over.

'Well, you've got to take a vacation sometime, right? When I get back, we're going to discuss it.'

'I promise,' I say. She's right. She loves to travel, and I owe it to her to take some time off.

She's satisfied with my promise, and she lays out her plans for tomorrow. She's going to the Museum of Modern Art and the de Young Museum. That's almost enticing enough to make me abandon the search for Maddy's killer and fly out to San Francisco.

As soon as I hang up, my phone rings again. It's Sandy LoPresto. 'Gabe told me you want to know who in town was acquainted with that woman who got killed. I think I might know who it was. I haven't seen you in a while. Why don't you come over for dinner and we'll chat? We eat early, so come at six. And bring that silly dog of yours. We'll put him in the backyard with our dogs.'

When I get home, I go down to see my cows. I'm feeling frustrated, and it always calms me to spend time with my herd. Dusty is with me, and he takes off as usual, scaring up a critter to chase. The heat of the day has mellowed, and the pen is in the shade, so the cows seem content. I've started putting out more feed now that the weather has gotten cooler, and they're crowding around the bins.

At five thirty, I get Dusty in my truck and we head out for the LoPrestos' place.

*   *   *

Gabe is the most successful building contractor in the area, but you wouldn't know it to look at his house. He and Sandy have always lived in the same place – a modest, sprawling one-story house tucked away off a gravel road a few blocks from my house. I asked Gabe once why he didn't have the road paved, and he said he never got around to it – he's always too busy.

Gabe greets me at the door, and I hand him the red wine I've brought. When I see Gabe during the day, he's always well dressed, if not in a suit, at least in slacks, a buttoned shirt, and tooled leather cowboy boots. At home, he's changed into jeans and a T-shirt. He's still wearing cowboy boots, but they're well-worn and comfortable looking. 'Glad you could join us,' he says. 'We don't get enough time to have real conversations.'

He takes me out to the back yard where we're greeted by a couple of mutts who welcome Dusty with yelps and leaps. There's a big grill out here and good smells are coming from it. 'I had some tri-tip marinating, so I thought we'd cook and eat out here,' he says.

Sandy sticks her head out the door. 'I'll be out there in a minute. I'm just whipping up the potato salad.'

Gabe picks up a beer sitting on the outdoor table. I'm going to finish this and have wine with dinner. You want a beer?'

I tell him that sounds good, and he takes the wine inside and brings out a beer.

By the time Sandy comes out with the side dishes, Gabe and I are deep in conversation concerning the prospects of this year's football team. 'I don't mind telling you,' he says, 'that I'm worried about Coach Winslow. He has a good reputation, but from what I've seen, he's awfully easy on the boys.'

I've heard that every year from LoPresto. 'Maybe you ought to take up coaching,' I say.

'That's all I need,' Sandy says as she sets the table. 'He'd have those boys trooping through this house, eating us out of house and home.'

It's only after dinner, which is some of the best barbecue I've had outside my favorite place, with sides to match, that I ask Sandy to tell me who she thinks Maddy Benson was acquainted with here in town.

'Her name is Becky Peltier. She and her husband moved here from Houston a year or so ago, and she told me she knew Maddy. But I don't think she knew her well.'

I know exactly who Becky Peltier is. She's the young woman whose dog the Baptist preacher's wife, Phyllis Dawkins, chased with a broom and reported as possibly rabid. 'How do you know Becky Peltier?'

'You know I have those exercise classes. I hold them right over there.' She points to a large, square building at the back of the lot. 'She looked me up as soon as she got settled.'

'Looked you up how?'

'I have website and a social media presence.'

Social media presence. I should know what that means. It sounds formal. 'So she found you that way?'

'That's right. It's the best way to advertise these days.'

'And she told you she knew Maddy Benson?'

'She actually didn't tell me specifically. She wrote it on Instagram.'

'What did she say?'

'It was just a quick post. She said someone she used to know got killed and she thought a small town would be safer than the city, but maybe not.'

She can't tell me anything more, but that's enough to have my brain buzzing. As soon as I get home, I'll call Becky Peltier and arrange to interview her tomorrow.

I leave shortly after eight. Dusty is so tired after his non-stop play with the LoPrestos' dogs that he flops down on the front seat on the way home and is instantly asleep. When we get home, he scoots up the steps ahead of me, probably as eager as I am to get to bed. I've just put my foot on the first step when I sense somebody behind me. Before I can react, a strong arm snakes around my throat, the other arm grabbing my wrist and pulling my arm up behind me. I strike backwards with my right foot and connect with the attacker's leg, and he grunts but doesn't loosen his grip. With my free arm, I jab my elbow into his solar plexus, but again he maintains control.

I try to holler, but he's holding my throat so tight that only a hoarse rasp comes out.

Dusty seems to have realized what's happening, and he comes charging down the steps, snarling and barking. The guy kicks at him, but Dusty dances out of range.

I kick backwards again, higher, and I connect with his knee. It's a better hit, and this time he loosens his grip enough for me to get in a good yell. But then, in a loud whisper, he says, 'You asked for it,' and something bashes the side of my head and I go down to my knees, seeing bright lights.

Dusty is hysterical now, and I'm worried that the guy will hurt him, but there's nothing I can do about it.

But his barking has brought the attention of one of my neighbors, who yells out, 'Shut that dog up.'

I try to yell for help, but the guy hits me again, and this time I'm out.

I don't know how long I'm unconscious, but I come to with Dusty licking my face. My first thought is that I'm glad my dog's OK. But then I realize I'm not OK. My head feels like it's been split in two. I feel the place where it's throbbing, and my hand comes away wet. I'm sure it's blood. I open my eyes and try to sit up, but it makes me too dizzy, so I lie back down. Meanwhile, Dusty continues to lick me.

I push him away, open my eyes, and when the world stops spinning, I try again to sit up. At least, whoever attacked me is gone. I wish Dusty would bark some more, maybe bring the neighbor back out so I can call for help. But then I realize I have my cell phone in my pocket. I have Jenny Sandstone, my next-door neighbor, on speed dial, and I call her.

She arrives within minutes, carrying a flashlight in one hand and a handgun in the other. She shines the light on my head. 'You need an ambulance,' she says.

'No,' I say. 'I'll be OK. I just need help getting into the house.'

'You can't fool around with a head wound,' she says. 'I'm calling them.'

'Goodness knows how long it will take for them to get here,' I say. 'Call Doc Bosco.'

'Now I know you need help. Bosco has been retired for ten years.'

'That doesn't mean he's stupid,' I say. 'He'll come out. And if he says I need a hospital, I'll go.'

Sure enough, fifteen minutes later Carl Bosco comes wheeling up in his big SUV. 'What the hell happened?' he asks as he bends over me with Jenny holding the flashlight so he can see.

I tell him I was attacked.

'Well, you're not killed, but I think this lady is right: you need to get to a hospital so they can do a CT scan, make sure you don't have a brain bleed. Instead of calling an ambulance, though, why don't I take you over there. It'll take less time. And you're not going to die right away.'

'That's a comfort,' I say. 'But I don't want to put you out. It's late.'

'Samuel, how long have we known each other? You know good and well I'm happy to be of service. And it isn't even ten o'clock. I'll be back home before midnight, and I never go to bed before then, anyway.'

Between the two of them, they get me into his car and on our way. He calls his wife to tell her he'll be a while. 'Don't wait up.'

TWENTY-TWO

Wednesday morning

The next morning, before the hospital releases me, the doctor tells me I should be glad I have a hard head, that there's no sign of a bleed, but that I'll have a headache for a few days. I call Maria to come and pick me up. When she arrives, she's brought Dusty. She says she picked him up from my place last night when Jenny called her. I get in the car, and the way he wriggles and climbs all over me, he must think I've been gone a month.

When we get to my place, Maria fusses over me like a nanny, which for once I don't mind. The pills the doctor prescribed have had enough effect that my head is only achy, not pounding, and I start pondering how I can identify my attacker.

'You said he spoke,' Maria says. 'What did his voice sound like? Specifically, high-pitched or low-pitched?'

'Neither extreme, but I can tell you he sounded youngish. Definitely not an older person.'

'Which leaves out most of the population of Jarrett Creek,' she says drily. 'You're sure you remember exactly what he said?'

'Oh yeah, it wasn't that many words. He said I asked for it.'

'Somebody connected to that note that was left? It said you should forget about investigating, right?'

I start to nod, but I wince. Not a good idea. 'Yes. So you're right – maybe the same person.'

'And that's somebody who thinks the same way that the Baptist preacher does. Could it have been him?'

'No, he's not that young. And besides, I would have recognized his voice. He has a particular tone. Like he's giving a speech.'

Suddenly, I remember it's Wednesday. 'You know Maddy's funeral is this afternoon. Four o'clock. I'd like us both to go.'

'You shouldn't go out in the afternoon. It's going to be hot.'

'I have to. I'll be fine. I'll rest until then.'

She sighs. 'I know you well enough to realize there's no arguing with you. But I'll pick you up and take you over there. You shouldn't be driving yet.'

There's no reasoning with her, and she also insists that I not come into the office today. I relent, but that doesn't mean I'm not going to make some phone calls.

I noticed when I was lying in the hospital bed this morning that late last night I had a phone call from Jason Schrage's sister, Karen. Her voice sounded frosty when she said, 'I'm calling you back because you said it was urgent. I guess you're not answering your phone, so it must not be that urgent.'

I need to call her back soon, and I also want to set up a time to meet with Becky Peltier to ask what her connection is with Maddy Benson. But all I can think about is lying down for a while.

The next thing I know, it's early afternoon, and I'm feeling better. My head still aches, but I don't feel like someone is driving a pickax into it. What I'm mostly feeling now is mad. Whoever hid out and attacked me last night must think I can be scared off easily. All they've done is redouble my determination to find out who shot Maddy.

Last night in the thick of things, when Dusty was barking, J.P. Roberts from next door came out and yelled for the dog to be quiet. I doubt he saw anything, but I want to go next door to ask him, and to apologize for the noise. I have time to go before I leave for the funeral.

J.P.'s wife Elaine answers the door. 'Samuel, I'm so sorry. I heard what happened. Are you OK?' She's in her late sixties, retired from forty years of working at a bank in Bryan. Her husband J.P. retired at the same time, and they moved from Bryan to Jarrett Creek, taking over old Mrs Summerville's house when she died and her daughter moved out to go live near her sister. I haven't gotten to know them, but I see them talking to various people in the neighborhood.

'Is J.P. here?'

'I think he's up from his nap. Let me go see. Come on inside. You don't need to stand outside in this heat. I swear I thought that rain would cool things off, but all it did was make it more humid.'

I step inside and hear the heavy footsteps of J.P. coming down the hallway. 'Samuel, glad to see you survived.' He shakes my hand. 'I'm sorry I yelled instead of coming to see what the fuss was about. I felt bad when I heard what happened.'

'Part of the reason I came was to apologize for the disturbance. He got awfully loud.'

'That's understandable. Like I said, I should have checked.'

'Don't just stand there, boys,' Elaine says. 'Come in and sit down. I can get you some iced tea.'

We move into their living room, a small room that's not too cluttered. Instead of a big sofa, they have a loveseat and a couple of moderate-size chairs positioned to look at a TV. It's a pleasant room, with family photos perched on tables and a spinet piano. 'Who plays the piano?' I ask. 'I never heard it being played.'

'Oh, I used to play,' Elaine says. 'But my hands don't work so well anymore. The arthritis, you know. But I like to think I might play again sometime.'

'I hope you do. I like piano music.' Not entirely true. I don't mind piano music, but I don't have much of an ear for music, so it doesn't matter to me whether she plays or not. I'm being polite.

Elaine goes off to get some tea, and J.P. says, 'You have any idea who attacked you?'

'I was hoping you might be able to help me out with that,' I say. 'When you went outside, did you see anything you took note of? An unfamiliar car? See anybody running away?'

'I wish I could help you with that, but I didn't see a thing. Soon as I called out about the dog, I came on back inside.'

'You notice anybody hanging around earlier in the day? Somebody you didn't expect to be here?'

He takes his glasses off and pinches the bridge of his nose. 'I didn't, but let me ask Elaine.'

She comes back carrying two big glasses of tea. 'Let me get some cookies,' she says and bustles out again. She's back in a minute with a plate of chocolate chip cookies and her own glass of tea. 'Excuse me, I'm not much of a baker, but these store-bought cookies are pretty good.'

When she sits down, J.P. repeats my question.

'Let me think,' she says. 'While you took your nap yesterday afternoon, I went to the grocery store. Took me a couple of trips to get the groceries in.' She takes a sip of tea. 'Oh, yes, I had to go out again because I had to deliver something. You know Loretta down the street? I'd seen her outside on my way to the store and asked if she wanted me to get anything. She said she was running low on sugar and would I get her some, so I took it down to her house.'

'You walked?' I ask.

'Of course I did, it's only a block away.'

'And you didn't see anybody around?'

She shakes her head slowly. 'Just the Baptist preacher's boy – what's his name? – Aaron. He was driving toward me when I was walking toward Loretta's. The only reason I remember is that I waved and he didn't wave back, even though I thought he saw me. He's a standoffish kid.'

'Are you Baptists?'

'In name,' J.P. says. 'We've been to church a few times here, but I don't much care for the preacher. He seems too full of himself. I guess that's where his son gets his attitude.'

Maybe I'm already inclined to be suspicious of Aaron Dawkins, but I can't help wondering why he was driving over this way? The Dawkinses don't live nearby. But would he attack me? Even if he did, how could I prove it? It makes my head hurt to think about it.

I thank the Robertses and arrive back to my place in time to intercept Loretta coming up my steps. She's got a bag in her hand, and I know what's up.

She's ruffled. I can tell by the way she's holding her shoulders high and tight. 'Why didn't you call and tell me what happened? Why did I have to find out from that nosy Jolene Ramsey? I came over this morning and you weren't home, and I didn't know where you'd gotten off to.'

'Loretta, I'm sorry I didn't call you. I just got home. Come on in. It's too hot to stand out here and fuss.'

She follows me inside and plunks the paper bag down on the table. 'I brought you some food so you wouldn't have to go to any trouble.'

'I appreciate that more than you know.'

She makes a humming sound, so I know she's mollified. 'Are you OK?' she asks.

I sit down. 'Passable. I would have called if I'd had my wits about me.'

She's still standing, hands on her hips. 'You've been home long enough to go over to talk to your neighbors.'

'Come on, sit down. I went over there first thing because I wanted to talk to them while it was fresh in their mind, to ask if they'd seen anything last night.' I tell her about Dusty making a racket and J.P. hollering for him to quiet down.

She eyes the dog and says, 'He's a good dog, then.'

Dusty gives a tentative wag of his tail.

She takes things out of the bag and says, 'Does Dusty bark like that a lot?'

'No, he doesn't.'

'Well, then J.P. should have known something was wrong.'

'I guess. What've you go there?'

She's brought a chicken and noodle casserole that she knows I like, and coleslaw and a dewberry pie.

'Dewberry pie! How'd you get that many dewberries? They're probably almost gone.'

She's pleased and eyes shine. 'I had some in the freezer. I hope the pie is fit to eat.'

'You know it will be.'

'You want a piece right now?'

I glance at my watch. It's two thirty and Maria is coming in an hour, so I don't have long. But I haven't eaten and I'm not feeling all that steady, so I tell her I'll have some pie.

By now she's not mad anymore. She likes to do things for people. Before she sits down she wants to examine my head wound.

'There's a big old lump,' she says. 'Who do you think hit you?'

'If I knew that, Maria would have arrested them, and they'd be in jail.' Suddenly, I remember the town meeting. 'How did the meeting go last night? I guess if I'd been ousted, I would have heard by now.'

She smirks. 'That's what I came over first this morning to tell you about. Let's just say Mr and Mrs Dawkins weren't too happy with the way it went. There were only a half-dozen people on their side and twenty of the rest of us. Not to say those half-dozen didn't have plenty to say. It went on for a good two hours. I was ready to drop by the time we got out of there, but in the end they were voted down.'

'That's a comfort, I suppose. But I hate to see it come to that.'

'I know, but it will settle down eventually.'

While I tuck into the pie, she quizzes me some more about my attack. I tell her what I remember of what happened.

'J.P. didn't see anything when he was outside yelling at Dusty?' she asks.

'Afraid not.' But then I remember Elaine saw the preacher's son driving by. 'Let me ask you, what kind of reputation does Aaron Dawkins have?'

'The preacher's boy?' She frowns. 'What makes you ask that?'

'I happened to think of it because Elaine said she saw him drive by yesterday. I had to have a talk with him last weekend.' I tell her about the boys 'borrowing' Dooley's boat and me having a come-to-Jesus talk with them. 'I don't want that getting around, you hear?'

'Why not? People ought to know when teenagers are up to no good.'

'I told them I wouldn't let it get back to their folks in exchange for behaving themselves.'

She snorts. 'You were too easy on those boys.'

'Not entirely.' I tell her they're pledged to do work for Dooley. 'So does Aaron have a reputation?'

'I never heard anything except that he's cocky with the girls, but if that was a crime, half the boys his age would be locked up.'

I look at my watch. It's time for me to get ready.

Loretta notices. 'I understand Maddy Benson's funeral is this afternoon. You're not planning to go, are you?'

'I have to. But Maria's taking me over there, so I don't have to drive.'

'Have you told Wendy what happened?'

'She's in San Francisco and I don't want to worry her.'

She cocks her head at me. 'She'd want to know. You ought to tell her.'

'Maybe tomorrow.'

By the time she leaves, I only have a half hour to get ready. I take a quick shower and dress, and have a few minutes to lie down. My head is tuned up again, so I take another round of pills.

TWENTY-THREE

Maria lets me off in front of the funeral home and goes off to park the car. Ernest Landau is at the door to greet people and send them into the chapel. He's been handling funerals for thirty years, having taken over the business when his daddy died. As he's aged, he's begun to look a bit like a cadaver himself, as thin as a rake, with skin that seems stretched over his bones. But he has maintained that air of kindness that people appreciate at these times.

Josh, Hannah, and Krista are standing outside the chapel greeting visitors.

'Nice of you to come,' Hannah says. She's dressed in an elegant gray dress and very high heels. You don't see shoes like that much around here. Krista has high heels on, too, and a figure-hugging black suit with a white blouse.

Funerals are usually held in a church, but Maddy's is in the funeral home chapel. It's a nice room with comfortable pews and tasteful stained-glass windows. It holds seventy-five people, but today it's only half full. Maria comes in and we take seats halfway down, on the aisle. In the front row, Eileen is sitting with a tall man that I expect is her husband. On her other side is an erect older couple, most likely Maddy's folks. I wonder whether Krista's parents will be here. I haven't heard them mentioned.

I get up and walk down to the front to introduce myself to Maddy's folks and to say hello to Eileen. I see that the casket is closed, with a photo of Maddy set on top. An unusual move. I wonder whose decision that was. Eileen gets to her feet when she spots me. I hope she isn't going to ask me again how close I am to finding out the identify of Maddy's killer. But it isn't her who asks that; it's her husband.

He stands up and moves too close, so I get a sense of aggression from him. He says, 'Eileen told me about you. Have you gotten anywhere on this investigation?' His voice is inappropriately loud for the surroundings. He's a large man with an oddly big head and a thick neck like a football linebacker. His physical presence does nothing to mitigate my first impression of him from when I spoke to him on the phone the day Maddy was killed. He's a boor.

'We can discuss this after the service,' I say.

He starts to say more, but I step over to address Maddy's folks. They get to their feet.

'Mr and Mrs Dillard?'

'Andrew,' he says, sticking out his hand to shake.

'And I'm Helen.' She has a determined look, as if the mere fact that her daughter has been killed won't pull her down.

'Samuel Craddock. We spoke on the phone. I'm sorry for your loss.'

Andrew nods and Helen takes hold of his arm. He covers her hand with his. 'It's been hard for us to process,' Andrew says. 'Denial. We didn't want to believe it.' The pain in his eyes tells me that's why they seemed so disinterested in their daughter's death. It wasn't disinterest; it was refusing to accept what had happened, pretending everything was OK.

'I understand.'

'May we talk to you after the service?' he asks.

'Of course.'

'There's going to be a reception back at the house. Hannah and Josh arranged it. I know they'll be glad to have you there.'

The reception is no doubt with the help of Landau's assistant, Belle. She always knows exactly what needs to be done to make people feel as if they've done right by their loved ones. She knows people can't think well when they are bereaved.

'I'll come over there and we can talk then.'

I see Helen looking at the bump on my head. 'What happened?' she asks. 'Someone walloped you. It didn't have to do with your investigation, did it?'

Before I have to think of a way to weasel out of answering, Ernest Landau strides down the aisle to the front of the chapel.

People have been chattering, and when he stops in front of the casket, everyone quiets down.

I nod to them and make my way back up to sit down beside Maria. On my way, I see a couple of familiar faces – Maddy's best friends, who have driven up from Houston. I also see a few faces that trouble me. I hope none of them is here to confront the family with rude comments.

Landau begins the service, welcoming everyone and then saying a few words about Maddy. Someone has directed him not to speak for too long, which I'm grateful for. I find that even the small amount of effort I made to greet the family has left me feeling the effects of my attack, not just the headache, but an overall shaky feeling that I've had a shock.

At the end of Landau's speech, he says, 'There will be no grave-side service. Josh and Hannah are inviting everyone in attendance to come to their home after this service. They each have a few words to say now, and they have requested that anyone else who wants to speak in remembrance of Ms Benson should come to the Benson home and they'll have a chance to speak there.'

Josh does himself proud with elegant words describing his loving mother, who had a caring nature, who did not complain when she had to nurse his father through his last days, although it was tough. And then he says, in a clear, strong voice, 'My mom did not deserve what happened to her. She was a good person whose life was dedicated to helping others.'

There's a sound like a subdued snort from someone behind me. If Josh heard it, he ignores it.

Hannah's words are much the same, but with more passion. 'In the darkest days of my life, my mother was there for me. No one could ask for a better mom.' Her voice breaks and she rushes off to sit down next to Josh, who puts his arm around her. She seems like a lonely person in that moment. I hope she knows people in Los Angeles who can comfort her.

When it's time to leave, Maria says, 'No one would blame you if you don't go to the reception.'

'I'll be there,' I say.

'I wonder why there isn't a graveside service?'

'Good question,' I say. It doesn't happen often in Jarrett Creek. People here go with tradition.

After people start leaving, I go to talk to Ernest Landau and ask him why. I have a feeling it wasn't on a whim. He looks uncomfortable, which is unusual for him. He's usually in complete control of the proceedings and always unruffled. 'Come in my office,' he says.

He has to stop to speak to several people on our way, so it's a few minutes before he closes the door behind us. 'The reason for no graveside service is that I had a call this morning. A threat, I guess you'd say.'

'A threat? Why didn't I know this?'

'I heard what happened to you, and I made the decision not to bother you with it. I decided to handle it myself, and I intended to tell you tomorrow.'

'What was the threat?'

'That the graveside service would be picketed.'

'Picketed? Who was the call from?'

'They didn't say, but they mentioned someone named Adam Johnson. Said they were modeling after him. I didn't know who that was, so I looked it up. He's a bad actor. The family doesn't need that kind of nonsense, so I called Josh and told him it was best if we held off and had a private graveside service later in the week if they want one.'

I'm stunned. I know who Adam Johnson is. He's based in Austin and is as nasty a piece of work as I've ever heard of. He's a conspiracy theorist who sends picketers to harass people who are grieving if they hold beliefs he disagrees with. He's detestable. But someone around here thinks otherwise and was planning to embarrass Maddy Benson's family at the graveside, the way Johnson has led his followers to do with regard to other issues.

I tell Landau he made the right call. 'How did the family take it?'

'They didn't argue with me, if that's what you're asking.'

Maria drops me at the door of the Benson place and goes to find a parking place.

I had half worried that there would be picketers here, but the only people I see are a few stragglers hurrying to the Benson home.

When I slip inside, it's quiet. I walk into the living room and see that Maddy's friend Joan is speaking about Maddy. Josh and Hannah are standing off to the side, with Krista a bit farther away from them. Maddy's kids look solemn, but it's nothing compared to Krista, who looks crushed. If I didn't know better, I would have thought it was her mamma who'd been killed. But I remember she said her own parents were difficult and Maddy was like a mother to her.

I'm glad everyone is focused on Joan, because it gives me a chance to get a look at the people attending. Most people are standing, but Maddy's folks are sitting at the perimeter of the crowd. Her mamma is crying, and her daddy has his arm around his wife. It has struck home that their daughter was murdered.

Maddy's other best friend, Carol Warren, is there with a man who looks like her, maybe a brother. There are also a few people who look Josh and Hannah's age – no doubt people they knew from their old life in Houston or maybe in college.

In fact, the only people I recognize from around here are the Bensons' neighbors, Kay Springer, who invited Maddy to coffee to meet the neighbors, and the Russells, who spotted the car driven by a man who seemed to be watching the house. I also see Isabella Lopez, standing ramrod straight with her arms crossed. Next to her is the woman I planned to call this afternoon, Becky Peltier. I want to know how she knew Maddy Benson before Maddy moved here. It looks like she is also acquainted with Isabella Lopez.

Maria slips inside and positions herself on the other side of the group from me. She can get a different perspective.

There are a few more testimonials, thankfully short. And then the neighbors all leave together. I follow them to the door. I ask the Russells if they've seen the suspicious car again, or if they've seen anyone else watching the house. It occurs to me that the people who threatened to picket could also plan to confront Maddy's family. But they say they haven't seen anyone else.

'Did you find out who the car belonged to?' Russell asks. He gave me the license number, which I imagine he thought would lead somewhere.

I tell him I did, but that it didn't lead to a suspect.

He frowns. 'Still seems odd that someone would watch the house and then the woman ended up dead.'

'I agree,' I say. 'I'm still pursuing it.'

'By the way,' Giselle Russell says, 'you remember I told you I saw Maddy walking with someone? She's here.' I ask her to point out the woman and she indicates Becky Peltier.

'I appreciate it. I'll have a chat with her,' I say.

So Becky is the person Maddy Benson took walks with. It seems strange that she didn't come forward when Maddy was killed.

I head back into the room and see Isabella talking to Carol and Joan. I go over to them. 'Can I have a word?'

They nod.

'Have any of you had anymore thoughts about who might have had a grudge against Maddy, or was angry enough with her to want her dead?'

As I might have expected, Isabella pipes up first. 'Nobody in particular, but there are so many crazy people with guns these days, it could be anybody. For that matter, it could have been a random shooting. Might not have been someone who targeted her at all.'

Joan looks annoyed at Isabella. 'I've gone over it again and again,' she says. 'I can't tell you any more than I did the first time we talked.'

Carol says the same. They both look deflated.

I walk into the dining room, where a spread of food and drinks have been put out, and find Becky Peltier pouring herself a glass of wine.

'Just the woman I'm looking for,' I say.

Her hand jerks and she spills a few drops of wine from the bottle. 'Me? Why do you want to talk to me? I did what you said. I saw Doc England. And my husband reinforced the fence. Duke won't get out again, I promise.'

I smile. She's very earnest. 'I'm glad to hear it's under control, but it's not the dog I want to talk about.'

She cocks her head. 'OK . . .what, then?'

'It seems you knew Maddy Benson before she moved here.'

'Yes, I did.' She doesn't seem to have trouble admitting it.

'Neighbors saw you taking walks with her.'

'That's right. Is there a problem?'

'Ms Peltier, Maddy Benson was murdered, and I'm investigating. I'm surprised that you didn't think to tell me you knew her. If you went on walks with her, she might have told you something that's relevant to my investigation.'

She casts her eyes down and her voice is small. 'My husband said I should have told you, but honestly I didn't think I knew anything that could help.'

I look at my watch. My head is beginning to throb, but I want to talk to this young woman. 'Is your husband here?'

'No, he had to work. And he didn't know Maddy.'

'But he knew you did.'

Her mouth turns down. She's not pouting. She's distressed. 'Of course he knew. She saved my life, and he knows it.' She's practically whispering.

'Look, it's late. I'd like to ask you some more questions. Can we meet at the police station tomorrow morning?'

'The police station?' She looks panicked. 'I swear I don't know anything. I had nothing to do with Maddy's death. She was my hero.'

I tamp my hands down. 'Relax, I'm not accusing you of anything. I just want to get a few details, find out what the two of you talked about, that kind of thing. Anything that might lead to me finding out who killed her. If you'd prefer that I come to your house, that's OK, too.'

'I guess I can come tomorrow morning. Ricky leaves for work early, so I can come down anytime.'

'Why don't we say nine?'

I hunt up Maria and tell her I'm ready to go anytime she is.

'I would be, too, but I'm curious about something and I'd like to stay a few minutes longer.'

'What is it?'

'Krista keeps looking at her watch and at the door, like she expects somebody to be here and they haven't shown up. It's probably nothing, but she really seems intent. I wonder who it is.'

'We can stick around longer in case whoever it is shows up.' If Maria thinks the matter is important, then I'll go with her intuition.

'You look tired. I could run you home and come back and keep an eye out.'

'I've got another idea. You mingle and I'll hide out for a while.'

I hunt up Josh and ask if he minds if I go into his mamma's apartment for a quick nap. 'I had a bump on the head and need to take it easy for a few minutes.'

'A bump? What happened?'

I forget that he doesn't know people here and that he wouldn't be well informed by the grapevine. 'Let's talk later. You have people to talk to.'

'Sure. Go ahead.' He waves me to the door to Maddy's apartment.

I lie down on the sofa and am immediately asleep, waking thirty minutes later feeling less ragged, but still exhausted.

It's after six, and I go back out to find that most people are gone. Eileen and Hannah are in the kitchen washing dishes. 'I imagine you're both tired and glad to see everyone cleared out.'

'I'm OK now, but it will probably hit me tomorrow that we buried my sister today,' Eileen says. 'And I don't think I'll really get a good night's sleep until I know whoever did this is behind bars.' For once, she doesn't seem to be aiming her hint at me.

'I want to sleep for a week,' Hannah says, 'but I'm going back to San Antonio tomorrow with Eileen so I can catch a plane back to LA.' I guess they've come to a truce.

I don't see Eileen's husband, so he must have gone home already. I ask, and Eileen says he left earlier.

Maddy's friends are gone. Josh is sitting on the sofa in the living room talking to a couple who were with the family in the chapel. Maybe cousins. Maddy's folks are sitting at a table in the backyard. They're holding hands over the table.

Maria is talking to Krista, so I go over to listen in, hoping that Maria has found out who Krista was looking out for.

'I didn't want them here,' Krista is saying. 'So I didn't tell them when the funeral was going to be. In fact, I didn't tell them what happened to Maddy.' She sounds forlorn.

'Are you talking about your folks?' I ask.

She nods. 'Are you feeling better? I heard what happened. Do you have any idea who hit you?'

'Not at the moment. Nobody saw anything and there was no weapon found at the scene.'

'Do you think it had to do with what happened to Maddy?' She seems anxious.

'Hard to say.'

Maria and I leave. On the way to my place, I ask if she picked up anything that might have a bearing on the case.

'All I know is that I don't like Jack Currey. He's arrogant and seemed disdainful of the whole affair. He didn't say a word to anyone but his wife, and I overheard him remark to her that Maddy wasn't the saint everyone thought she was. This is his sister-in-law who got killed. You'd think he'd have some respect.'

'What did his wife say?'

'She said if he didn't like being here, he could leave. So he did. Without saying goodbye to Josh or Hannah. That was rude.'

'Did you happen to ask Krista who she was on the lookout for?'

'I did. I wasn't sure whether I should, but I figured the only way I'd find out was if I asked. And she said she thought a friend was coming, but he never showed up.'

'Huh. Could it be her old boyfriend? You think she'd invite him here?'

'She didn't say one way or another, and I didn't push it. She seems really fragile.'

I'm glad to get home. I'm not hungry, but I heat up a scoop of the casserole Loretta brought for me. I take pills for my headache and sit down on the sofa to eat and watch TV, with Dusty next to me and my cat Zelda frowning at us from an armchair that is her domain.

I finish the soup, set the bowl on the floor, and lay my head back. The next thing I know, I hear a spoon rattle in the dish, and I wake to find Dusty cleaning the bowl.

I want to call Wendy, but I'm not up for it. Instead, I text her and tell her it has been a strange couple of days and I'll call her tomorrow.

I usually take Dusty out, but instead tonight I open the screen door and give him a few minutes to tend to business. He's back in five minutes, and ten minutes later I'm in bed.

TWENTY-FOUR

Thursday morning

I sleep later than usual, and for the first time since the attack, I wake up with only a mild headache.

When I get to headquarters, Becky Peltier is waiting in the parking lot. Connor is supposed to be on duty this morning, but the office is locked up tight. Becky follows me inside. Connor has left a note that he had to go deal with a car that's run into a ditch north of town. That's the third car mishap this week. Is it something in the air?

Becky accepts a cup of coffee and pronounces it perfect.

'You're one of the few people who doesn't complain that my coffee is too strong,' I say.

'No, I like it that way.' She seems cheery, and not as nervous as she was yesterday when I asked her to come in today.

'This won't take long,' I say. 'Can you tell me how you met Maddy?'

She takes a deep breath. 'I figured you'd want to know. At first, I didn't want to tell you, but Ricky said I should. He reminded me that without Maddy, I probably would be dead, or at the very least unable to get pregnant again. It was a problem pregnancy and the doctor said I was at risk if I didn't have a D and C.' She pauses. 'You know what that is, right?'

I nod.

'But of course that wasn't legal. So I had to figure out what to do. We had just moved here, and we were broke. We couldn't afford for me to fly out of state. So I looked online for help and found Haven. They hooked me up with Maddy.' She swallows, and I see that she's fighting back tears. But she straightens her shoulders and says, 'That woman personally drove up from Houston to take me to New Mexico. She stayed by me, paid for my motel and my meals, and drove me back home.' Her voice is shaking by the time she finishes. 'Mr Craddock, when you catch whoever did this, I'd like you to give me five minutes alone in a room with him – and I'm sure it's a him. He'll be begging for you to rescue him.'

She's so fierce that I have no doubt she'd do exactly what she says. 'I imagine there are more than one of you who'd like a crack at him. But first I have to find him.'

'How can I help?'

'You spent plenty of time driving with Maddy. What did you talk about?'

She smiles wistfully. 'All kinds of things. Her family had decided to move out of Houston, and she was considering where she should go. She said her husband needed a good oncologist, but that they didn't want to live in a big city. They wanted a quiet place. I told her Jarrett Creek was a sweet town, and the lake was really nice, and people were welcoming. She realized that it was central, so she could serve people from all over. And I told her that Bryan/College Station was thirty minutes away so her husband could get good care. We stayed in touch, and she decided to move here.'

'You're closer in age to Maddy's kids, so did you ever meet them?'

She sighs. 'Maddy wanted me to meet them, but as soon as she and her husband moved, he got really sick, and she never had time to do much but take care of him. Every now and then, she'd call and we'd go for a walk together. She said it did her good to get out of the house and be around someone young – someone who wasn't a relative.'

'Did she get along with her kids?'

'Oh, yes, it wasn't that there was a problem. She said when she was with them, they always had family things to discuss, so it was easier to talk with me because she could listen to me describe my life and not feel like she had to get involved. She liked hearing what I was up to. You know, I guess Sandy told you I'm taking that exercise class with her. I tried to get Maddy to come, but she said that wasn't her thing. She didn't have the patience for it. But she liked walking with me. She said I cheered her up.' She wipes away a tear that's escaped.

'When you were on your trip with her, did the matter of her kids moving with her come up?'

She nods. 'Sure. You spend twenty hours in a car with somebody and you end up talking about everything. She told me there was a problem between her son and daughter-and-law. I don't know if I should tell you what she said. It was private.'

'I suspect I already know what you mean, but whatever it is, I assure you I won't be tattling. Unless it has to do with her murder, that is.'

She tells me that Maddy said her daughter-in-law had had an affair. 'Maddy wanted to get them out of town to get Krista away from her lover. That's one reason I didn't want to meet Krista and Josh. I thought I'd be embarrassed to know so much about them.'

'When you went for walks with Maddy, did she seem happy here?'

'Happy? I don't know. She liked it OK, but she was so busy that she hardly had time to make friends. After the Supreme Court decision, she threw herself into helping girls and women, and I don't think she had much time to think about where she was. She was always running off to Houston or Austin, for meetings.'

'What kind of meetings?'

She shrugs. 'Strategy meetings. You know, like, how to approach the next state elections, lawsuits to challenge the state's abortion laws. That sort of thing.' Her face is flushed. 'I just have a high school education, so I'm not as up on things as she was. She told me, but I didn't always understand. That's one thing I liked about her, though. She acted as if she thought I knew exactly what she was talking about. I learned so much from her!'

'Did she ever tell you anything that made you think she was in danger?'

She puts a hand to her mouth, and I can see that she's trying to hold back tears. 'No. If she had, I would have done anything to help her.'

'No one threatening her?'

'One time she did say that she was helping someone whose boyfriend was really angry. But she wasn't worried for her own safety; she was worried about the girl.'

'Did she ever mention her relationship with her sister?'

'I didn't even know she had a sister until I met her at the funeral yesterday.'

'And you're sure things were OK at home?'

She hesitates. 'I think so. She did tell me that she thought the move hadn't fixed things between Josh and Krista. And I have to agree. When I met them yesterday, they didn't look like a couple that cared much for each other. Not like Ricky and me.'

'But she hadn't had arguments with them?'

'Are you thinking they might have had something to do with Maddy's death?'

'Just asking.'

'She didn't say they had arguments. She really loved both of them and she was sad that they weren't going to make it. She said she thought Krista was seeing her old boyfriend again, and she wasn't happy about that, but she said there was nothing she could do to fix it, that they had to figure out what was best for them.'

'She thought Krista was seeing the guy again?'

'Yeah. I don't think she liked him.'

I thank Becky for her time and tell her to be sure and get in touch if she thinks of anything else I should know.

No sooner has Becky gone than Connor comes in, looking disgruntled.

'What's up?'

'One more reason I'm not long for this job. This guy drove off into a ditch, and when the tow truck came to pull him out, he treated the driver like he was a fool, even though it was his own fault. I just don't get people.'

'Who was the tow truck driver? Was it Skippy?'

'No, his name was Ricky something, but he works for Skippy. Nice guy. It didn't seem to bother him that the guy was rude to him. He shrugged it off like it was nothing.'

'Good thing it wasn't Skippy. He would have had a thing or two to say to the guy.'

'I guess.'

Connor is probably right. He's too thin-skinned to deal with the kind of people cops have to deal with all the time. 'Connor, people who've done something stupid often feel embarrassed and they take it out on anyone handy. You have to ignore it.'

'That's what I'm saying. I have a hard time doing that.'

'Have you looked into taking courses at the college, like we discussed?'

'I have an appointment next week.'

'Good. Don't forget, I'm happy to give you a good reference. I'd hate to lose you, but I think you're doing the right thing.' The problem is finding someone else. I have a revolving door here. Only Maria has stuck with it, and I'm always worried that she'll come in one day and say someone has made her an offer she can't turn down.

My cell phone rings, a number I've dialed several times.

'This is Chief Craddock,' I say. 'Is this Karen Schrage?'

'This is Ms Schrage's assistant. Can you hold please?'

'I'll be glad to.' I must admit I'm impressed that this young woman has an assistant to arrange her phone calls.

It's a five-minute wait before a peremptory voice starts speaking. 'This is Karen Schrage. How can I help you?'

'Ms Schrage, I'm happy we made contact.' I put on my 'good old boy' voice. 'I'm chief of police in Jarrett Creek, Texas, and I have some questions concerning your daddy's car.'

'My father? That's what you're calling about? He passed away a few months ago.'

'My condolences. The thing is, your daddy's car was seen near the house of a woman who was killed here in Jarrett Creek, and I'm trying to find out who was driving it.'

She hesitates, but I don't know if that's because she is considering the question or if someone else has grabbed her attention. 'You'd have to ask my brother. He's the one who has charge of the car.'

'Have you ever driven it?'

'Once or twice when I was visiting. I've been living in Seattle for the past few months, and I don't get home often.'

'Your brother said you were in town for a few days a week or so ago. Did you drive it then?'

'No. I didn't have time. I spent all my time trying to clear things out of Daddy's house. We're putting it up for sale.'

'Would your brother have any reason to come to Jarrett Creek?'

She makes an impatient sound. 'Not that I know of. Why not ask him?'

'He told me hadn't been here, but I wanted to corroborate that.'

'You mean you think he might be lying?' Her voice goes up an octave.

'Or maybe forgot.'

'Not likely. Look, I don't know how to help you with this.' She wants to get me off the phone.

'Your brother did say he lent the car to a friend.'

'Oh, well, then that's who was probably in your town. Who was it he lent it to?'

'Man by the name of Craig Presley. You know him?'

'Yes. Not the most reliable guy.'

'Interesting. Your brother said the opposite.'

'He would. They're bros. They'd stick up for each other.'

Even though he has an alibi, her comment strikes me as worth pursuing. 'What makes you say Craig is unreliable?'

'He's sort of a flake. Jared shouldn't have lent him the car, but that's his business.'

'When you say he's a flake, can you elaborate? Is he a deadbeat? A liar? A cheat?'

Unexpectedly, she chuckles. 'I wouldn't go that far. But I also wouldn't lend him a car. He's the kind of person who might put a dent in the car and not tell you, and then deny it if you confronted him. He has trouble holding down a job, so he's always out to make a quick buck, and I've always thought he was a little shady. So if he says he wasn't in Jarrett Creek, I'm not sure I'd believe him. But like I said, you should pursue this with my brother. Now, if you don't mind, I've got a meeting to get to.'

I ignore her. My wheels are spinning. Make a quick buck. 'You think he'd rent the car to someone else while he was out of town?'

'That's sounds like him.'

'I appreciate your time. And, Ms Schrage, I'm investigating a murder and I can use all the help I can get. If you think of anything that might help me pin this down, or if your brother mentions anything, please give me a call. I'd really like to find whoever killed the woman.'

'I wish you luck.' And she's gone.

Maria has come in while I've been on the phone. I tell her I was talking to Karen Schrage.

'She wasn't any help?'

'I'm not sure. I don't know why that car sitting out on the road keeps nagging at me.' I tell her what Karen Schrage said. 'I think I have to push this. It may come to nothing, but when I talked to this man Craig Presley, I wasn't altogether sure he was telling me the truth. I asked him if anybody else had driven the car while he was in Dallas, and he said no, but I don't know . . .' I'm remembering the conversation. Am I right that he took too long answering that question? Karen has rekindled the doubt in my mind.

The office phone rings, and Maria answers it and tells whoever is calling to wait just a minute. She has a sour look on her face. 'It's Reagan.'

I take the call. 'Reagan, how can I help?'

'It's not how you can help me, but how I can help you. The FBI wants to set up a meeting with you to discuss the case. Seems like there have been threats to the organization your victim was working with – Haven. You told me you'd talked to the head of the organization and that they were worried they had a mole. They'd like to get any information you have.'

'It's not much. Have they talked to Isabella Lopez?'

'I don't know. They haven't shared much with me. Is it possible for you to come and meet them here? I'd like to sit in. They've suggested tomorrow afternoon.'

'I could do that. And there's one more thing you might want to know.' I tell him about the attack on me.

'And you didn't think to tell me this?'

'Reagan, what would you do that I can't do?'

He's silent for a minute. 'Send in reinforcements for one thing. First someone leaves you a suspicious package, then you get threatened with your job, and then you get attacked. This is not looking good. And by the way, I suppose you're still on the job? You didn't get ousted?'

'The movement fizzled.'

'You think they'll try again?'

'Never can tell. They don't seem like the kind of people who will give up easily. But I may have an advantage to work with.'

'What do you mean?'

'The preacher's son has been appropriating a boat at night from a local marina without the owner's permission. We came to an agreement that if he did some work for the owner, I wouldn't tell his folks. But he didn't seem all that contrite. If I need to use gentle persuasion on the preacher to back off, I might have to tell him that his son could be in trouble with the law.'

He snorts. 'Small-town arm-twisting. But hold on. You said the boy wasn't contrite. You think he might have been the person who attacked you?'

'Anything's possible. Someone saw him drive by my house earlier that day, but it's a small town; he could have been driving by for any reason.'

He asks the boy's name. 'Won't hurt to check him out.'

'I'd be surprised if he's gotten into trouble that I don't know about.'

'We'll see.'

He's right to hesitate. The boy has been in college for a year, so it's possible he got involved in something there that I wouldn't have uncovered. It's a Baptist college, though, and I don't know how much hell-raising goes on in a religious institution. I tell Reagan that.

'Oh, you'd be surprised,' he says dryly. 'Anyway, we'll look into it. So you can come over at two o'clock tomorrow?'

I tell him I'll be there. When I hang up, I ask Maria if she wants to join me.

'I'm tempted. It would be interesting to see what the FBI has to say, but I'm not sure I want to be in Sergeant Reagan's presence.'

'Maria, you have to get over that. We need to work with him at various times. He's not a bad guy, even if he got off on the wrong foot with you.'

'The wrong foot? You mean calling me "your girl"?'

'I agree that was uncalled for, but this will give him a chance to see that I trust you to be professional.'

She grudgingly agrees to go.

TWENTY-FIVE

I need to talk to Jason Schrage again, and I don't think I can I get the job done on the phone. It's a lot easier to tell if someone is lying if you see them in person. But what do I think Schrage is lying about? He lent his car to someone who drove it during the time the car was spotted in Jarrett Creek. The story checked out. So why would he lie?

Maybe it's actually the friend, Craig Presley, that I need to be concerned with, especially after my conversation with Karen Schrage. Last time I talked to Presley, he was in Dallas. I assume he's back by now. I'll call him to find out. And if he's in Houston, do I tell him I want to speak to him in person, or do I quiz him by phone? His alibi checked out, so the only thing he might be lying about is if he lent (or rented) the car to someone else while he was gone.

Before I can make a decision, my phone rings.

'Chief, this is Tom Gainer. You in the office?' He sounds grim.

'Sure. Are you in town?'

'I just drove here. I need to talk to you.'

'I'll be in the office.'

'Can we talk privately, the two of us?'

'I can make that happen.' It's an odd request, but to honor it I send Maria to Bobtail to pick up office supplies.

Gainer walks in looking as grim as he sounded on the phone. He sits down with a weary sigh.

'Want some coffee?' I ask.

'Just what I need.'

I get him seated next to my desk, pour us a cup, and sit down. 'What can I help you with?'

'Something I'm not happy about. It concerns my son.'

'I see.' I hope he's not going to tell me that his son attacked me. Or, worse, that he shot Maddy Benson.

He sighs again. 'Dell called me yesterday and said he wanted to come home. I asked him what was wrong, but he gave me a vague answer, said he needed to get ready for school. So I came and got him. He didn't talk to me a lot, but I could tell he had something on his mind. Then all evening he wasn't fit to tie up and throw in the river. He was sulky and snapped at my wife and me.' He hunches forward with his forearms on his knees, hands clasped between his knees. 'The thing is he's not usually like that. So . . .' He chuckles unexpectedly. 'This is down to my wife, mind you. She and my son are very close, but she doesn't put up with a lot of guff from anybody, including him.'

I settle back and sip my coffee. I don't know Tom well, but I do know he's not chatty as a rule, and whatever is bothering him is especially hard for him to get to.

'So the second time he made some smart-mouth remark, she asked him what was wrong. He said nothing, and she said if he wanted to continue to live on this planet, he'd better tell us what was on his mind. Not that she'd kill him, but that he'd wish he was dead.'

I laugh. 'Pretty straightforward.'

He looks up at me and then back down. 'Yeah, well, he knows she meant it. Anyway, he hedged at first. He told us that he wasn't a participant in what happened, but neither did he intervene, and that he couldn't tell us exactly what it was because he didn't want to rat out his buddy.'

I'm beginning to get the gist.

'That's when Bonnie went into high gear. She told him that we weren't gangsters and that was stupid talk. She said any friend who did something he was ashamed of and couldn't tell us about was not a good person to hang out with. You should have heard her. She could convince the devil that hell is cold. She told Dell that if the guy had done something bad, it was better that he got caught now, before he did something *really* bad.' He shakes his head. 'So he told us. He said his friend Aaron attacked you.'

'Whoa.' I sit up. 'It's good to know who did it. I appreciate your son confessing his part.'

'He was relieved to get it off his chest. But I couldn't let that be the end of it. I told him he's going to have to come in and talk to you, but that I'd pave the way. You OK?'

'I'm fine, but you know I won't be able to let this go. You can't attack a lawman and walk away from it.'

'I know that. I told Dell the same thing. What do you think will happen to him?'

'Dell? Has he ever been in trouble before?'

'No, sir. He's a good kid.'

'The worst that will happen is that he may have to testify, and maybe do some community service. So tell me what he told you.'

'First, he told me they had been sneaking one of Dooley's boats out at night and joyriding and that you confronted them. I told him it was stealing, but he said you had given them a talking-to and set them up with Dooley to do some work. And that you said as long as it didn't happen again, you weren't going to do anything more. I don't mind telling you, I would have handled it differently. They'd be spending some time in jail.'

'Tom, teenage boys are always messing around at the edge of the law. If I ran in every teenaged boy who got out of line, I'd have to build a bigger jail. Dooley agreed that having them do some work for him was good enough.'

'It might have been, but wait until you hear what I have to say.'

I nod.

'Dell said he was relieved, but that Aaron got all riled up and wanted to get back at you. Dell said they had to let it go, but Aaron didn't want to. He told Dell his parents had been talking, and said they had a problem with you, and he thought you needed to be taught a lesson.'

'Aaron said that?'

'I know. Harsh. And cocky. I'm surprised. I always thought Aaron was a nice enough kid. But this puts a different light on it.'

'Continue.'

Dell said he rode with Aaron the night he attacked you. He said he couldn't believe what Aaron did and that he knew he should have jumped out of the car and yelled or honked the horn, but he was too shocked. I don't mind telling you, Craddock, I'm ashamed of that. I thought I taught him better.'

'He's a teenager, Tom. Like I said, they get all mixed up sometimes. Maybe this is a lesson he needs to learn.'

'That's kind of you, but Bonnie and I . . . well, we're trying to figure out what to do as punishment. If you have any ideas, I'd like to hear them.'

'The first thing is to find out if Dell is willing to sign a statement. Is he with you?'

'I left him out at my place.'

'Let's go on out there and I'll talk to him.'

'All right.' He stands. 'But, Craddock, I don't want you coddling him. He needs to know he's done the wrong thing.'

At Gainer's place, we find Dell sitting at the edge of the porch, head in his hands. He looks up as we approach, and then stands, shoving his hands into his pockets.

I stick my hand out for him to shake. For a second, he freezes, but then takes his hand out of his pocket and extends it to me.

'I believe Dell has something to say to you,' Tom says.

The boy swallows, looking like words are too big for his mouth. 'Chief Craddock, I'm awful sorry what happened. It . . . I . . . I wish I could go back and do better.'

'Dell, I appreciate your apology. I know what you mean. We all have things we wish we could undo. The thing is, no matter how much I appreciate your apology, I have to follow up. Your friend Aaron Dawkins lay in wait and attacked me, and he has to answer for that.'

He winces. 'And what about me? Will I be punished? I should have stopped him.'

'Yes, you should have. And there will be a consequence for you, but as I told your daddy, the fact that you've come forward counts for a lot, and you'll likely get no more than a slap on the wrist. Maybe some community service.'

He looks away to hide the fact that relief has brought him almost to tears.

'I need to ask you a few questions,' I say. 'Why don't we sit down?'

Tom goes inside and comes back out with folding chairs. We take them in the shade of the trees near the tank, where it isn't so hot.

'First, I want to ask you what led up to the attack? Tell it in your own words, from the time the idea came up.'

He tells it the way Tom did, that Aaron Dawkins was upset that I had confronted them. 'I told him he shouldn't be mad, that you could have taken us to jail, and we could have been in a lot more trouble.' He glances at Tom, who is sitting like a statue.

'But he didn't agree?'

'No, sir, he told me that his folks thought you ought to be fired, that you weren't upholding the law the way you should.'

'Did they tell him why they thought that?'

He shrugs. 'He didn't say. Anyway, he said he was going to get back at you. At first, I swear I didn't know what he meant. We drove to your place, and I thought he was going to confront you face to face. You know, tell you to go to hell or something like that. I didn't like it, but he said I shouldn't be a coward, that taking that boat out wasn't a big deal and you shouldn't have made so much of it.

'Anyway, when we got there, he went to the door and you weren't there, so he came back. But before he got in the car, he got something out of the trunk. When he got back in, I saw that it was a tire iron.'

'A tire iron.' I can't help releasing a big breath. I might have gotten off lucky. The weapon could have done more damage.

'Yes, sir. I asked him what he was planning to do, and he said he was going to teach you a lesson. I said, "What do you mean?" and he said I'd find out.'

This is sounding worse and worse. I had hoped it was a spur-of-the-moment thing, an impulse, but this was premeditated. Aaron Dawkins might spend time in prison. 'So I came home, and then what?'

'No, that's not exactly how it was. After a few minutes, he said he was going to go wait in the yard for you. By now, I was getting worried. He was acting – I don't know – kind of crazy. Hyped up. I know he has a temper, I've seen him throw stuff or yell, but this was different. I said I thought we ought to leave, and he said I could walk back to his house if I wanted to. I should have. I wish I had.'

'I'm glad you didn't, Dell. If you hadn't been a witness, he might have done worse than he did.'

He frowns. 'I never thought of that.'

And there's more that I don't say. If Dell hadn't stayed, he wouldn't be able to testify to what happened. I'm not sure he knows yet that his story is going to have to go on record and he may have to tell a judge and jury. 'How long was he out in the yard there before I came home?'

'Not long. Maybe five minutes. The whole time I was wondering if I ought to leave, but I kept thinking no way he was going to attack you. I thought maybe he'd threaten you or . . .' His shoulders slump. 'But then you walked in, and I saw him rush over to you and grab you, and you fought him, and he clobbered you.' He shudders. 'You see stuff like that in the movies or on TV, but you don't think you'll see it in person.'

'How did he act when he got back in the car?'

Dell chews his lip. 'He was, like, proud of himself. He was laughing and pounding on the steering wheel. I asked him if he thought you were OK, and he said you'd have a bad headache but that he didn't hit you hard.'

'Hard enough. Dell, did Aaron tell you if he'd ever done anything to me before?'

'Like what?'

'Somebody left a package on my doorstep last week with a threatening note in it. I wondered if it might have been him?'

'If it was, he didn't tell me.'

'OK, here's what's going to happen. We're going back to headquarters, and I'm going to write up your statement, and I'm going to have you and your dad look it over to make sure I got it right, and then you'll sign it.'

He looks uneasy. 'Can I ask you something?'

'Sure.'

'Will Aaron know I told you this?'

'I'm afraid there's no way to keep him from finding out. Unless there was another witness?'

He shakes his head.

I lean closer. 'Son, what Aaron Dawkins did was not just a crime; it was an outrage. You don't need friends like him. I'm sure you had some good times together, but he's not a good person. My guess is he was the one who instigated stealing that boat at night. Now, I can tell you, you've got your whole life ahead of you, and you're going to meet other people, and one day you'll look back and not even remember Aaron. But I assure you, you're better off leaving him in the dust.'

He looks pained. Teenage boys don't like to be lectured.

'And one more thing. You're lucky to have the parents you have. To give you good advice. Your daddy told me he's trying to figure out what kind of punishment you deserve, and whatever he decides, I hope you take it like a man, follow through, and don't pout.'

He gives a half-grin at my admonition not to pout. 'Yes, sir,' he says.

I drive Dell to headquarters in the squad car, with Tom following. I figure it doesn't hurt for Dell to get a dose of what it's like to be transported as if he were going to be arrested. As soon as we're done with the statement, I'll be heading to Aaron Dawkins's place and then a real arrest will take place.

When we arrive, both Maria and Connor are there. It occurs to me that it's probably a good thing for Dell to have to give his statement in front of my two officers. It will get him used to having a public hearing. It may not be necessary, but I have a feeling Reverend Dawkins may kick up a fuss and insist on a trial. If that happens, Dell will have to testify.

I introduce Dell, telling Maria and Connor that Dell has come forward as an eyewitness to my attack.

'That must have been hard,' Maria says to him. 'But in the long run, you'll be glad you stepped up.'

'I guess.' He sits down and hunches forward, looking miserable.

After I've typed in the statement, I ask him to read and sign it. His face is bright red by the time he finishes reading it. He sets it down without signing it. I'm afraid he's going to balk, but Tom says, 'Son, if what's written there is what happened, you need to sign it.'

He picks up the pen and signs it, fast.

'Thank you,' I say to him. 'I'll do everything I can to make this easy on you.'

'Whatever,' he says. He gets up. 'Can I go now?'

'Yes. I'm sure I don't have to tell you not to leave the state.' Normally, I'd tell him not to leave town, but I trust Tom Gainer to bring him back when we need him. 'And it's important that you don't have any contact with Aaron Dawkins. Do you understand that? Do I need to confiscate your phone?'

He looks startled. 'No, sir, I understand.'

TWENTY-SIX

I don't call the Dawkinses in advance. After their condemnation of me, I know I have to have a witness to any conversations I have with them, so I take Maria along.

I considered whether I ought to call Sheriff Hedges in Bobtail to tell him what's happening. I didn't tell him I was attacked, and now I realize I should have. Hedges gives me free rein, but he does like to be kept informed.

Aaron Dawkins himself answers the door. He looks startled when he sees me. 'Mamma and Daddy aren't here,' he says. He's dressed in baggy shorts and a plain, white T-shirt. His hair is tousled, as if he was sleeping.

'It's you I came to talk to,' I say.

'What about?'

'Mind if we come in?'

He shrugs and steps back so we can come in.

'Let's sit in the living room,' I say. We follow him into the living room, and I notice that he's favoring his right knee. That's the knee I gave a good kick to when I was attacked.

Without indicating where we should he sit, Aaron sprawls in the middle of the couch with his legs spread and his arms draped across the back. 'What do you want to talk about?' There's a confrontational edge to the question.

Maria and I sit in armchairs facing him. 'You're limping,' I say. 'What did you do to your leg?'

'Tweaked it.'

'How?'

He looks annoyed. 'I don't know, getting into the boat when we were going fishing.'

'When was that?'

'Couple of days ago.' His eyes are watchful. My questions are making him wary.

'Hmm,' I say. 'Should have been more careful.' I sit forward. 'Here's what I wanted to discuss. A few nights ago, I was attacked in my yard.'

'Oh yeah?'

'There was an eyewitness to the attack.'

He takes his arms from the back of the sofa and crosses them across his chest. 'Who?'

'That's not important. What is important is that the witness named you as the attacker.'

He snickers. 'I don't know who this eyewitness is, but they've got the wrong guy.'

'Can you tell me where you were Tuesday night?'

'This week? Home with my folks.'

'Really? Was your friend Dell here, too?'

His eyes narrow. 'Dell? Yeah, as a matter of fact he was. He was staying with me, and we went fishing that day. We were tired and didn't want to go out that night.'

'So if I ask Dell, he'll confirm that he was with you?'

'Sure.'

'Is he here now? Can I talk to him?' I know perfectly well where he is, but I want Aaron Dawkins to be nervous.

'He's, uh, not here.'

'But he's in town?'

'He was supposed to spend the week, but he had to go home early. His mom called and said he needed to come home.' Another lie. Tom Gainer told me his son called him and asked him to come pick him up.

'When was that?'

'That would have been Wednesday.'

'So yesterday.'

'That's right.' He's fidgeting. I'll bet he's itching to get to a phone to tell Dell he needs to cover for him for Tuesday night. 'Say, aren't you supposed to talk to me with my parents?'

'You're over eighteen, right?'

'I guess. Nineteen.'

I'm looking at his knee. It's swollen. 'Here's the thing, Aaron, I got in a hard kick to the guy who attacked me. Same knee as the one you're favoring.' I nod toward it. 'And with that eyewitness, I'm fairly sure you're not telling me the truth.'

'You can ask my folks. They'll tell you I was right here.'

'You sure?' I know where his folks were Tuesday night. They were holding a meeting, trying to convince some of their congregation to have me thrown out of office.

'You don't believe me?'

'Matter of fact, I don't.'

He couldn't look more affronted if I slapped him. 'You calling me a liar?'

'I'm suggesting you have the wrong night. Your folks were at a meeting Tuesday night that lasted until after I was attacked.'

He snorts. 'Well, I was right here anyway. You can't prove otherwise.'

I stand up. 'Actually, I can. Like I said, I have an eyewitness. I want you to stand up. I'm going to have to take you into police headquarters in Bobtail. The sheriff will want to have a few questions for you.'

He leaps to his feet. 'You can't do that. You have no proof.'

I snort. 'What do you think an eyewitness is?'

'Whoever that is, they're lying. They want to get me in trouble.'

'If that's the case, we'll get to the bottom of it, but right now, you need to come with us.'

Maria rises and takes out her handcuffs. He stares at them with horror. For a minute, I think he's going to cut and run. 'You don't have to put cuffs on me.'

'In fact,, we do,' Maria says. 'Now hold out your hands. It'll be easier if you cooperate.'

When he's cuffed, he makes one last stab. 'Don't you have to read me my rights?'

'We're not arresting you, we're taking you in for questioning.' He'll get his rights read soon enough.

'Can I call my folks and tell them what's happening? They'll want to get me a lawyer.' Finally, he sounds cowed.

'Soon as we get to headquarters in Bobtail, they'll let you make a call.'

'Can I at least leave them a note? My mamma will worry if I'm not here.'

'I doubt that. You're old enough so that I expect you come and go as you please.'

Unfortunately, when we leave the house with Aaron in handcuffs, the next-door neighbor is out on the lawn. Her eyes get big as she sees what's happening, and she scurries inside. It will be all over town in ten minutes.

On the way to Bobtail, I call Hedges and tell him the story, leaving out the identity of the witness. I have him on speaker phone so Aaron can hear the whole exchange.

'You should have told me you were attacked,' he says.

'I know that. I guess the blow to my head was worse than I thought.'

'Not funny. Do you think he's the same guy who left the threatening note on your doorstep?'

'No idea. We'll get to that.'

From the backseat I hear, 'What? No, no way. I didn't leave any note.'

Hedges says, 'I hope you told the suspect that attacking a lawman brings an extra penalty.'

'I didn't tell him, but you can tell him all about that when we bring him in.'

I glance into the rearview mirror to see how the sheriff's words have affected Aaron Dawkins. He's not so cocky now. He's pale and his leg is bouncing up and down. I think of calling his folks to tell them where he is, but I prefer to have someone from Hedges's office do it. I don't need to annoy them any more than I already have.

When we get to the Bobtail PD, it takes an hour to get all the paperwork done and have photos taken – mugshots and photos of his lame knee. It's after two by the time Aaron Dawkins is tucked into a cell. During the proceedings, he alternates between being a smart-mouth and pleading that he's innocent.

I'm in Hedges's office when he personally calls the Dawkinses to tell them their son has been arrested. He puts the phone on speaker and the outrage is palpable. Dawkins sputters that he's coming to the station right now, that he'll be hiring a lawyer immediately, and that his son will be out on bail within the hour.

'That's fine,' Hedges says. 'He'll be here.'

When he hangs up, he says, 'I expect Dawkins is going to be surprised that his son has to spend the night in jail. The wheels of justice don't spin quite as fast as he seems to think.'

'Won't hurt the kid to spend a night in jail. Because if he's convicted, he's going to be spending a lot longer than that in prison.'

'Are you sure you can get the kid who witnessed the crime to testify? Because I imagine it will come to that, since he's the only witness.'

'He'll testify.'

On the drive home, Maria asks if I think Dell Gainer will step up.

'His folks are intent on making sure he does the right thing. And he was contrite. I think he'll do it. Especially if I can get the DA to agree to let him off light if he does.'

'Changing the subject,' she says, 'what's going on with Connor? He seems mopey. Did something happen?'

I don't intend to tell her that he is rethinking his commitment to being a cop. They don't get along well, and I don't want her to poke him. 'He's considering some life decisions, like maybe going back to school part-time. It's on his mind.'

We're almost back to headquarters when my phone rings. It's Wendy. 'Let me call you back,' I say.

'You'd better. Something's going on. And I want to know what it is.'

As soon as we get back to headquarters, I leave Maria in charge and go home. I know this will be a tough phone call. Sure enough, Wendy starts talking as soon as she answers the phone. She sounds ruffled.

'Every day, I keep thinking you're going to call and tell me you've solved the case and you're getting on a plane to come join me. And then I got that odd text from you last night which said you'd had a strange couple of days, but explaining nothing. What's going on?'

'I'm sorry I didn't call this morning. It has been an odd couple of days. Maddy Benson's funeral was yesterday afternoon.'

'Was there a problem there?'

'No.' I realize I'm not going to get away with putting her off. 'Did Maria call you? Or Loretta?'

'Why would they call me?'

'Just wondered how you knew something was wrong.' I don't believe in sixth sense, but it seems like that may be in play here.

'Stop fooling around and tell me what happened. Are you OK?'

'Yes. But there was an incident.' I lay it out for her, the blow to the head, the doctor giving me a clear report. 'I'm fine now. I'll have a headache for a couple of days. And then this morning there was a break in the case.'

'Which case? The woman being shot or you being bashed on the head?'

'That bash on the head.' I tell her that Tom Gainer brought his son in to confess his part in the attack and who he pointed the finger at.

'Samuel, I think I should come home.'

'Absolutely not. I'm fine, and there's a good chance the DPS is going to take over the case of Maddy Benson, along with the FBI.'

'FBI? Wow. You'll have to tell me all about that. Because when you turn it over to them, you're coming here to be with me, right?'

I laugh. 'That would be the silver lining.'

She quizzes me for another half hour, and I'm happy to stay on the phone with her.

But when I get off the phone, I feel deflated. I don't want to turn the case over to anyone. I'm stubborn that way. So I sit back with a glass of good red wine and the rest of Loretta's chicken noodle casserole and think.

The day got away from me with the arrest of Aaron Dawkins. I had planned to call Jason Schrage again today. Early on I asked him whether he thought Craig Presley might have lent Schrage's car to someone while he was in Dallas. He said no, but the way Karen Schrage described Presley, he could well have done so. She even suggested he might have rented it to someone. So when I asked if he'd lent it, he could have said no without actually telling me a lie. There's something slippery going on here.

I wish I could go to Houston to talk to Schrage in person. But it's too late for that. Tomorrow afternoon, I have an appointment with the FBI and Leland Reagan. No time to go to Houston. And I have to admit it seems far-fetched that Presley lent or rented the car to some random person who then killed Maddy Benson.

Still, someone was close to Maddy's house, watching, in Jason Schrage's car. Or, rather, his dead daddy's car. It's only six o'clock. I might as well call Schrage to press him on the subject, just to clear my doubts.

I dial the number I have for him. No answer. I tell him to call me back right away, that I have a quick question. To my surprise, he calls back in minutes. 'Sorry, I was parking when you called. You had a question?'

'I told you I spoke with your friend Craig Presley and that he verified that you lent him your daddy's car, and that he was in Dallas at the time the car was seen in Jarrett Creek. And I verified that fact for myself. But let me ask you this. You said Presley was a good guy. You trust him?'

'What? Trust him? Yeah, I guess. Why?'

'I want to clear up one thing that's been bothering me. I asked Craig if he lent the car to anyone while he was away, and he said no, but I had the feeling he might have been hedging. Do you have any reason to think he wasn't telling the truth?'

'Not really. I mean, why would he lie?'

'Maybe because he didn't think you'd like it? But let me put it a different way. Can you think of anyone he might have lent it to? A buddy? A relative?'

'I suppose he could have lent it to his brother. But he would have told me.'

'Except your sister suggested he might have rented it to someone, and if he made money doing it, he might not tell you.'

'Ha. I should have known you'd talked to my sister. She never liked Craig. She thinks he's sneaky and greedy.'

'Is he?'

'Look, maybe he's not always the most reliable, but Craig and I, we go way back. Known each other since grade school. So I don't have the same kind of charge on it that she does.'

'I'd like you to do something for me. Call him and ask him if he lent it to anyone while he was in Dallas.'

'I guess I can do that. Seems like it would be a weird question, though.'

'Tell him you noticed a dent in it. Ask him if he put the dent in it, and then when he says no, ask if he lent to anybody.'

'That could work.'

'And if you could get right back to me.'

'Will do.'

I can't help pacing while I wait for him to call me back, even though I know it could take a day or two for him to reach Presley. But twenty minutes later, my phone rings.

'OK, you called it. He did lend the car to his brother.'

'Tell me about his brother.'

'Loren? What do you want to know?'

Loren. The name stops my breath. It can't be, can it? But of course it can. My thoughts are racing as pieces fall into place almost too fast.

'Hello?'

'Yeah, sorry, I was thinking. What does Loren do for a living?'

'I don't know him well; he's a couple of years younger than Craig. I think Craig said he works in catering.'

'Married?'

'Why are you asking these questions?'

'I want to know if he ever had a reason to be in Jarrett Creek.'

'You think he staked out and watched the house of the woman who died? Or that he killed her? That's damn far-fetched.'

'Maybe, maybe not. What else can you tell me?'

'Look, I don't know the guy. Call Craig. You have his number. I don't have anything else to say.'

The phone clicks off, but that's just as well. I don't need to ask him anything else, or call Craig Presley. The person I need to talk to is right here in Jarrett Creek.

I call Josh Benson. 'Sorry to call so late. Is Krista there?'

'Yeah, you want to talk to her?' He sounds surly.

'No, that's all right. I'm going to come there.'

'Now?'

'Half hour or so.'

'It's not exactly the best time. What do you want with her?' He definitely sounds odd. Has he been drinking?

'It's pertaining to a new lead I have on who might have killed your mother.'

'And you need to talk to Krista?'

'That's right.'

'Wait a minute. You think *Krista* had something to do with it? No way.'

'I just need to ask her some questions. I'll be there soon.'

He sighs. 'OK, OK, come on.'

'And, Josh, don't tell anyone I called. Including Krista.'

'Whatever.'

On the way to the Benson house, I stop by headquarters and log on to the computer. I search to find out if Loren Presley has a criminal record. What I find is a lot more than I bargained for.

I call Maria and tell her what I've found out. 'I'm going over to question Krista. I'd like you to come with me.'

I don't have to ask twice. I pick her up and on the way over she says, 'Do you think Krista knows her boyfriend was arrested for assault? Twice?'

'We're going to find out.'

TWENTY-SEVEN

J osh greets us at the door, and I was right: he's been drinking. His eyes are glazed, his mouth slack. He's holding a glass with nothing but a few ice cubes in it.

Without a word, he leads us into the living room, stumbling before he plops into a chair. There's a bottle of bourbon in front of him. 'Have a seat,' he mutters.

'Is Krista around?'

'She's here, and it's a good thing you came tonight.' He's slurring his words.

'Why is that?'

'Because tomorrow morning she's leaving. Said she's going back to Houston. Leaving me here in this big old house.' He waves his hand around.

'I'm sorry to hear that,' I say. 'Did your sister and your aunt get off this morning?'

'They did. Ol' Hannah is probably back in Los Angeles right now, whooping it up.'

'Is Krista upstairs?'

'Yep. Packing. I can call her to come down if you'd like.'

'We'll go upstairs to talk to her.' I get up.

'Be my guest.' He pours a hefty amount of bourbon into his glass and then lifts the bottle to ask if we'd like some. We decline.

Maria and I head up the stairs. I hear the sound of crying. This is going to be even tougher than I thought.

'Hello?' I call out. 'Krista, it's Chief Craddock and Deputy Trevino. We need to talk with you.'

There's silence for a minute, and then she walks out into the hallway. Her eyes are swollen and she's clutching a tissue. She's in her pajamas. 'This is not a good time. I'm sorry.'

'I'm afraid we have to insist. You want to come downstairs, or shall we go into your office?'

'What do you want? I'm sure Josh told you what's going on. Can't you leave me alone? I'm having a hard time.'

'I do apologize. We'll be as quick as we can, but there's a

development in Maddy's case. I need to talk to ask you some questions.'

'Oh, for heaven's sake! Just a minute.' She whirls around and heads back into the bedroom and comes back out a few minutes later dressed in long pants and a T-shirt. 'Come into my office. I've finished packing in there.'

She's been busy. The room is bare except for dozens of boxes stacked against the walls. The bookshelves gape empty, and the desk is cleared of all but a few stray paperclips and a calendar. The walls have been stripped of the photos and awards that were displayed. There are only two chairs in the room, so she goes to get another one. Before she sits down, she asks if we want anything. 'I'm getting myself a glass of wine.'

Maria and I decline. She's back in a minute with a wineglass almost full to the brim with white wine. She plops down at the chair behind her desk. 'OK, let's get this done.'

I stretch out the silence, giving her a chance to catch on that this is serious. 'Krista, do you know a man by the name of Loren Presley?'

I couldn't have startled her more if I'd told her a snake was dangling from the ceiling behind her. She pulls in a sharp breath. 'Yes, of course I know Loren.'

'How do you know him?'

Her lips form a thin line as she glares at me. 'I suspect you know the answer to that.'

'I'd like to hear it from you.'

'He's the man I had – am having – an affair with.'

'When was the last time you saw him?'

She takes a gulp of wine.

'Recently?' I ask.

She nods.

'When?'

'Last week.'

'Where was this?'

'We were in a motel in Bobtail. What a ridiculous name for a town.' She practically spits the words. It isn't the town she's mad at; it's her situation.

'That's where you were last week when you ran away?'

'It wasn't exactly running away. It was more like running to. I can't take it here anymore.'

'Did you call Loren or did he get in touch with you?'

'We've been talking a lot, so I don't remember which of us suggested that we meet there.'

'You had broken up with him, so when did you start up again?'

She sighs. 'I called him when Maddy was killed. I was so upset, and Josh simply isn't capable of providing emotional support. Loren was so kind. I don't know what I would have done without him.'

Next to me, Maria shifts in her chair. I don't dare look at her. This romantic scenario is like a bad movie.

'How did you meet Mr Presley?'

'What? Why do you care? We met at a party. He was one of the catering crew.'

'How long ago was that?'

She frowns. 'A year before we moved here. Why are you asking about Loren?'

I ignore the question. 'How much do you know about his background?'

'Not so much, but I know that he's kind, that he loves me, that he's got a lot of interests. That's all I need to know really.' Her demeanor is different when she talks about him. She's in love.

'Know anything about his family?'

'You mean . . . what exactly? I know he has a brother and that his folks live in Lubbock.'

'What are his interests? Sports? Artistic pursuits? Politics?'

She huffs impatiently. 'He's not a sports nut, if that's what you mean. We would sometimes watch a football game on TV.'

'Is he a fan of your books?'

She giggles unexpectedly. 'I wouldn't think so. He's proud of my success, unlike my husband, but I suspect he's never read any of them.'

'Did he serve in the armed forces?'

'As a matter of fact, he did. He was in the army for two years. He flunked out of college and decided he should go into the military while he tried to figure out what to do with his life.'

'That's what he told you?'

She gives a short, sharp bark of laughter. 'Yes, that's what he told me. How else would I know?'

'Suppose I told you that he joined the army because a judge gave him the choice of going to jail for assault or enlisting?'

'Where did you hear that?'

'It's in his police record.'

'Police record!' Now she's paying attention. 'Are you sure it's him?'

'Loren Christopher Presley, born in Lubbock, Texas. Parents still live in Lubbock. One brother, Craig Presley, and sister, Deborah Presley. No record of college attendance, but Loren did two years in the U.S. Army. Currently lives in Houston, where he was formerly employed by the Taste of Houston Catering Company. Does that sound like him?'

'Yes, but I never heard he assaulted anyone. Who did he assault?'

'Depends on which time you're talking about. The first time was right out of high school, in a bar fight. Attacked a guy with a broken bottle and cut him up. He was convicted of assault but was given probation since he was a teenager and, according to witnesses, the guy had provoked him. The second time he was at a political rally and attacked someone whose politics he disagreed with. Hit them with their own sign. Since it was his second conviction, this time he was given the choice of jail or military. He wisely chose the military.'

She has downed her wine and is fiddling with the glass. Her face is flushed, whether from the wine or emotion, I can't say. 'Well, he was young. Maybe a little wild. But I've never seen him lose his temper that way.'

Maria clears her throat. She's waiting for me to spring the big one.

'Krista, when you and Loren split up, was he angry?'

'Of course he was. He thought we ought to be together. He knew Josh didn't treat me with respect, and that I was just going back to Josh to please his folks.'

'Did he threaten you when you said you were breaking up with him?'

'No! He . . . he was frustrated, and he might have been angry, but he didn't threaten me. He never would!'

'Then who was he angry with?'

Her face goes blank. 'I guess Josh.'

'And Maddy?'

She swallows. 'OK, yes, he was mad at her, too. He didn't like her interference.'

'Did Loren tell you any details of his time in the military?'

'Not really.' She's puzzled by the switch of subject.

'He had some impressive medals from when he was in the army.'

'Really? He told me he didn't get sent to any hotspots, so I don't know what he would have gotten medals for.'

'You're right, he didn't get sent overseas. He spent the whole time in Georgia because he showed proficiency with a rifle, and they put him on the Service Rifle Team. He won a couple of shooting medals. He never mentioned that?'

'No. I mean, why would he?'

'Was he proud of his service?'

'I wouldn't say proud. He didn't dwell on it.'

'That may be because he ended up with a dishonorable discharge. He got into an altercation with his superior officer, and he spent time in the brig before they decided to boot him out.'

She has brought her hand to her mouth. She stands. 'I think I need more wine for this.'

She leaves and comes back with the bottle. She pours herself a glass. 'I suppose not knowing all that stuff about Loren makes me sound like a fool.'

'I wouldn't say that. Careless, maybe.'

'You think?' she sneers. 'He for sure has some explaining to do.'

Maria and I exchange glances. Krista hasn't quite grasped the enormity of what I'm getting at. 'Krista, when you were with Loren in the motel in Bobtail, did he mention to you that he'd been here watching you?'

She sits up very straight, indignant, and tipsy now. 'You mean like spying on me?'

'Yes.'

'Ugh, no. I don't believe he would do that.'

'He did. We have an eyewitness. But I have another question.' The heart of the matter. 'Did Loren know that your mother-in-law was helping girls go across the state line to procure abortions?'

She sits as still as a deer, eyes bouncing back and forth between Maria and me. 'I might have mentioned it.'

'What was his reaction?'

She blinks a couple of times. 'I can't remember.'

'Would it surprise you to know that the assault he committed that sent him into the military was on a pro-choice marcher? And that he is in a database of people who have threatened activists?'

'Threatened? Like, how?'

'Like sending letters saying they deserve to be killed. Threatening enough to be in the sights of the FBI.'

She whimpers. 'You're not saying what I think you're saying?'

I let her sit with it for a good thirty seconds before I say, 'Looks like it.'

She lets out a sorrowful wail and buries her face in her hands, shoulders heaving. 'Oh, please don't tell me that. He would never. He wouldn't.'

But I think he would and did.

'Krista, when you leave here, are you planning to meet him?'

She's rocking back and forth, keening. 'Oh God. Oh God.' She sits up and speaks as if she's in a trance. 'I'm supposed to meet him tomorrow. I'm going to his brother's house. That's where he's staying. And then we're going to find a place to rent together. We're going to do that this weekend. We don't want to stay there with his brother. It would be too awkward. I mean his brother is OK, but . . .' She stops babbling and looks from me to Maria. 'That's not going to happen, is it?' she whispers.

'Not likely,' I say. 'For one thing, I'm going to ask you to stay here another day or two. I'll be going to Houston to question Loren. So I need you to stay here. And I need to know where you were going to meet him.'

She shivers and looks around the room. 'I can't stay here, though. After what I've said to Josh. I can't stay here.'

'We have a motel here in town. It's not the Marriott, but it's comfortable.'

'Can I go tonight? I can't face Josh.'

I wonder if she's thinking of driving to Houston and warning her lover that he's been found out. Even though he killed her beloved mother-in-law, is his hold on her still strong? I can't take that risk.

'Tell you what. I'll arrange a room for you tonight.'

'No, that's OK, I can do it.'

'It's my pleasure.' I can't muster a smile. 'Maria and I will stay here at the house until you get packed and then we'll help you load your bags into the car.' I gesture to the boxes. 'What's going to happen with all this?'

'I hired someone to bring them when I tell them my new address.'

'I'll go downstairs and give you some time to get your goods together. Maria will stay up here to help.'

'I don't need any help.'

'I don't mind,' Maria says. 'I'm really good at packing.' Maria knows she needs to keep an eye on Krista to make sure she doesn't warn her lover that we're on to him. I'll take her cell phone, but they may also have a landline.

'Sure.' Krista's smile is as false as a wooden doll.

'And by the way, I need to take your cell phone,' I say.

'What? Why?'

'Standard procedure.' Not really, but I find that phrase works well in all kinds of situations.

She hands it over reluctantly. 'When will I get it back?'

'Soon.' Not as soon as she wants it.

Downstairs, before I go into the living room to face Josh, I call Brick. 'I need you to stand guard at the motel outside someone's room tonight. Is that a problem?'

'Not at all. What's the deal?'

I explain the situation to him. 'And Connor can take over in the morning.'

'What's Maria going to do?'

'She's coming with me. We'll be leaving for Houston early tomorrow morning.'

'Sounds like big doings.'

'You might say that.'

We have to leave early because we need to be back in time to meet with Reagan and the FBI tomorrow afternoon.

Josh is asleep in the living room – or passed out, more like it – sprawled back on the sofa, with his mouth open.

I go into the kitchen to make some coffee. While it drips through, I call to make a reservation at the better of the two motels south of town.

I sit down with my coffee and I'm getting sleepy, lulled by Josh's snores, when Krista wakes me banging her suitcases down the stairs. Maria follows with another bag. I jump up to help. Krista has spruced up since I last saw her, put on jeans and a clean T-shirt and make-up. I suspect she thinks she's going to make a run for it with Loren Presley. She's got a rude awakening.

'Wha—?' Josh snorts awake, peering around with alcohol-dulled eyes. 'What time is it?'

'It's nine thirty,' I say.

'Krista, what . . . you mean you're really going?' He sounds unbearably sad.

'Josh, I'm sorry, I have to go.' She bites her lip and tears form in her eyes.

Josh groans. 'Why so late? You could wait until tomorrow. You could sleep in Mamma's apartment.'

'No, I can't stay,' Krista says. She hesitates a moment longer as if she has more to say, but then turns and walks away.

Maria follows Krista to the front door, but I stay back to talk to Josh. 'You going to be all right?'

He groans. 'Hungover probably.'

'I'm sorry how things worked out.' I do feel bad for him. He looks bereft.

'No surprise. It's been coming for a while. I'll be OK. I've got my work.'

Outside, we stow Krista's luggage in her car. She gets into the driver's seat, and Maria tucks into the passenger side. 'I'll ride over there with you,' she says.

Krista looks like she's going to protest, but snaps her mouth shut.

I follow them over to the Best Value Motel, where we find Brick sitting in the lobby. 'Hey, Chief, how's your head?'

I tell him I'm fine, and I send him out to help Krista bring in her bags. He comes in carrying only one small bag, with Krista behind him, looking furtive, and Maria bringing up the rear.

'You don't want to bring in your other bags?' I ask.

'I won't need those. I'll be heading for Houston first thing tomorrow.'

'Maybe not first thing,' I say. I introduce her to Brick. 'I'm sorry I have to do this, but Brick is going to make sure you stay put until I tell him it's OK for you to leave.'

'Why? Am I under arrest?'

'You're being detained to avoid you contacting your friend Loren.'

'I'm not going to call him!' She's raised her voice, and I see the desk clerk come alert.

'I can't take the chance. Sorry. As soon as I have him in custody, you'll be free to go. If this is a problem, I can always take you to our jail, but I don't think you'd find it all that comfortable.'

'This is ridiculous,' she snaps.

'I'm really sorry, ma'am,' Brick says, with that gleam of smile. But its effect seems lost on her.

We go into her room, and I check to make sure the windows are secure so she can't climb out of them. It's on the first floor, and sure enough, the windows can only open six inches, too skinny for anyone to get out or in. I unplug the room's land phone and take it out to the front desk. 'Don't give her a phone if she asks for it,' I tell the desk clerk, a kid who looks barely out of high school.

'What's going on?' he asks. 'Is she, like, dangerous?'

'No, there are people I don't want her to contact so I need her to stay here. A deputy will be outside her door. She ought to be free to go by tomorrow noon at the latest.'

After Krista is in her room with Brick set up outside, I take Maria home.

'I'll pick you up at six o'clock,' I say. 'I'll bring a thermos of coffee.'

TWENTY-EIGHT

Friday morning

Maria and I don't talk much on our way to Houston. She's driving, since she says she knows how to drive in a city better than I do. I can't argue with her. Her family lives in San Antonio and the traffic there is epic.

We make good time and are on the outskirts of the city before eight. We head for the nearest police station to check in with the officer in charge and to tell him what we're up to.

The chief, Larry Fitch, is amiable and has no problem with our arresting someone in his jurisdiction if it comes to that. 'We'll send a squad car out for backup,' he says.

Craig Presley lives in a working-class neighborhood with small houses and sparse yards. As we drive down the street toward the house, we see several people scurrying to their cars, leaving for work, and a few mothers hustling kids off to school.

The house Presley rents is one-story with gray siding and a gray-tiled roof. There are two cars in the driveway. One has a flat tire and looks like it has been there a while; the other one looks only slightly more functional.

We park in front. 'I suppose we ought to wait for that squad car.'

We've waited ten minutes when the front door opens. 'Uh-oh,' I say. 'We're going to have to get into action now. You ready?'

She nods.

We get out of the car and walk up to meet the young guy who has come out and is walking toward his car. He looks up, startled, when we approach.

'Can I help you?' He's dressed in jeans and a T-shirt that shows off a wealth of tattoos. He looks disreputable – hair longish, in need of a shave, and posture in a slouch.

'We're looking for Loren Presley. Is that you?'

'No, that's my brother.' He takes off his sunglasses and eyes our uniforms. 'What's this about?'

'Is your brother here?'

'No. He's already gone. Said he had somewhere to be.'

'Did he say where?'

'No, I didn't ask. And he was in hurry, so I didn't want to bug him.' He looks at me curiously. 'I recognize your voice. I talked to you on the phone. You're that cop that called me when I was in Dallas.'

'That's right.'

He looks back and forth between Maria and me. 'You need me for anything? I ought to get going. I don't want to be late for work.'

A squad car drives up and stops across the street. I raise a hand to them. The one on the driver's side rolls his window down. 'Everything good?'

'Yeah.'

'Wait a minute,' Craig says. 'Why are they here? What's going on?'

'Like I said, we're here to talk to your brother.'

'About what?' He's getting suspicious.

'I'd like to go into your house to be certain your brother isn't there.'

'You think I'd lie? I'm telling you he's not here.'

I walk over and introduce myself to the cops and tell them I'm going inside to make sure the suspect isn't there. 'Keep an eye on this guy. We need him to stick around for a few minutes.'

One of the cops, a hefty older Black guy climbs out of the passenger side of the squad car. He introduces himself as Officer Neary. 'I need to stretch my legs anyway, so I'll stroll over and say hello.'

Maria and I proceed to the front door and ring the doorbell and knock. After a minute, I repeat it. Still no answer. I turn to Craig. 'I'd like you to unlock the door for us.'

'Don't you need a search warrant?'

'Not if we're here to take the subject into custody. If you'd prefer, we can break the door down. That should be entertaining.' I nod toward the street, where neighbors have come out on to their porches to see what the cops are doing here.

He comes over with his key. 'What do you mean take him into custody? What has he done?'

'We need to question him about an incident that happened in Jarrett Creek.'

'You talking about that murder? My brother? No, you've got the wrong guy.'

I gesture toward his key. He relents and unlocks the door and follows us inside.

'Loren Presley?' I call out. Silence greets me.

'I'm telling you he's not here.'

I send Maria to make sure.

'What time does he usually leave for work?' I ask.

'Not until after I'm gone. But that's not where he was going today.'

'Why not?'

'He was laid off last week.'

'Does he have a car?'

'Yeah, he just bought it.' He gives us the make and model. 'It's old, but he had to replace the one in the driveway.'

'A couple of weeks ago, you borrowed Jason Schrage's car. When I asked you if you had lent it to anyone while you were in Dallas, you said you hadn't. That's not true, is it? Your brother borrowed it.'

'I didn't lie intentionally. I didn't know at the time. When I got back, Loren said he'd driven it.'

Maria comes back and says it's all clear.

'So he did drive Schrage's car. Did he say where he went?'

'No, I didn't ask. Why would I?'

'Did he know anyone in Jarrett Creek? Please don't lie to me.'

'Yeah, his ex-girlfriend lives there.'

'Krista Benson?'

'That's right.'

'Mr Presley, do you have any idea where your brother might be?' He shakes his head.

'If I find out you're not telling me the truth, I'll bring charges against you for obstruction. That would be jail time.'

He throws his hands up. 'I swear I don't know.'

'How long ago did he leave?'

'I don't know, a half hour? Not long before you got here.'

'I'd like you to call him, see if he picks up.'

'What should I tell him if he does pick up?'

'Tell your brother your car won't start and ask if he can come pick you up.'

He dials the number. I tell him to put it on speaker.

'Oh, hey, Loren. Where are you?' He sounds nervous. 'I need a favor.'

'What kind of favor?' Loren asks.

He tells him what I suggested. 'I need a ride.'

'Sorry, bro, I'm not close by.'

'Well, where are you?'

There's a long silence. 'Do you have the phone on speaker?'

'Yeah. I was making some coffee.'

'You're going to have to call an Uber. I'm out of town. I'll call you when I get back.'

He hangs up. Craig stares at the phone as if there might be more to come.

'Craig, does your brother own a firearm?'

'He's got a few. A rifle and a shotgun, and handgun.'

'Does he keep them here?'

'Yeah. In his closet.'

'I'd like to accompany you to check and see if the firearms are there. For that I *would* need a warrant, unless I get your OK.'

He's starting to look alarmed. 'Yeah, of course it's OK. Christ!'

I follow him into his brother's room. It's relatively neat; the bed made, although it was clearly done in haste; most clothes put away; and a pair of running shoes on the floor near the bed.

Craig seems to steel himself, hesitating before he opens the door to the closet. There aren't many clothes on the hangers – a few pairs of pants and a couple of shirts. To one side is a standing gun rack. It contains only a shotgun. Craig stands there looking at it as if mesmerized. Then he jerks himself into action and goes over to the bedside stand and yanks it open.

He gazes into it and then slams it shut and hits the wall with his fist. 'Shit. He's taken the rifle and the pistol.' He searches my face. 'What do you think he's going to do?'

'I wish I knew.'

Back in the front room, I tell Maria to get Craig's work information and cell number. 'I have some phone calls to make. And you,' I address Craig, 'if you hear from your brother again, I need to know right away. Again, I'm warning you that obstruction is a serious charge.'

I walk outside to call Brick. 'How are things there?'

'Connor's on his way over.'

'Have you heard Ms Benson stirring this morning?'

'Yeah, I heard the shower.'

'I'd like to speak to her.'

I hear him knock on the door. Then I hear the door open and Krista's voice. 'What do you want?'

'Chief Craddock wants to talk to you.'

'Yes?' she says to me, her voice testy.

'Krista, I'm at Loren Presley's place and he isn't here. Do you have any idea where he might be?'

'How would I know?' She sounds surly.

'You were supposed to drive to Houston this morning, so I'm surprised that he isn't here if he was expecting you.'

She's quiet for a minute. Then she exhales. 'I really don't know. Maybe he went out for coffee?'

'Craig said his brother was in a hurry. Is there any way he would know you aren't coming today?'

'How would I get in touch with him? I don't have a phone.'

'Were you supposed to call him this morning?'

'No, but maybe he called me to check and he's worried that I've changed my mind.'

Uh-oh, she's right.

'OK, can you give the phone back to Brick?'

'Hey, Chief, what do you need?'

'First, are you sure Krista didn't leave the room last night?'

'Absolutely.'

'Brick, when Connor gets there, I'd like you to take a few minutes to get a cup of coffee and stretch your legs, and then I'd like you to relieve Connor again until we get there. Is that a problem?'

'Not at all.'

I like that he doesn't ask any questions. The fact is that if somehow Loren gets there, I don't want Connor to have to deal with him.

I get Maria and tell her we need to leave, now. Outside, I ask the two officers if they can stick around for a while to make sure Loren doesn't come back. But if my hunch is correct, he's not coming back here anytime soon.

They clear it with their boss, and I tell them I'll call them when I can release them. I hand the older one my card and tell him to call me if anything comes up.

In the car, I tell Maria we need to get to Jarrett Creek fast. 'I have a hunch Loren is on his way there to get Krista. Somehow, he knows she's not coming, or maybe he tried to call her, and when she didn't answer, he thinks she might have changed her mind. Which I hope is true at this point.'

'I'm not so sure,' Maria says. 'She writes those romance novels. She's got romance in her blood. I can imagine her thinking we're wrong and that he's innocent, and she's going to save him.'

'I hope not.' I dial Connor's number.

'Hey, Chief, I'm on my way to relieve Brick. I'm almost there.'

'I need you to make a detour by the office. There's a phone in my desk drawer. I want you to see if there have been any calls to it.'

'Do you have a password?'

'If there was a call, it will show up without actually opening the phone. I want to know the number the call came from and the time. Call me as soon as you get it.'

'Will do.'

I've got a new worry. If Loren is on his way to get Krista, he won't know she's at the motel, and he'll go straight to her house. He has a half hour head start. I need to warn Josh.

I dial Josh's number, but he doesn't pick up. I'm not surprised. He's probably in a hungover stupor.

In five minutes, Connor calls back. 'Chief, you're right. There were two calls last night.'

'What time?'

'One at ten, and another at eleven. And then there was one this morning at seven.' He gives me the number. It's Loren Presley's.

'Connor, we've got a situation. Maria and I are on our way to Jarrett Creek. I need you to call Brick and tell him you won't be there right away. And then I want you to drive over to Josh Benson's house.' I give him the address. 'When you get there, do whatever it takes to wake him. He was on a bender last night and might be out cold, so it might take some doing. When you get him awake, have him call me.'

'OK, I'll do that.'

It occurs to me that Craig could have underestimated the time when his brother left. And if Loren drives fast, he could already be there. It's not likely, but I have to keep Connor safe. 'Connor, I'm going to give you the make and model of a car. If it's in the driveway at the Benson place, don't go in. Just call me and let me know.'

The traffic is abysmal. I tell Maria we need to tune up, and I switch on the lights and siren and Maria hits the gas.

Twenty minutes later, we're halfway to Jarrett Creek, and Connor hasn't called. I call his cell phone and there's no reply. Then I call Brick. 'Have you heard from Connor?'

'Just to say he was going on errand for you and that he'd be here as soon as he could.'

'I'll get back to you.'

I dial Josh's number. No reply. Connor is timid. Surely he didn't decide to ignore my instruction not to go to the Benson house if Loren's car was outside. But another scenario has me worried. Suppose Connor was there trying to rouse Josh when Loren drove up. I tell Maria what I'm thinking.

'Oh no, Connor . . .' She doesn't get along with him, but that doesn't mean she wants anything to happen to him.

TWENTY-NINE

'm trying to decide the best way to proceed when Brick calls. 'Boss, do you want me to go try to find Connor?'

'No. We'll be there soon. Have you and Krista had any breakfast?'

'I offered to go get food, but she said she isn't hungry. I brought her a cup of coffee from the lobby, and I got a cup of tea. I'll be OK.'

Maria and I discussed whether I should call Bobtail PD and ask them to go check out the Benson house, but we agreed that if Loren is there, having a bunch of cops show up could set him off and be a danger to Josh and Connor.

It seems like it takes a lot longer than an hour, but in fact with Maria driving with the lights and siren, it takes only fifty minutes to reach the outskirts of town. I switch off the bells and whistles, and tell Maria to go straight to headquarters. 'I have an idea.'

I dial Connor's phone once more. Still no answer. Same with Josh.

Maria stays in the car, and I run inside. I am glad to see that Connor didn't take Krista's phone with him. I grab it and head back to the car.

'We have to get to the Benson house, and then we'll have two choices.' I describe them on the way.

Sure enough, Loren Presley's car is in the driveway behind Connor's small pickup. Maria drives on past, clutching the wheel.

One hundred yards past the driveway, I tell Maria to pull over to the side of the road. 'What do you think?' I ask.

'In theory, I like the idea of having Krista call Loren Presley,' she says. 'But too many things can go wrong. We don't know if she can pull off luring him somewhere. And what excuse would she have for not calling him sooner?'

I nod. 'I'm with you. We've got to get into the house without alerting Presley.' The bottom line is that this is a man who has firearms with him. We can't risk knocking on the door and being greeted with a blast from a gun.

'Maybe we can go through Maddy's apartment,' she says. 'But how?'

'There wasn't a key in Maddy's backpack. She might have a key hidden outside somewhere. Or maybe she didn't bother to lock the door.'

We move the car farther off the side of the road and head back on foot.

We stop at the driveway. It's a problem to get around the back of the house to Maddy's apartment. The front and back yards are bare of bushes. There's absolutely no cover. If Presley were to look outside for any reason, he'd spy us.

'I could go knock on the door and ask to speak to Connor as if there's nothing wrong and that will give you cover to get around back,' Maria says.

'Or we could do it the other way.'

'I'm more expendable than you,' she says.

As we're arguing, the front door opens. We lunge for the cover of trees to the side of the driveway. Connor comes out on to the front steps, followed by Loren Presley, who's holding a handgun on him. Presley is a muscular guy with a tawny mane of hair that reaches his collar. Even from this far away, I see that Connor's face is bright red. Stress always makes his face flush. But his voice rings out surprisingly loud and clear. 'You're not going to get away with this.'

Maria pokes me. I look at her. Her eyes are wide. Is that really our Connor? The two men head for Loren's car, Loren directing Connor to get in the driver's seat.

We need to get out of sight range, so we hustle up the road, sticking to the trees to provide cover, and dash into the driveway of the house next door.

Loren's car drives off toward town. We make a run for the squad car. I'm driving and when I turn around, Maria says, 'Should we check on Josh?'

I hesitate, picturing Josh Benson shot, losing blood. 'I'll call to see if he answers.' I dial the number, but he doesn't reply.

'I'll call Hedges and he'll send someone to check on him.' I hadn't wanted to call Hedges earlier because I didn't want Connor put in danger, but that time is past.

When I reach Hedges, I tell him I need a couple of squad cars, one at the motel where Krista is being held, and one to check on a possible victim at the Benson house. 'Do you have the manpower or should I call DPS to send some patrol officers?'

'It'll be faster from here,' he says. 'They're on their way.'

I know he's as good as his word.

Now I call Brick. I tell him who Loren Presley is. 'He's here in Jarrett Creek and is on his way to the motel to get Krista. He's got Connor and he's armed with a pistol and maybe a rifle. Go into Krista's room and keep her safe. We're on our way.'

'What do you mean he's got Connor?'

'Probably intending to use him as a hostage. I'm not sure of the situation. But you need to get out of sight.'

'Shouldn't I go to the front to protect the desk clerk? I wouldn't let this guy get past me.'

'We don't know what he plans to do. Best to stay out of sight for now. I'll phone and tell the desk clerk to hide in the back room.'

He hangs up and I call the motel. A woman answers. 'There's a situation,' I say. 'A man is coming there to the motel to find the woman we have under guard. I want you to go into the back room and don't come out.'

'Wait, what? You told Oliver last night this situation wasn't dangerous!'

'You'll be fine if you don't show yourself. I'll be there in five minutes.'

'What if one of the guests comes out and sees him?'

'Is there any way from the back room that you can call their rooms and tell them to stay inside?'

'No. The room phone is in the front.' She's sounding increasingly stressed.

'We'll have to hope they don't come out. This guy is not going to be after them.'

'But . . .'

'Into the back room, now.'

'Oh,' she moans, 'the manager is going to kill me.' She hangs up.

As we get near to the motel, Maria slows down. Loren's car is in the drive-up in front of the motel, blocking the front entrance.

'Now what?' Maria asks.

'Let's see if there's a back entrance.'

She pulls around the side of the motel. I see Brick waving from a window in one of the units along the side. 'There's Brick,' I say.

Maria parks near the window and we get out, guns drawn.

Brick has opened the curtains and the window. 'I'm going to try to force this window open wider,' he says, 'so we can get out of here.'

'No. Krista should stay where she is,' I say. 'Loren is out front.'

I peer into the room and see Krista huddled on the bed, knees drawn up to her chin.

'But we have to get inside the building,' I say. 'Is there a back door?' Brick goes to the door of the room, opens it, and sticks his head out and looks both ways. He nods vigorously and gestures with his hand that he's going down to the end of the hallway.

Maria and I drive around to the back. My phone rings and I take a look at it, but it's a number I don't recognize. I send it to voicemail. We get out and wait for Brick to open the back door. It takes longer than I expected. When he does, he steps out and whispers, 'I had to disengage the alarm system so it wouldn't go off when I opened the door.'

We hear shouting from the front of the motel. 'Hey, get your ass out here!' A desk bell is banged again and again. Clearly, the clerk has done as I said and is hiding, and Presley is impatient.

One of the doors along the corridor opens and someone sticks his head out. He sees us. 'What's all that racket?'

'Sir, get back inside,' I order. 'Stay there until we give the all clear.'

'But . . .'

'Now!' Brick says.

The guy ducks back inside.

'Brick,' I say quietly, 'I'd like you to go around front and provide cover for Maria and me. I'm not sure what you'll have to do, but don't put yourself in danger of being shot.'

'I'll figure it out when I see what's going on.'

'We'll come up the corridor and get him from behind.'

'On it,' Brick says. He starts out the door.

'Don't be a hero,' I add. 'I'm worried that when he sees you, he'll use Connor as a shield. Just show your face to distract him and then get out of sight.'

Sticking close to the inside wall, I inch down the hallway, Maria behind me. Presley is still yelling for the desk clerk to come out. I hear him banging on the door to the room behind the counter. That puts us at an awkward angle. He can cover both

Brick and me if he stays back behind the counter. I wonder where Connor is.

Then I hear Connor's voice, strong and firm. 'Dude, you need to calm down. There's no need for all this.'

Maria pokes me. I look at her and she whispers, 'Dude?'

She's right. That doesn't sound like Connor.

'Don't tell me to calm down, asshole.'

'Look,' Connor says, 'this motel is not that big. Go bang on the doors and call her name. If your girlfriend is here, she'll come out.'

'OK, I'll take you . . . whoa! Who are you?'

'Hey, Connor,' Brick says. 'What's going on here? I thought we were going to have breakfast.'

'Uh, well, I got held up.'

'Hi, I'm Brick Freeman. Oh, wait, hey. What's with the gun?'

'Listen, cowboy, I don't know what you're doing here, but . . .'

He doesn't get to finish, because I hear a scuffle, and then a shot goes off and there's more noise of a ruckus. I run into the foyer and stop cold. I'm not needed. Loren Presley is on the floor with Connor sitting on his chest. Brick is standing over them, with a gun trained on Presley. Since I can see that Brick's weapon is still holstered, he must have wrestled Presley's away from him.

'Get off me,' Presley snarls.

'Chief, I don't have any cuffs,' Connor says. 'You got any?'

I can't help laughing. That's more like the Connor I know.

Maria steps over, yanks her cuffs off her belt, and hands them to Connor. 'I'll let you do the honors,' she says.

Connor gets off Presley and jumps up faster than I thought possible. He leans down and heaves Presley to his feet, and wrenches his arm behind him, cuffing one wrist and grabbing the other arm before Presley can react.

The desk clerk opens the door to the back room and pokes her head out. 'Is everything all right?'

'It is now,' I say.

'I heard a shot. Do you need an ambulance?'

Brick points to the ceiling. We all look and see a nick in the ceiling where a bullet penetrated. 'I think we're good.'

But then a body rockets past me and crashes into Presley, knocking him off his feet and onto his back. Krista straddles him, pummeling him with her fists. 'What the hell is wrong with you? Chief Craddock told me what you did! Where is Josh? Did you hurt him?' She's screaming her questions.

'Hey, baby, no! Ow, ow!' He's trying to buck her off him. 'I didn't do anything! Ow! I would never hurt anybody. Get off me!'

'Oh, yeah?' Connor says. 'Then why were you holding a gun on me?'

Maria, Brick, and I are all taking in this new version of Connor.

Brick and I haul Krista off Loren Presley. 'Steady now,' I say to her. 'We've got this. You need to back off.'

She spits at Presley, hitting him in the face.

A squad car comes squealing into the parking lot, and two Bobtail officers hop out. 'Brick, go tell them we've got it under control, so they don't start shooting.'

He goes outside.

'Connor,' I say, 'Is Josh Benson OK? The sheriff sent a squad car to check on him.'

'He's OK. Tied up, though, so he'll be glad for somebody to come and let him go.'

'Krista,' I ask, 'do you have a key to the house so the officers over there don't have to bash the door in?'

'I'll get it.' She runs toward her room and comes back with the key. 'What happens now?' She's wild-eyed, looking rattled, and is trying hard not to look at Presley. He's keeping up a steady, low string of curses.

I call Sheriff Hedges to tell him to call the officers that went out to the Benson house and tell them not to break the door down. 'I'm sending somebody there with a key to get into the house. The guy isn't hurt, but he's tied up.'

'Everything under control there?'

'Yes, we got our man. We'll be bringing him in this afternoon. I want to have a chat with him first.'

'I understand.'

Brick has had a long night, but I need him to do one more thing before he goes home. I look into Presley's car and see that the key is still in the ignition. I tell him to bring the car to the station and then search it. I want Presley's rifle.

'And, Connor, go with Krista to take the key to her place.'

He looks different, standing straighter, as if he's proud of himself.

He should be. He's had a trial by fire and has acquitted himself admirably. I'm curious to know if this has affected his decision to leave law enforcement.

'And when you're done there, stop by and get the two of you a bite to eat. Then bring her back to the station. I need to question her as well.'

Connor swaggers as he walks Krista out to her car.

At that moment, my phone rings. When I see who it is, I look at my watch. It's not time for the meeting yet, so I wonder why Reagan is calling.

'Craddock, two things,' he says without preamble.

'Yeah?'

'First, the meeting has been postponed. FBI guy couldn't make it. But the second thing is he has a suspect he's taking a look at. Name is Loren Presley. He's threatened some protestors, and they suspect he might have been involved in a shooting last spring. And it seems he has a connection to someone close to your shooting victim. The FBI is putting out a BOLO, and I thought I'd give you a heads-up.'

'No need for the BOLO. We just arrested Presley.'

He's quiet for a second. 'What do you mean arrested him? You want to explain how you managed that?'

I tell him the short version. I don't know when I've gotten more satisfaction from an explanation.

Reagan's chuckle turns into a full-blown laugh, a sound I've never heard coming from him. 'Well, if that doesn't beat everything,' he says. 'Let me know if you need any help, although that doesn't seem likely.'

'You can help me with one thing. Give me the FBI guy's name so I can call him myself and tell him the news.'

Another laugh. 'That suits me fine. It's nice to beat the Feds for a change. Let me give you his phone number.'

THIRTY

As soon as we get to headquarters, Maria and I stick Presley into a cell. I need a minute to cool down, get myself a cup of coffee, and decide how I'm going to approach Presley. I don't have any doubt that we've got our man, but my question is: why did he kill Maddy Benson? Was it because of her work helping women get out of state, or was it because she stood between him and Krista? Or both.

By the time I brew a pot of coffee and Maria goes off and comes back with donuts, Brick comes in to say he's finished searching Presley's car. He shakes his head. 'Sorry, boss, the rifle isn't there.'

That's a blow. Unless we can get a confession out of Presley, without the rifle there's not enough evidence to tie him to the murder.

When Maria gets back, I tell her, and she grimaces. 'Not good.'

We go to the cells to question Presley.

I go into the cell with him and take a chair, while Maria sits outside. I've brought him a donut and a cup of coffee, which I set on the square metal table next to the cot. 'You probably didn't have time for breakfast,' I say.

'What am I doing here? What is it you think I've done?' he snarls. Up close, I see how a woman would find him attractive. Intense blue eyes, shaggy hair, and a strong jaw. And a sense of arrogance that oozes off him. A bad boy. Some women find that attractive.

I see no reason to mince words. 'I think you killed your girl-friend's mother-in-law.'

'You can't prove that!'

I stare at him. Interesting that he didn't say he's innocent. He says we can't prove it. He can't know what I'm thinking: that half the people I arrest tell me I can't prove things. 'Proof is overrated,' I say.

'What the hell does that mean? What kind of a cop are you? You can't charge me without proof.'

'I didn't say I don't have proof. I said it's overrated. What I mean is, if somebody confesses, that's the big one. So you want to get it over with, or do we have to do the song and dance?'

He looks at me like I've lost my mind. 'I'm not going to confess to something I didn't do.'

'Krista thinks you did it.'

'She doesn't know what she thinks.'

Maria snorts. 'I bet she'd love to hear you say that.'

'So you're going to arrest me because Krista Benson believes I killed somebody?'

'Why do you think she believes that?'

'How the hell do I know? She gets these ideas.'

'Not that her opinion is particularly important, but I wonder what makes her think you'd be capable of killing somebody.'

He looks confused. 'So if her opinion doesn't matter, are you going to let me go?'

'Not likely. Because what does matter is if the bullet casing we found matches your rifle.'

He lets out a bark of laughter. 'What rifle?'

'Your brother said you have a rifle.'

'He must mean the one I sold a few weeks ago.'

'I'll need to know who you sold it to.'

'I don't have the information on me. And besides, even if you find the guy, your shell casing won't match that rifle.'

'How do you know? Maybe the guy you sold it to came here and killed her.'

He shrugs. 'Doesn't have anything to do with me.'

'One other question. Are you the person who called the Baptist church to tell them that Maddy Benson was helping women get out of state for their healthcare?'

'Healthcare! You mean to kill their unborn babies?'

'So you are the person who called?'

'I certainly did. I thought it was important for people to know what kind of person she was.'

'So they could divert people's attention from the fact that she was murdered and get them to argue that she deserved it?'

'I knew they'd agree her death was no great loss.'

'Did you ever tell Krista that's how you felt? Did you tell her you made that phone call?'

'It didn't come up between us.'

'And did you also leave a package on my doorstep with a note warning me off the investigation?'

'I don't know what you're talking about.'

'I think you do. And I think when we match fingerprints found on the package and the note, you'll be a match.'

'I wouldn't be so sure.' He's gloating. He wore gloves.

'So take me through how this happened. You'd been watching the Benson house. Why was that?'

'I did no such thing.'

I sigh. 'Look, you were seen. There was a witness, the person who got the license number and make of the car you were driving saw you. Like you said, it doesn't prove anything. It just means you were watching the house. I want to know why. Would Krista not call you back?' I'm stretching the truth here. No one actually saw him, but sometimes it's necessary to nudge things along.

'OK, so I did go to her place. I wanted to see where she was living, that's all. No harm in that.'

'Not a bit. Unless you took the opportunity to follow Maddy when she left that morning.'

'Why would I do that?'

I take a sip of my coffee. It's gone cold. 'Hold on while I get a fresh cup of coffee.' I let myself out of the cell and take my time getting my coffee, giving Presley a while to consider how much I know.

When I walk back in, I sit down and smile at Presley. 'I do love coffee,' I say.

'Well, good for you,' he says. 'Now, can we get this over with?'

'Sure. So the morning Ms Benson was killed, you were there watching her house and you saw her get in the car with somebody, and you followed them out to the farm-to-market road. Have I got it right so far?'

He stays quiet.

'So you passed them and . . . take me through this . . . did you already know you were going to shoot her? Did you come armed? Or did the idea just strike you, and you made a hasty decision?'

'I didn't—'

I interrupt his protest. 'The reason I'm asking is it could make a big difference in sentencing. You know if it was premeditated, that's first-degree murder. You could get the death sentence for that. But if it was—'

'What the hell are you saying? I told you, I didn't do any such thing.'

'Well, if you were watching the house, you at least had to see Maddy leave. So maybe you can tell me if you saw anything.'

'OK, I admit that. I saw her leave. But I didn't follow her.'

'So back to the murder sentencing. I want to be clear. If it was spur of the moment, that's second-degree murder and the sentence is lighter. And I expect if you get a good lawyer and make the case that Maddy was somebody who deserved to be shot, the sentence might be even lighter. Who knows?'

'Well, she did deserve it, that's for sure.'

'For what? For helping women or for keeping you from your girlfriend? You know, interfering.'

'Meddling.'

'You were unhappy with that, weren't you? Maddy keeping you from Krista. Tell me, I'm curious. Krista Benson makes a lot of money from those romance novels she writes. Was it her money you were after, or was it true love?'

'I don't care about her money.'

'The reason it occurred to me is that I know you had some trouble holding down a job, and maybe you thought it would be nice to have a cash cow – you know, a sugar momma.'

'Sugar momma,' Maria says. 'I like that.'

He shoots a glare at her. 'I told you, I don't care about her money.'

'When you were holed up in the motel with Krista, did you tell her what you'd done?'

'There's something wrong with you, you know that? You've got a – what do you call it? – an obsession, thinking I killed that woman.'

'I do have sort of an obsession, but here's what we've got. We have the bullet casing that will match your rifle. We have the tire prints from the car that drove out into the driveway where she was killed – that's the car you were driving – we have the eyewitness of the woman who was driving the car Maddy was riding in, who saw you when you passed them . . . I think that's enough.' Of course, I don't have those things, but I don't have any qualms about lying to him. He's a killer. I'm stretching for a confession. Without the rifle, we don't have enough.

I get up. 'And then I've got your statement that she deserved to die. I think it's good enough. Maria, what do you think?'

She shrugs. 'A confession would be better. Maybe some statement of contrition, maybe Mr Presley saying he momentarily lost his bearings when he decided to shoot her, or maybe he didn't mean to kill her. I think things would work better if he said that. But without that, I guess a jury will have to decide.'

I've been waiting to hear Connor come in with Krista, and I hear the front door open and two sets of steps. 'OK, well I guess we're done for now.'

Presley leaps up. 'What do you mean "for now"? I want out of here. Do I need to get a lawyer? You've got nothing on me.'

Maria gets up and stretches. 'Sounds like Connor and Krista have gotten here. It will be interesting to hear what Krista has to say.'

'We'll talk to you again in a bit,' I say to Presley as I let myself out of the cell.

'Hold on a minute,' Presley says. 'I want you to know something. Krista might say anything. You can't go on what she says.'

'I'll bear that in mind.' I act like I'm going to walk away and then I turn around. 'What do you think she might say?'

'Who knows? She's got an active imagination.'

THIRTY-ONE

Krista is sitting next to my desk, and she looks completely drained. Connor is leaning against the wall nearby. He comes to attention when we enter the room.

'Did you get her some breakfast?' I ask Connor.

'Yeah, but she wouldn't eat much.'

'You want to sit in on this chat with her?'

He shrugs. 'I guess.' I can tell by the way he looks at her that he feels sorry for her. But no more sorry than she feels for herself. He pulls up a chair and sits down. Maria sits down at her desk.

Krista looks at me with a hopeless expression. 'Is he here?' she asks.

I nod.

'Did he confess?'

'I'm not sure he's the confessing kind. So that's where you come in.' I draw up a chair close to her.

'Me? I don't know anything.'

'You might know more than you think.'

'Can I see him?'

'Maybe later. First, let's talk. Tell me how you came to go stay with him at the motel in Bobtail. Did he call you? Did you call him?'

She bites her lower lip. 'He called me.'

'Was this before or after your mother-in-law was killed?'

'He called me a lot, so I'm not sure. Can I look at the calendar on my phone?'

'Sorry, I forgot I had it.' I take it out of my pocket and hand it to her. 'It should still have some juice.'

She fiddles with the phone, nodding a few times. Her jaw is clenched. 'OK, it's in here. I sent in the synopsis of my next book a couple of days before Maddy was killed, and Loren called me that day. But now I see that he called me the day after she was killed, but I didn't pick up. He left a message.' She looks up at me, her expression distraught. 'I never listened to it. That day was so awful that I didn't look at my messages.'

'Let's hear it. Put it on speaker.'

She seems to hold her breath as she keys the voicemail. Loren's voice is cheery. 'Hey, babe, how's it going? Listen, between you and me, I think from now on things are going to go better for us. Let's have a secret rendezvous. If you can tear yourself away from your old man.' He chuckles suggestively. 'What do you think? Call me back. I gotta see you. I gotta get some of your crazy love.'

Krista switches off the phone. 'That bastard. Did you hear what he said? Things are going to go better for us. It has to mean he killed her.'

'Maybe. It could also mean he had just heard that she was killed.'

'How? How would he have heard that?' She's at the edge of her seat, practically spitting her words. 'Was it information that was on the news in Houston? I doubt it.'

'I'll find out eventually.'

'No. Let me ask him. Maybe he'll talk to me.'

I shake my head. 'I'm sorry, I can't do that. Let's go over the timeline. He called you again a couple of days after that message, and this time you agreed to meet him?'

She nods.

Sometimes stringing together small details can jog people's memories. 'What time of day did he call?'

She looks at the phone, frowning. 'Mid-morning. Maybe ten, eleven? After we talked, I packed and decided to go meet him.' She hangs her head. 'I can't believe I've been so stupid. I got caught up in the romance of it. He's . . . I don't know, sexy and attentive. Romantic. Everything Josh isn't. Except Josh at least has a conscience.' She bangs the sides of her head with her fists.

'Settle down. You're not the only person who ever let romance cloud their judgment.'

She grimaces. 'I thought I was smarter than that.'

There's nothing to say. She's got some regrets ahead of her. 'Let's continue. You were with Loren in the motel for a few days. Try to recall if he said anything that struck you as odd. Anything that, when you think back on it, made you wonder what he meant, that might suggest he was involved in Maddy's murder.'

'Give me a minute.' She draws a shaky breath.

'I'll get you some coffee.'

'Oh God, that's the last thing I need. I'm already a wreck.'

Maria goes to the coffee stand where there are still a couple of

donuts left. She puts one on a napkin and sets it down next to Krista.
'You need to eat. Your blood sugar is probably in the pits. And let's
face it, you've had a hard couple of days.'

Krista takes a bite of the pastry and obviously struggles to get it
down, but then she takes another one. 'This is good. You're right,
I needed some food.' She gives Maria a wan smile.

I try more questions, but Krista is unable, or perhaps unwilling,
to remember anything incriminating that Presley might have said
while they were together.

We're still no closer to getting the evidence we need to charge
him. We have the sighting of the car Presley was sitting in while
he watched Maddy's house, and now we have the suggestive voicemail he sent to Krista. And then there's his declaration that Maddy
deserved to be killed. It's not enough. Where could he have ditched
his rifle? I'll contact the police in Houston and arrange a thorough
search of his place. But we may never find it.

I'm not quite ready to give up on getting a confession. Before I
take Presley to Bobtail, I want one more pass at him.

I send Connor to take Krista home, but before we can walk into
the next room to start on Presley again, my phone rings. It's the
same number that called earlier when we were at the motel and that
I sent to voicemail.

'Craddock,' I say.

'Hey, Chief Craddock, this is Officer Neary from Houston PD.
Did you get my message earlier?'

'I'm sorry, I didn't check it. We had a hairy situation here.'

He chuckles. 'I have something that might make your situation
less hairy. We recovered a rifle.'

It's too much to hope for. 'Tell me everything.'

'Well, sir, right after you left, the young man you were talking
to got a phone call while he was still standing next to his car. He
got in and took off like he had a burr in his saddle. I know you told
us to stay at the house, but I've been at this awhile, and I had a
hunch we ought to follow him.'

'And I assume you're going to tell me it was the right
decision.'

'I think you'll agree it was. Our guy drove around a bit and kept
checking his rearview mirror, and it looked an awful lot to me like
he had some nefarious intent and was hoping to lose us. It occurred
to me that we needed to put an unmarked car on him.'

'Good call.' He's a rambler, and I'm trying hard to stay patient. 'So we arranged to swap out with an unmarked. We took off, gave him a big wave and another couple of officers picked him up on the next block. And that's when the boy made his move. He drove around some more and finally found a dumpster. According to the boys who took over from us, he retrieved something out of his trunk and threw it into the dumpster. Thank goodness they were younger than I am; one of them climbed up in there and found an object wrapped up that turned out to be a rather fine rifle. You know, the kind of thing you're surprised somebody would want to get rid of.'

'Neary, you've made my day, maybe my whole month. Where is the rifle now?'

'It's here at our station all safe and sound anytime you want to come get it. Or we could send it your way with a highway patrol crew. Whatever you prefer.'

'I'll be sending one of my deputies there. Man by the name of Connor Loving.'

'Oh, now there's a name for history books – Loving.'

I'm sure he could go on and on spouting the history of the Goodnight–Loving trail, but I cut it short, telling him I'd appreciate it if somebody could pick up Craig Presley as a person of interest.

'Well, sir, we're ahead of you on that one. It seemed Mr Presley made himself so nervous that on the next block he had a fender bender, so the guys who retrieved the rifle were able to bring him in for questioning. We figured if you didn't need him, we could always let him go.'

'I do need him. I'll get back to you.'

It gives me great pleasure to go into the next room. 'Come on, Presley. We're leaving.'

'You're letting me go? I told you I didn't do anything.' His voice is gleeful.

'No, I didn't say you're leaving. I said we're leaving. Deputy Trevino and I will be transporting you to the Sheriff's Office in Bobtail for further questioning.'

I don't tell him we found the rifle. I want to hear what Loren's brother has to say first.

We don't talk much on the way to Bobtail. I've been thinking and realized that I have to go to Houston with Connor to pick up the weapon, and that will give me a chance to ask Craig Presley how it went down. The way Neary described it, I expect Loren called his brother to tell him he'd stashed the rifle in Craig's car and asked him to get rid of it. We'll get a court order to examine Loren's phone and find out if he did make that call. Having seen Craig's alarmed response when he found the rifle gone from his brother's closet, I don't think it will take much to persuade him not to incriminate himself, even for his brother.

When we get Loren signed in at the Bobtail PD and into his cell, Maria and I go in to debrief Hedges. I tell him all the details and that I'll be going down to Houston to question Presley's brother and to retrieve the rifle.

'It's a funny case,' I say. 'All this time we thought Maddy Benson was killed because she was active in helping women get abortions, when it was actually a matter of selfishness. Presley wanted his girlfriend back and was mad because her mother-in-law interfered.'

'It's murder either way,' Hedges says.

When we get up to leave, I say, 'How's our preacher's boy doing?'

Hedges shakes his head, disgusted. 'He's out on bail. He had to spend the night, but the lawyer sprung him this morning. He'll be back here tomorrow for an arraignment.'

'Let me know if you need me to bring him in again.'

'Will do.'

THIRTY-TWO

I haven't been back to San Francisco since my wife Jeanne died, and I worried that it would make me feel nostalgic to see all the places she and I used to go. But the sight of Wendy running across the lobby of the hotel to greet me dispels that notion. She turns her face up to me and I kiss her.

'I can't wait to hear your story,' she says.

'Let's go upstairs so I can get rid of this bag, and then we'll go out for lunch and I'll tell you everything.'

We don't get out of the room quite as fast as I might have thought, because Wendy surprises me with champagne on ice and other ideas on how to spend some time before we head off.

It's two o'clock before we end up at the Embarcadero at an outside table of a restaurant near the Ferry Building. 'I love it here so much,' she says. 'I'm so happy you could get away. How long can you stay?'

'As long as we want to.'

Examination of the rifle and the bullet casing will take some time, but I have no doubt it's the weapon used to kill Maddy Benson. As I suspected, Craig Presley didn't take much persuading to admit that his brother called him and told him he'd stashed the rifle in Craig's car and asked Craig to ditch it somewhere.

I left Maria in charge, with instructions to treat Connor like royalty. She didn't protest. She's keeping Dusty while I'm gone, and the young man who usually takes care of my cows when I go away was happy to do it, even on short notice.

'You're going to miss all the excitement,' Wendy says. 'The whole town must be thrilled with all the action that went on.'

Not exactly thrilled. I haven't heard the last from Reverend Dawkins, especially since I've been instrumental in arresting his son for assault. And I'm sure he's got parishioners who will take his side in thinking that somehow Maddy Benson got what she deserved. But I'm not going to bring that up with Wendy right now.

'Let the young cops have the glory,' I say. 'They've earned it.' I don't mention that I put in a request for a commendation for Connor

for his actions. If it goes through, I'll be back in time to present it
to him.

Wendy and I eat fried calamari and French fries and decide to
stroll down the Embarcadero for a while before we have dessert.
It's a beautiful day, cool and clear, which I remember was often the
case in San Francisco. Tomorrow, we'll go to some art galleries. I
wouldn't mind finding a piece of work from a new artist.

'Can we go to the wine country?' Wendy asks. 'Or . . . while
she was here, my friend and I went to Fisherman's Wharf and rode
a cable car. It was fun. We could do that instead, if you want.'

I tell her I've done that, and I'd rather go to the wine country.
And maybe go out to the beach in Marin County.

She puts her arm through mine and snuggles close. And makes
me wonder if it's time to give up my job and spend time traveling
with her. But right away I think, not yet.

ACKNOWLEDGEMENTS

I owe a debt of gratitude to my Bay Area and Beyond writer's group: Brad Balukjian, Sandi Char, Laird Harrison, Karen Laws, and Robert Luhn. They closely read every book I write, and always make astute suggestions. A good writer's groups is golden. So if you are a writer who hesitates to join such a group, I urge you to try it. How do you tell if it's a good group? First of all they read your work. And everyone in the group doesn't gush over your every word. They also don't criticize your every word. They praise the parts they enjoy and they tell you what they think could be improved. They give you their honest opinion. And they expect the same from you. You job is to take their comments and sift out the ones that seem true to your vision of what you're writing.

I want to acknowledge my generous, smart agent, Kimberley Cameron. She knows when to perk me up! And my editing team at Severn House Publishing, Sara Porter and Shayna Holmes. The whole team at SH makes me feel like they are really pulling for me as an author. You can't beat that!

Thank you to David, who took me to the Bahamas again and again so that the adventures in this book could come to life for me before I put them on the page. Happily, not all the adventures were as harrowing as Jessie's, but there were some doozies!

I want to acknowledge the women of Texas who have been crushed by the political whims of their government, and those who are fighting hard to change the draconian laws they've enacted. Right on!

One last note: the publishing world lost a good pal when agent Janet Reid died. She was a champion for writers, and taught me a lot. I still hear her voice: "You're not done yet. You need one more twist!" She was right!

ACKNOWLEDGEMENTS